Tivaja

*A stolen soul, a civil war,
a father's secret.*

A woman hunted.

Venessa Giunta

http://www.VenessaGiunta.com/

Jivaja
Copyright © 2018 by Venessa Giunta

Image/art disclaimer: Licensed material is being used for illustrative purposes only. Any person depicted in the licensed material is a model.

eBook ISBN: 978-1-7326860-1-4
Print ISBN: 978-0-9910778-9-2

Cover Artist: The Book Brander
Logo: Quill & Scale Designs
Published in the United States of America by Fictionvale Publishing, LLC.

http://www.VenessaGiunta.com

Dedication

For my husband, my muse.
And all the things.

Prologue

"You have to be very careful when you touch people, Mecca," her father murmurs as he kneels on the warm ground pulling weeds out of the flowerbed. He brushes the back of his glove-covered hand over his forehead, wiping away a faint gleam of sweat. "You're still learning to use your Gift and you could hurt people."

She nods. The plastic beads on the ends of her braids click against each other with a muted sound. "That's why you don't want me to touch Mom."

He exhales and leans back on his ankles as he looks up at her. She wishes her eyes were like his. When he looks at her, his love shows in his bright, dark blue eyes.

"Yes," he says. "Mom is sick, and she needs all her energy. I know you're careful, and I know you love her very much, but you can't control it yet. You wouldn't mean to but could accidentally make her worse. Do you understand what I mean?"

Even at eleven, she gets how much it hurts him to forbid her to touch her mother. She understands why too, but she hates it. She hates it more than peas, more than cleaning her room, and more than cough medicine. And she hates herself for having the "Gift" that keeps her from her mom.

"Yes, I understand," she replies. "I get it. I wish — I just wish there was a way…"

He grabs her arm and pulls her into a bear hug. "I know, baby. I'm so sorry. I hate doing this to you. When you're older. When you learn more…"

Her tears spill onto his thin white T-shirt as she wraps her arms around his neck and weeps into his shoulder. He smells of earth and sweat. She stays with him for a while after she stops crying. Watching him work in the earth, planting new flowers, she can pretend her life isn't the freak show it really is. She can imagine running home and hugging her mom without having to make sure there is something between their skin. In her thoughts, in her wishes, skin to skin means nothing.

Later, she wanders behind the house and down to the pond. It's large enough to be home to many fish, birds and animals, but not so big that a bunch of people come to play in it. She never sees boats or even swimmers, here. That's why she comes. It is quiet.

An expanse of trees backs up along the pond's bank, and she catches sight of a doe with her fawn just as they catch sight of her. They dart into the safety of the trees, leaving her behind. Where the pathway goes into the trees, she continues along the water's edge, until she reaches the flat, smooth boulder at the water line.

She loves this rock. Surrounded by trees and brush, this is her spot, her rock. She scrambles to the top and sits, her legs stretched in front of her. A magnificent bird swoops across the still water, looking for fish, she guesses. It had rained earlier and her Keds are dirty from the walk through the woods. With one finger, she flicks a spot of mud from her toe.

"Stupid Gift. Why couldn't it skip me like it did Dad?" A ladybug flutters past her nose and lands on the tip of her shoelace. It crawls along until it comes to the end where her lace leans against her ankle. The bug hesitates a moment and then creeps onto her soft brown skin, a tiny red spot moving along her leg.

She watches and feels the tiny tickle from its movement. Her anger at her life still bubbles below the surface, but she is happy to watch this small, pretty thing living its life carefree, in a way hers would never be.

She sighs and then a sharp little tingle slips from that tiny bug's spot and up through her body, a feeling that reminded her of putting her tongue on a nine volt battery. The tickle stops and she watches, wide-eyed as the ladybug slides down her leg, bounces off the tongue of her shoe and falls to the hard surface of the rock.

It is dead.

She clamps her palm over her mouth and cries into it. She scoots away on her backside, then draws her knees up to her chest, bends her head, and sobs.

Chapter One: Mecca

Darkness cloaked the back parking lot in Little Five Points. On the asphalt, the man shuddered and gasped, his dusky blue eyes wide in his confusion. Mecca Trenow, her fingers wrapped around his wrist, held her own fear at bay by the need for survival. A confused grimace transformed the man's face into an ugly, alabaster mask.

Mecca's heart thumped hard against her breastbone. Everything had happened so fast! His attack. Her response. Now, crouched over him, she found the arm in her grasp thinning, becoming more frail, until she could feel the actual bone between her fingers. His dark hair greyed and then wafted to the concrete like so many delicate feathers.

He withered.

Superimposed over his form, like a double-exposed negative, the Cavern where his soul would have resided spread before her. It should have been bathed in golden light. Instead, a small ball of gold looked to be tethered to the walls with thick, silver-grey tendrils.

She closed her eyes to block out the reality behind the image of the Cavern. She tugged at the golden life force within him. Its colored fringes had already washed out to a pale pink. The silver tethers which held it stretched and then popped, one by one. Mecca surrounded the sad little ball with her own energy, gold with blue fringes, as it began to come away.

The captive energy swung free from its bonds, momentarily bathing the cold, dank Cavern in light. It hurled into Mecca. Her own life force, the little part of her soul she'd sent into him, crashed back to her, breaking her hold on his frail arm. She toppled onto her ass between the cars, sharp pain vibrating up her spine.

Energy tore through her, mixing with her adrenaline. The red-hot spike shuddered through her body and along her limbs. It reached her toes and then bounced back and shot through her entire body again. Her skin tingled electric.

She had no concept of how long she lay on the gravel lot. The acidic smell of piss coming from the ground made her queasy. The energy waned and ebbed until it settled into her and became familiar, became a part of her own soul. With a long, deep breath, she pulled herself up from between the cars, leaning against the cool door of a Toyota Camry.

As the energy finally began to level out, she realized that she felt drunk. Her fuzzy brain had trouble registering things around her, or even thinking, for that matter. So it took a moment to realize that the blob she stared at now was actually a man. He stood near the Dumpster, across the parking lot.

Tall, with dark, tousled hair, he watched her with wide eyes. What she'd done began to sink in. Panic edged her thoughts. She looked down at the withered corpse, at herself.

Dark droplets dusted her blouse. She touched the side of her neck and her fingertips came away bloody. The *thump-thump* of her pulse pounded in her ears.

At her feet, the shrunken carcass looked nothing like the sexy man in the coffee shop who'd approached her so many times over the last few weeks. His energy had been strange, which had kept her from engaging. But today, she'd said yes to a chat. And she'd ended up a murderer.

She stared at the dead thing. The fear she'd been holding back crashed over her like a flood.

She turned on her heel and ran.

Chapter Two: Claude

The young Visci half-breed male— smelling of a sweet, rotten scent, much like day-old milk — who showed Claude into Emilia's quarters had been more interested in his telephone than in courtesy. But there was no accounting for manners.

Emilia's rooms encompassed half of the lowest level of the sub-basement in her compound. Situated at the end of an extended hallway, it would be defensible in case of a breach; Claude felt sure that Emilia had installed escape tunnels leading from her rooms to a safe location. He would have, in her shoes. Good defense means nothing if one is trapped like a rat in a corner.

Claude crossed the threshold into Emilia's quarters and the door closed behind him with a muted click. Rich moss-green carpet swallowed his footfalls as he made his way through the small ante-chamber to the main living area. The scent of cinnamon incense caressed him.

Emilia's love for all things aged and European showed in her design tastes. The Queen Anne style writing table that flanked him on the right held a pale cream colored porcelain pitcher beside a chipped washing basin, both settled on a lace table runner. A tapestry on the opposite wall displayed an English fox hunt with braying dogs, noblemen and pretty women riding side saddle. Claude had always found Emilia's affection for European history charming.

Through an open archway, he entered the sitting room. The green on the floor gave way to a thick, merlot carpet, which accented russet walls hung with various light colored paintings framed in dark woods. Emilia's passion gave way to practicality with the smoke grey, leather sectional in the corner and the glass-topped desk which faced the room near the far wall, flanked by two ultra-modern chairs.

Emilia sat at the desk, glow from the LCD computer monitor highlighting her almond skin tone. When she looked up at him, Claude saw the girl he'd taken from a battlefield in what is now Cambodia. Her face, her expression when she smiled, those were the same. But her eyes had changed. Darker now. Harder, perhaps. Claude supposed he'd done that to her.

"Thank you for coming," Emilia said as she rose, a smile spread across her face. "Things have gotten complicated and I am eager to have your counsel, if you would stay for a bit."

Claude affected a short bow. "I am happy to assist." The conflict between the pure blood Visci and the half-breeds roiled below the surface of every interaction these days, in every city he'd visited, so Atlanta seemed no different. It had only been a matter of time.

Commotion just outside the arched doorway caught both their attention. A tall, thin man bustled through, followed directly by the rotten-milk half-breed, who sputtered apologies to Emilia.

"What is going on?" she said, moving from behind her desk. "James?" She stared the new arrival down, but to his credit, he did not fluster under her gaze.

"My apologies for bursting in," James said, tilting a nod in Claude's direction.

Claude could detect no scent coming from him, though he was a distance away. Pure blood? *Interesting*.

"You need to hear what happened to Hayden."

Emilia waved a hand of dismissal to the half-breed from the doorway and he stepped back, a scowl on his face.

"All right," Emilia said as she leaned against the desk. She crossed her arms over her chest. "Who did Hayden kill this time?"

Claude didn't know who this Hayden was, but listened with interest. James shook his head, but seemed unable to talk for a moment. When he finally did speak, it came out all in a rush, with barely any breath between words.

"He didn't kill anyone. Someone killed him."

"What?" Emilia rarely showed excessive emotion, but the surprise traveled across her features for a moment before she regained control. "Was it Visci? A pure blood killed him?"

James shook his head. "I don't know *what* she is. But she isn't Visci."

This conversation had gotten exponentially more interesting.

"Then how?" Emilia asked.

"He was at the college campus, down at Little Five Points. He hunts — hunted there pretty often. He liked the college kids."

"Yes, yes, I know." Emilia waved her hand. "Go on."

"He was in the coffee shop and had zeroed in on one girl. He'd targeted her before, several times, actually, but she always shut him down."

"Who is she?"

"I don't know. She's a student — she's always in one of the coffee shops, working on things — light-skinned, African-American, young. I've been in the same room with her too and I get why he wanted her. She pulled at me, but I have no idea why. I suppose that's why he kept going back to her every time he saw her."

"But this time, she accepted him." Emilia's jaw had tightened and set in a hard line.

"She let him walk her to her car but then... Then..." James looked down and Claude realized suddenly that although James might have been a full blood Visci, he was very young. That made him wonder who the boy's parents were. Who had been lucky enough to procreate without a human? Claude would have to make inquiries.

"Enough with the theatrics," Emilia said. "What happened?"

"He went to feed from her and when he leaned in, he died."

Emilia caught Claude's gaze for a moment and the exasperation evident in her tone flashed through her eyes. She looked back to the young Visci in front of her. "James, I swear to you, if you don't tell me what happened, you're going to be an offering in the Maze Gathering, rather than a potential contestant."

"Yes, I'm sorry. When he went to feed, she grabbed his arm and he just suddenly started withering. He tried to pull away, but not until he was too weak to do it. It's like she was sucking everything out of his body and he just shriveled up and died."

Something in the back recesses of Claude's mind pinged on James's words, but he set aside the strange memory-like feeling for now. He'd search his past later. Now, he wanted more information, and he hoped Emilia would ask the questions he wanted answers to.

"I don't understand," Emilia said. "What actually killed him?"

James shook his head, but didn't respond immediately. Claude wondered whether James feared for his own safety because he was unable to answer. When James did find his voice again, he said, "I don't know how she killed him. There was no blood, and I saw no injury when I retrieved his body."

"What did you do with it?"

"It's still in my car. I thought you would want to see it."

"Yes. Take it to the medical suite and we'll see what we can make of things." Emilia moved behind her desk again. "You can go. You did well, James. Thank you."

James furrowed his brow and shifted his weight from one foot to the other and back again. "There's something else."

Emilia looked up from the paper she'd lifted and begun to study. "What?"

"She saw me."

Claude could all but feel Emilia's temper, though her face remained stoic. She'd always been hot-headed, but it seemed she'd finally learned to control her immediate outbursts. Likely a skill learned as she solidified her hold over Atlanta. It's difficult to govern Visci effectively without a huge measure of self-control.

"Go on," Emilia said, her tone quiet and calm.

"She saw me, but I think she was terrified. She ran in the direction of the university."

Claude wondered, briefly, whether Emilia had misgivings about having heard all of this news with him in the room. He had the sort of feeling that created something like a live wire beneath his skin, as if he had information that he didn't yet understand, but that would be indelibly useful in the future.

"Is there anything else?" Clearly, Emilia was ready to dismiss James. Her attention returned to the things in front of her eyes, though Claude was sure that she didn't even know what she looked at.

"No, Lady."

"Very well. Please take the body to the medical suite."

"Yes, Lady." To his credit, James left on silent feet.

When he closed the door behind him, Emilia raised her gaze to Claude. "I'd like to postpone our discussion until tomorrow. I have a few things that I must address."

Claude tilted his head in a respectful bow. "Of course. As you wish. Please send for me at your convenience."

She gave him a smile and for barely a moment, he saw the girl she had once been — slow to smile, but with a twinkle when she did. "I'm glad you're here," she said.

"It is my pleasure," he replied. "Until later, then."

—➤➤◄◄◄—

The death of this Hayden weighed heavy in Claude's thoughts. There was something about it...something about how it happened. He knew there was something in his past — probably in the early part of his life, judging from the difficulty he had recalling it — that called to him.

It took longer than he expected to find the medical suite. James was just entering with a black back slung over his shoulder. Not the most graceful way to transport a body surely.

Claude followed the man into the medical suite and stood near the door as James dumped the bag onto a flat thin-mattressed gurney. Claude had expected it to be something like a body bag — though he had no idea why he would think a Visci traveled around with a body bag in his car — but it turned out to be a plain black garbage bag. James ripped the plastic, as if he were unpacking a pound of store-bought beef.

The body inside looked more like a mummy than a recently-dead man. The memory in Claude's mind that hadn't wanted to come forward before, slammed to the forefront now.

Claude's uncle — a man named Politus — had been found just like this in a copse of olive trees a few leagues from where Claude had grown up. Claude couldn't remember specifics. He'd only been a boy then. But he recalled his father organizing a party of Visci — they'd all been full blood then — to hunt down the...

Claude couldn't remember the name of the person, or maybe it was a group name. He would have to think on it for longer.

Claude stepped up silently behind the young full blood. "James." He got a bit of satisfaction at the startled jerk and turn when James faced him.

"Yeah...?" Even this close, James had no scent. He must have come from a strong bloodline.

"You said, in Emilia's quarters, that this girl only touched him and he became..." Claude motioned to the corpse.

James narrowed his eyes, obviously suspicious. "Yeah."

A man of many and varied words. "Only one small question, if you please. I see he wears a long-sleeved shirt. Do you recall whether she touched him over the shirt or on his skin?"

James glanced at the corpse and looked back to Claude. Claude imagined he was weighing the pros and cons of sharing something now that he hadn't shared with Emilia. That's what Claude would be doing. But all things considered, this was a seemingly innocuous piece of information.

"Does it mean something to you?"

Claude didn't show his surprise, but he hadn't expected the question. "Perhaps. But I can't know without some research. And there's no need to do the research without an answer to the question."

"Did Emilia send you?"

Claude didn't answer, but didn't release the man's gaze.

James licked his lips and pulled in a breath. Then he turned to the corpse and pointed to what would have been a strong arm. "There. At the wrist. She grabbed it when he'd leaned in to feed from her."

"So the clothes weren't in the way?"

"No."

"Thank you, James." Claude left the man to whatever he would be doing now that he had the body on the slab.

The skin to skin contact meant something. Now Claude just needed to remember what that was.

Chapter Three: Mecca

Mecca clutched the steering wheel in two tight fists, her cell phone pinched between her head and shoulder. On the dashboard, the speed needle had slipped past eighty. She eased her foot off the gas. The buzzing ring in her ear stopped as the line clicked on the other end.

"Dad?" The fear in her words scared her even more.

His sleep-roughened voice came across the line. "Mecca? It's almost 1 a.m. What's wrong?"

She took a deep breath, releasing some of her panic. "Dad, something really bad's happened. I think I killed someone." She blurted it before she chickened out. *I know I killed someone.* Her words hung in the air like a heavy winter fog.

"Are you with the police?"

"No. I ran."

Moments crawled by. A giant black Lincoln Navigator blew past her, windows open, bass thumping. Her seat vibrated with the beat.

Her father finally responded, his tone tight and clipped. "Come home."

She pulled into the driveway and cut the headlights. The foyer's chandelier dropped a warm glow through the open front door. Her father's silhouette appeared in the door frame. Relief welled up in her.

She closed the space between them. When he opened his arms, memories of her childhood overtook her. She fell into his hug and let her defenses down for the first time since she'd met Hayden at the Brew-haha.

He brushed a hand over her hair. Tall and strong, with broad shoulders and thick arms, her father made her feel safer than she had all night. When she looked up at him, she found more comfort in his electric blue eyes which looked at her now with worry.

The little scar over his left eyebrow twitched, as it always did when he got stressed out or upset. Her Uncle Ken had nailed him with a baseball bat by accident when he was eight. As a kid, she'd thought that was one of the funniest stories of his childhood, because while he stood bleeding from the head, Uncle Ken ran around crying hysterically.

"Come on." He kicked the door shut and turned her in the direction of the kitchen. "I made coffee. I figured we'd both need it."

Mecca let him guide her through the contemporary living room and into the bright kitchen with its glass cabinetry and slate tile floor. Beneath the wall where the phone hung, a tiny black laptop lay closed on the countertop.

Visions of Saturday morning breakfasts superimposed themselves over the empty room. Dad settled her at the table and then went about putting together two cups of coffee. Another twinge of nostalgia tugged at her, seeing him in the blue terrycloth robe with its red piping. Mom had given him that robe the Christmas before she died. Guilt curled up in a little pit in her belly.

"So what happened?"

She didn't answer right away. She couldn't. Where would she start?

"Mec?"

"I'm still not really sure. "

In the bright light of the kitchen, his gaze flicked down to the blood drops on her blouse, then back to her face. "You're hurt?"

Mecca flushed and then berated herself for being embarrassed. She hadn't invited Hayden to chomp on her neck. But the intimacy of the bite — was it a bite? It had seemed more like a sting when she'd felt it with her fingertips. But it was the location that made her uncomfortable sharing with her dad.

"Only a little," she said. "I'm fine."

He set a mug in front of her. On its side, Winnie the Pooh and Piglet tromped through a field. It had been her favorite mug in high school. Her coffee, creamed and sugared as it was, seemed very close in color to the skin of her hand. She shook her head to focus.

"Just start at the beginning," her father said as he dropped into the seat beside her, his own mug palmed in his hand.

"This is going to sound nuts, but it's true, I swear." She didn't continue until he nodded, but then everything came out in a ridiculous rush. "I didn't want to go clubbing with the girls tonight, so I went to the Brew-haha to work on a paper. The coffee house I took you to in Little Five after the play last month, remember? Anyway, there was this guy there and — Well, he'd been asking me out for weeks. His energy was weird though and so I've been avoiding him. I guess tonight I just got curious." Mecca shrugged. It was the truth.

He raised his eyebrows. "You used your Gift?"

Yes." Mecca looked down into her cup.

She hadn't wanted to. She *never* wanted to use the Gift. When she looked up again, the surprise on his face hadn't faded. Did she see accusation there too?

"I couldn't avoid feeling his crazy energy, whether I used the Gift or not. And if he hadn't attacked me, I never would have used it." The whine in her voice made her cringe.

"It doesn't matter."

Mecca couldn't read his expression. And she didn't understand why he wasn't more accusatory. She'd *killed* someone, for fuck's sake.

"What was different about him?" he asked, raising his mug to his lips. It was almost as if the question were academic. As if she hadn't killed a man.

She pushed on. "From a distance, he seemed like he wasn't part of his energy. Like he was wearing a glove. I know it doesn't make sense, but that's the best way I can describe it."

"Did you touch him?"

"Not until…" She shook her head to get rid of the sudden image of the withered husk on the ground. "I haven't used the Gift in any real way in so long. I mean, I always feel how people are — like you might hear background music and be aware of it, but not actually paying attention."

He nodded but didn't push her.

"It was getting late and he offered to walk me out." She saw the upcoming scolding in his eyes and pre-empted his protest with a raised hand. "Don't yell at me and tell me it was stupid. I know it was stupid. But we'd been talking a long time, and I wanted to know why he felt different."

"All right," he said, his blue eyes clouded with a mix of emotions. Mecca couldn't tell which, though. "So what was it that made him different?"

Mecca hesitated before answering. She thought about what happened. About what she saw. About what she experienced. She tried to break it down. Finally, she said, "It was stolen. The energy he was using."

Her father's forehead crinkled and Mecca watched him try to process the information.

"I found it bound in his Cavern with these silver… ties. They looked like rope, but stretchy and gross-looking. Like membranes."

Her dad wrinkled his nose to match his forehead.

"So this ball of energy was held to the walls of his Cavern with those things. It was like looking at an insect in a spider's web." She shuddered again, because that was *exactly* what it had been like, she realized. A sticky, gross spider's web.

He shook his head and ran a thick palm over his buzz-cut. "That's not how it works."

"Before I explored the Cavern, he'd touched me on the arm and I felt emptiness. Cold. Nothing like a normal person. I know you've never experienced it, but he didn't have the warm, soft feeling that a person's Cavern has."

"He can't live and not have a life force. Even when you borrow energy —"

"I *don't* borrow energy." Mecca's cheeks warmed and her pulse beat heavy in her ears. She hadn't used her Gift since just after Mom died. She didn't borrow energy. She *didn't*.

"I know. I'm sorry. My point was that even if *someone* were to borrow energy, the life force diminishes in one and increases in the other. It just adds to what's already there. Capturing, binding it is unnecessary. And, in theory, if you — if *someone* took all the energy from another, that other would die."

"Yes." Mecca's hand hurt. She looked down to find herself gripping the coffee mug so hard her knuckles had paled.

"You think that's what he did? He killed someone?"

"I don't know. I just know that when I was able to touch him and send my energy into him, he didn't have anything of his own. I found a ball of gold light, small. Diminished."

He shook his head. "Let me make sure I understand," he said, his words punctuated by an exasperated sigh. "You meet this guy at the coffee shop. He seems just like a normal person, except for the weird feeling. Aside from that, he's like anyone else, right? But he doesn't have any energy of his own. No life source. Only a small bit he stole from—from who?"

Mecca shrugged. "I don't know. All I know is that the Cavern was cold and the color of the energy was fading. He must have been living off it, like food."

Her father leaned back in the kitchen chair, confusion playing along his features. He didn't look like he believed her. "Living off stolen energy. Okay, then what?"

"I took it. I pulled it right out of him. And he died." Mecca swiped a tear from her cheek, her fingers warm from the cup. When had she started crying? "I killed him."

He only watched her, his forehead creased in worry or in thought. Why didn't he react? Mecca didn't know. He sat rigid.

"The police didn't come?"

"I don't know. I ran."

"Did anyone see you?"

Mecca looked down again. The face of the man near the Dumpster came up, unbidden. "Yes. One guy. He looked terrified."

"Shit."

"I should have called 911."

Her dad didn't say anything for a minute. Then, "Are you sure he's dead?"

Mecca stared at him, unbelieving. Why wasn't he appalled at her? Why didn't he look surprised or scared? Or even freaked out, for that matter?

"Yes." A vision of the emaciated head flashed through her mind's eye. It reminded her of Mom, just before... She pulled in a breath. "He's dead."

The corners of his mouth tugged downward. He stood abruptly. "I'm going to go see if anyone found the body."

Mecca reeled back in the chair, as if he'd hit her.

"What? Are you crazy?" The police would be there.

"We need to know, Mecca. Let me go put on clothes. I'll only be a minute."

"I'm going with you," she said. The chair scraped against the tile floor as she stood. Her nerves ratcheted up, making her skin feel hot.

"Don't be ridiculous. You don't need to go."

"I'm not just gonna sit here and pace the floor." This whole thing was batshit crazy, but she wasn't going to bounce around the house, making *herself* crazy. "I'm going."

He stared at her and then gave her a curt nod. "All right."

Mecca jerked her head up. She'd slid into sleep again. The rocking of the BMW and the familiar scent of leather and old cigarette smoke had lulled her. Her dad claimed he'd quit, but she knew he snuck a smoke here and there. Outside, the city moved by at a quick clip. They hadn't gotten off the interstate yet.

"Where did the blood come from?" her father asked. The blue light from the dashboard added a gruesome element to his features. Mecca looked away.

"He bit me. Or something. I don't know exactly. It happened really fast." She pulled the visor down and flipped the cover off the mirror. The brash light made her blink several times before she could see again. Her face looked haggard. Little red veins lined her eyes, brown irises against a pink backdrop.

When she tilted her head, just looking at the angry puncture mark on her neck made her flinch. A single wound, it looked like a bee sting, slightly raised and swollen, the tiny opening puckered like a mouth. If there'd been two, it would have looked like Dracula had come calling. She brushed a fingertip along the skin, bracing herself for a stab of pain. Instead, the flesh beneath the skin was sore, but the puncture itself felt tingly, something like when pins and needles set in after her arm fell asleep.

"That looks pretty ugly."

Mecca let the mirror cover snap shut and put the visor back in place. "It's okay."

"We should have cleaned it up before we left."

"It's fine, Dad."

She couldn't believe they were going back. What if the police questioned them? What would she say?

Would she lie? Would she even be able to? Her belly churned. She was going to give herself an ulcer.

A chirp came from her purse. Her cell phone showed four missed calls and one incoming. "Hey, Jo."

"Where *are* you?" Josie said. Her roommate's voice came through shrill and filled with worry, loud enough to get her dad's attention. He raised an eyebrow and looked at her sidelong.

"I'm with my dad. I'm going to crash at his place tonight."

"Jesus, Mecca, I came home and you weren't here. I was getting ready to call the cops!"

"I'm sorry. I didn't mean to worry you."

Josie took in a deep sigh. "I tried to call you a bunch of times. Why didn't you answer?"

"I forgot my purse in the car when I got to Dad's."

"Don't do this shit again. I'm too young to have a heart attack."

"I won't. I'll be back in the morning." She paused, unsure for a moment whether to ask. "What was Little Five like when you drove through?"

"One of the clubs had closed, so everyone was heading back."

"Anything else?"

"Nope. Usual Friday night."

"Okay, thanks. I'll see you tomorrow."

Less than ten minutes later, they arrived. Mecca directed him around to the parking lot in the back, tucked between a four story apartment building and the backsides of the shops along Euclid. The lot spread out like a dull, grey sea, its smoothness broken only by the dark blue Jeep Wrangler parked near the Dumpster in the back. The Dumpster where the man had been.

No police. No news vans.

No body.

Chapter Four: Mecca

The library lights flickered for the second time. Mecca frowned and clicked the link for "More Life-Suckers." A somewhat dubious website but it contained a lot of interesting information on the vampire mythos. The idea of vampires seemed ridiculous. But Mecca couldn't ignore the bite, or sting, or whatever it was on her neck. So researching vampires seemed the best place to start. Maybe she'd run across something more plausible than the undead.

For the third night since the incident at the Brew-haha, she'd spent the entire evening parked in front of a computer. She usually used her laptop, but found she needed to print a lot. Not having a printer meant relying on the terminals in the main library.

Sunday, she'd checked out half the books on the shelves relating to vampire legends. That got her some interesting looks from the librarian. Monday, she'd stayed in the dorm, reading and researching. This afternoon, when she'd gotten out of class, she stopped by the library to print out some things from the Internet.

She hadn't realized so much time had gone by. Now the library was closing and she hadn't left yet. Her stomach rumbled.

There wasn't much out there on what vampires could and couldn't do. Not anything concrete, anyway. Hundreds of powers and skills were attributed to vampires and most of them seemed to have their basis in fiction. But of course they would. Vampires were fictional, right?

What could be believed? The only things she counted on to be real were the things she'd seen and experienced herself. And that wasn't much. The entire attack, once it started, had happened faster than she could have imagined. When he'd concentrated his attention on her, he tugged at her consciousness. And when he'd made the wound in her neck, it was like the sweetest electric shock slipping through her veins. She shivered. So those things she knew.

And so her hunt for information continued.

"Hey." A low, rumbly, unfamiliar voice.

Mecca looked up, past the monitor she'd been studying. Approaching, she saw a guy, younger than her, with wiry blond hair tumbling over his forehead, obscuring his eyes. Even so, she thought those eyes might be focused on her. He pulled up short three feet from the computer desk she occupied.

"Hey, you know the library's closing. Didn't you see the lights? You need to be shutting down." The deep octave didn't match the whiny tone of his voice.

Entitlement via work-study.

"I am. Just give me two minutes."

He looked from Mecca, to the back of the monitor, then to her again. "Just hurry it up."

Mecca nodded gravely at him, trying hard not to laugh. She turned her attention back to the computer. She hadn't had much luck this evening, anyway. She scanned the dodgy website in front of her, about to shut the whole thing down, when she reached the bottom and found a small, grainy photo of a young man.

Is this man a White Widower? Three wives dead of unexplained causes. Coincidence?

Mecca's breath caught in her throat.

The blurred image had been scanned from a newspaper photo; that much was obvious. The pained look in his eyes would have touched her if not for the caption. And for the fact that she would have recognized those eyes anywhere.

The lights wavered again. Any minute, the work-study guy would be coming around to herd her away and shut down the computer. Mecca hit the print icon on the browser and watched the screen as the printer spun to life. She studied the picture, her mind numb.

Her father stared back at her.

Mecca bounded down the great stone steps of the library, her mind racing. A chilly gust of wind slid against her skin. October in Atlanta brought the cooler days that people wished for in the August humidity. Mecca hadn't thought to bring a jacket this afternoon and the cool night breeze skimmed along her skin.

As she strode down the darkened campus sidewalk, her satchel, stuffed with her class notebooks and the articles, banged against her hip. She fought the urge to stop and pull out the printed website with her dad's picture on it. Walking across the quad at one in the morning wouldn't be the best time or place.

Silence blanketed the campus. The hairs on the back of her neck prickled. Usually, students wandered around at all hours. She wasn't the only one who had to be ushered out of the library, but not many people milled about now. She welcomed the solitude tonight, even though it was eerie.

That photo kept creeping into her mind. Her father's eyes.

The overcast sky locked away the moon and stars, casting the pathway in shadow. Streetlamps scattered throughout the quad created circular pools of light, like island oases in the darkness, soft and inviting. Mecca moved from one to the other hardly seeing them.

The chirp of her cell phone jerked her out of her thoughts. With a sigh, she answered and put some false cheer into her voice. "Hey, Josie."

"Mecca, where the hell have you been? I've left you five hundred messages!" Usually, Josie was the most laid back person in their little group, made up mostly of track people. She was the first person Mecca had met at college. Roommates their freshman year, they'd been inseparable and their relationship remained close through their sophomore and junior years as well.

Lately, though, Josie was acting more like a mom than a roommate.

"Sorry," Mecca said. "I forgot about a paper, so I'm really behind. I've spent most of my time in the library this week." Not a complete lie.

"You've been blowing off practice for a paper? Coach is pissed at you. He thinks you won't be ready for the meet on Saturday. He's ready to throw you off the team."

Mecca hiked her bag up farther on her shoulder. "I'll be ready. Tell him I'll be ready."

"You're not going to practice tomorrow either?"

"Look, this is a big paper. I'm almost done. A couple more days and things will get back to normal." *I hope.*

"What is going on with you lately?" Mecca could almost see Josie's pale eyebrows knitting into a worried furrow. "Mecca—"

"Jo, I need to go, okay? I'll call you tomorrow." She disconnected without waiting for a response, too worn out to deal with Josie or the track coach.

As much as she tried to avoid it, her mind kept going back to that fuzzy photo of her dad. Mecca had always loved hearing the stories about him — an older widower — meeting her mother and their whirlwind romance. Mecca had been on the way before they'd even been married.

Some of her favorite stories had been the Romeo and Juliet-like family tensions. Dad's side didn't have a problem with Mom. But Mom's side... He just didn't fit in with his flat-top hair-cut, bright blue eyes and the tanned skin of an Ivy League college athlete. It was no family secret that Gram and Grandpa Stone hated that their daughter had married a white man.

That act had caused a great deal of turmoil at the Stone family gatherings. But within their own immediate family circle, they'd been picture-perfect. Until her mom got sick.

How could that website say such terrible things? Her dad couldn't have done anything to those women. He didn't even *have* the Gift. It skipped him. Uncle Ken had it, her grandfather had it. But her dad didn't.

She entered The Tunnel, built under Moreland Avenue so that students wouldn't have to cross the busy, four-lane road to get to the dorms at Atlanta State University. The Tunnel had an actual name, but no one ever remembered it. Everyone just called it the Tunnel.

Fluorescents on the ceiling lit the round walls, making the explicit graffiti easier to read. One light near the far opening flickered. Moreland fed into Little Five Points a few miles down and even at one in the morning, the sounds of traffic overhead rumbled through the Tunnel's walls.

With heavy steps, she trudged on. She planned to read the strange article and mull over that picture when she got to the dorm. She wanted to know what it said, yet… she didn't.

Sometimes things happen in life that throw you off a cliff, making your world careen out of sync. Mecca couldn't keep back the feeling that she was about to take a flying dive.

As she reached the dorm end of the Tunnel, three dark figures stepped in from the sides, blocking the exit. She stopped, her heart pounding double-time. Who were they?

"Hello?" Mecca hitched her satchel farther up on her shoulder, dread and fear mingling in her veins. None of the figures replied.

She could backtrack and outrun them. At least running she'd have a chance.

She glanced over her shoulder. Two more figures approached from where she'd just come, each in black, long sleeves and gloves. Ski masks covered their faces. Ski masks.

How long had they been behind her? Had she just walked into their trap, oblivious?

Mecca's heart banged inside her rib cage. She searched for a way out. If she could break through, she could put distance between herself and them. She moved in a slow circle, trying to keep an eye on all of them, and waited for an opportunity. They crept toward her, keeping their distance, but that couldn't last.

As they drew closer, the guy on her left moved farther into the Tunnel, creating a small gap between him and the wall. If he just moved a little bit more, she might be able to make a run for it. Her bag weighed heavy on her shoulder, but she couldn't drop it. She couldn't leave it.

Who are they? This seemed so surreal.

There. An opening. She could make it if she moved fast enough.

The gap widened another foot and she darted forward, her gaze fixed on the darkness she knew was her freedom. Her assailants shouted as she passed the guy on her left. Her shoulder slammed into him. The collision threw her off balance only momentarily. It was enough. They fell onto her in a flash.

Being on the track team for six years, counting high school, had made her strong and fast, but they seemed faster. Hands scooped her up; arms wrapped around her waist and lifted her from the ground like a child. She kicked and pushed at them, trying to shove her attackers away, trying to find another out. A scream burst from her lungs.

She twisted violently. Her feet slammed to the ground and sent a jarring rattle up her legs. Her bag dropped to the cement with a thud as they hoisted her up again.

"Don't touch her skin! Get the needle in her!" A man's voice. An accent.

White hot pain seared the side of her neck, and then cold radiated through her body. Ice slipped into her veins. They let her feet drop to the ground and she willed her leaden legs to run. But she couldn't get any of her limbs to move the way she wanted.

Run, damn it!

The figures in her vision doubled and she staggered, blinking hard in an effort to clear her gaze. Everything went soft around the edges. Fuzzy. They all stepped back, watching her as she stumbled. They removed their masks, but she couldn't focus on details of their faces. Her knees hit the ground and she groaned. Then one of the black figures heaved her up and dragged her arm over his shoulders. He began to walk with her as if she'd gotten drunk. Her head lolled. That same voice with the strange accent spoke. Was it Irish?

"This'll make Emilia happy."

Mecca jerked awake and struggled to sit up, her head fuzzy and aching. She'd dreamt about a Christmas when she'd been small, five or six at the most. Mom had been coughing on Christmas Day. For the first time, Mecca had realized that her mother was sick.

The room's bright light hurt her eyes. She tried to raise her hand to her head, but couldn't. Thick leather restraints circled her wrists, fixing them to a hospital bedrail. An I.V. hung nearby, the plastic tube leading to the top of her hand. She stared at the restraints. *What the hell?* Curling her fists, Mecca yanked. The rattle of the chain tethering her to the bed rang out sharply in the quiet room. She pulled until the leather bit into her wrists.

They (*who?*) had dressed her in a stark, white gown which reached to her knees. Matching cuffs held her legs tight and a wide belt extended across her hips and fastened somewhere under the bed, pinning her lower half down. She thrashed against the leather, trying not to let panic overtake her. Bile rose to her throat, and a wave of nausea roiled through her belly.

A firm hand pressed against the middle of her chest and pushed her back down. Mecca jumped. The room had been so silent. She hadn't realized someone was here.

"Stay still. Too much movement will make you ill."

Mecca followed the deep and gentle voice into eyes the color of walnuts. A dark brown circle, almost black, rimmed the irises and thick, long lashes framed them. His eyes complemented his dark honey complexion and wavy chestnut hair.

"How are you feeling?" he asked.

Mecca yanked against the wrist restraints again and immediately regretted it. A bolt of pain shot through her head and perched above her eyes like a vulture in a tree. "Let me go." She'd meant to yell, but her voice came out small and hoarse.

"Sorry. I don't have that ability." He took her wrist in his hand and slid two warm fingers beneath the cuff, rubbing gently until he found her pulse.

The headache beating at her eased by a degree or two. She'd drawn energy from his touch without meaning to. Not much, but a little. Were whatever drugs they had dumped into her screwing up her control? She clamped down on her Gift. A sickly stab of nausea again poked at her belly.

"Are you all right?" he asked. "You look a bit green." He felt her forehead.

He didn't look like a kidnapper. He didn't look like he meant her harm. Of course, neither had

Hayden. And Mecca was a lot more vulnerable bound to the bed than she'd been in the coffee house.

"Why am I here? Who are you?"

"I'm Will. The rest of your questions will have to wait. I can't give you the answers. Emilia will be here soon. She wants to speak with you." Will unfolded a crisp ivory sheet and draped it over her, the fabric billowing down over her legs and torso. "Sorry about the lack of privacy."

"Who undressed me?" Blood rushed to her cheeks and warmed them.

"And sorry again. That would be me. But your clothes weren't damaged at all and are safely put away." He smiled, showing even, but slightly yellowed teeth as he picked up a clipboard and made a note.

"You can't keep me here."

"Sadly, we can." Will's smile didn't fade as he turned away.

Her head throbbed. She wasn't in a proper hospital, that was for sure. A chair rail bisected the room, dividing the burgundy upper walls from the rich velveted lower walls. She'd never seen velvet wallpaper. Thick-framed paintings hung on each wall, depicting sun-washed scenes of family outings. Crown molding highlighted the tall ceiling. A small crystal chandelier lit the room, sometimes throwing colored rays along the walls.

In the far corner, a narrow door, stained a rich brown to match the chair rail, was closed. Above the doorknob, a black electronic scanner. Her unease threatened to take her over. Mecca drew in a deep breath and tried to settle herself.

Against the wall near the door, Mecca's satchel laid beneath a pine writing desk, propped against a heavily engraved leg. A burgundy upholstered Queen Anne wing chair was tucked against the desk. Papers lay scattered across the desk's surface. She couldn't see the writing on the papers from her bed. Were those the things she'd printed out at the library?

"How long have I been here?"

Will didn't reply, his attention focused on sucking some liquid into a syringe.

"My dad will call the police. They'll find me."

Will turned back to her with the syringe poised in one hand. "They'll find you if Emilia wants them to find you." He slipped the needle into the butterfly portal of the I.V. and pushed the plunger. It only took moments before Mecca's eyelids became heavy.

"What do you want with me?" She knew her words were jumbled, but she kept trying to speak, even as darkness clouded in. "Let me go."

When she came out of the darkness, Mecca lay silent, her eyes closed.

The rough leather cuffs still held her wrists, but the pressure of the belt over her hips was gone. That was something, at least. Though she couldn't feel it, she assumed the I.V. still had a home in her hand. She tried to shift her foot.

Damn it. Her legs remained immobile.

Why did they snatch her, and who kept her strapped to a bed in a windowless room?

Of course, there could only be one answer. She'd spent the last two days and nights researching vampires on the assumption that they— or something like them — existed. Apparently, that theory panned out way more than she'd expected. She'd found them.

Or rather, they'd found her. She still doubted the actual vampire theory. Which was more plausible, that vampires existed or that a bunch of crazy people *thought* they were vampires?

But why did they keep her here, drugged? She knew the secret of their existence — regardless of whether they were vampires or not. She supposed it made her a liability. She understood that. So why didn't they just kill her and be done with it?

Not that she wanted to die. Not that she wouldn't fight with everything she had. But they had plenty of opportunities to get rid of her. Why hadn't they?

And, more important, where was *here* and how was she going to get away?

Some part of her recognized that she was being a lot more analytical than she would have expected of herself.

The door opened. The soft clack of a shoe meeting the hardwood floor coupled with a sudden electric jolt that flashed through Mecca's belly. For a moment, every sense heightened. Sounds came clear and distinct. Will's breathing and the skitter of the shoes seemed to rise and become more distinct. The air brushed against her exposed skin like calm waves on a sun-drenched, sandy shore. Mecca barely kept from gasping at the overwhelming sensations.

"Has she come around?" The woman's smooth and throaty voice raised gooseflesh on Mecca's arms.

"She hasn't opened her eyes since the last dose," Will said, "but her breathing changed a while ago, so I suspect she's awake."

"Very good. Go eat. Be back in an hour."

Mecca heard Will leave the room with quiet steps. She slowed her breathing and concentrated her attention on listening. This was her enemy. Only the sound of the stranger's footfalls alerted her to the woman's movements. And then those sounds stopped. Silence ruled her small prison cell, but an electric current continued to pulse in her veins.

"Why do you lie there, feigning sleep?" the woman asked.

Mecca made no reply.

"Look at me."

The urge to obey rose up, shocking and unpalatable, sour in her mind, like the taste of bile at the back of her throat. She struggled to keep from opening her eyes.

"Very well. Keep them closed for now."

The need to obey swept away in a wind, and Mecca released her breath slowly, unaware that she'd been holding it. Her senses settled down as well. Sounds, the air, everything finally registered as it should.

What just happened?

"You're an interesting young woman, Ms. Trenow. That's why I brought you here. Yet imagine my surprise when your bag was opened to reveal your research abilities. If I didn't have other plans for your more unique talents, I'd consider bringing you on as an information gatherer."

The soft rustle of paper reached Mecca's ears.

"But that's not where your *real* strength lies, is it?" She waited a short moment before continuing. "I did some digging based on a bit of information you'd already gathered. I hope you don't mind." The woman barked a quiet cough. It sounded staged. "There were more women than these, you know."

The print out. That grainy photo. *White Widower.*

Mecca finally opened her eyes to look at the owner of this voice, her heart strumming a wild tattoo in her chest. That website contained awful, terrible insinuations about Dad, and she didn't believe them. She wouldn't even believe in the *possibility* of it being truth. He wasn't a murderer. He was her father. But still, she opened her eyes.

"You're lying," Mecca said. She twisted her wrists in the cuffs. "I don't know why, but you are."

"No, I'm most definitely not."

The woman sat in the chair beside the bed with one leg draped over the other, a stack of papers resting on her knee. She had Asian features: a small nose, almond-shaped eyes and high cheekbones. Black hair cut in a severe pageboy style framed her round face. She looked tiny in that chair and younger than Mecca would have expected. She could imagine having a class at the university with this woman.

"You're Emilia?"

"Yes."

"Why am I here? Why didn't you just kill me?" Did she really want to know this?

The corners of Emilia's mouth curled as she smiled. Some part of Mecca expected her teeth to be long and thin. They turned out to be small, square, and compact. Just teeth. Not fangs.

"There is information you have that I want. Keeping you this way" —she waved a hand at the room— "seemed much more conducive to getting that information."

"What information?"

"You killed someone recently."

How could she know that? Mecca's face grew hot, and she looked across the room at the wooden door with its electronic lock. This woman knew she killed that Hayden guy. How? Had she seen? Shame threatened to overwhelm her. She fought to keep tears from her eyes.

"Tell me how you did it."

Again, that need to speak pushed at her mind. Mecca knew how she'd killed him, though she had no idea how she would explain it to someone, even if she wanted to explain it. Emilia watched with her eyes like black marbles and the urge to spill everything about that night in the parking lot hit harder. Mecca closed her eyes. "I don't know what you mean."

The pressure to speak came stronger and then passed. Mecca gasped, relieved, feeling like a stone had been lifted from her chest. When she opened her eyes, Emilia still watched her, but a smile flitted along her thin pink lips. After a moment, she stood and dropped a news clipping onto Mecca's lap.

"That is Susan Harrington — or, rather *was* Susan Harrington."

Mecca couldn't keep from looking at the newspaper copy. A small article mourned the death of a local Chicago philanthropist to a mystery illness. A statuesque woman in her fifties, with dark hair, smiled out at her. Beside the photo was another candid shot, this one of her husband, a non-local twenty years her junior. According to the caption, they'd wed the summer before, after a whirlwind romance on the tennis court of the local country club.

That young husband had Mecca's smile. On his head grew the same unruly curls that her father now fought with a flat top haircut. In the photo, he wore a black suit and a frown.

Emilia continued. "She was a very well respected woman in the Chicago area. Her first husband died of prostate cancer, I believe, and left her extremely well off." She slid the article into a manila folder at the bottom of her stack and then laid another clipping in the same place on Mecca's leg. "Carol Dodson. Her mother was heir to a coffee dynasty and had already left her more money than she could possibly have spent in her own lifetime. Your father was twenty-four when he met her."

Mecca grimaced, but couldn't keep her eyes from being drawn to the clip. She hated that she wanted to read. But wasn't it better to know the truth? Part of her screamed, "No!" but she read the clip anyway.

There stood her father again with those same curls. He didn't look as old as in the previous photo. A young woman's arm looped through his, and they both wore formalwear. A glittering diamond necklace graced her throat, a facet reflecting the flash from the camera.

According to the article, Carol Dodson also died of a mysterious wasting disease that doctors and researchers had since been studying diligently. Mecca leaned back and glared at the ceiling. She didn't even want to touch the tangle of feelings surging through her. Disbelief, confusion, fear, anger.

Emilia made an amused sound, before she gathered up the clipping. "Unfortunately, I have some business to attend to and I don't yet trust you. So I am going to direct Will to administer another sedative. When you wake, you will be allowed limited movement and all of this paperwork will be available to you." She dropped the folder onto the table, before she turned to look at Mecca again. "Where would I find your father?"

Mecca's raised her head to meet Emilia's gaze. She whispered, "Fuck you."

Chapter Five: David

David paced his office. It wasn't like Mecca not to answer her phone. She'd missed their breakfast plans, and he couldn't get hold of her all day. He'd called the friends he knew about and none of them had been able to help. Josie hadn't even seen her. And those two were joined at the hip.

He couldn't shake the thought that Mecca being missing had something to do with what happened the night before. Dread crawled through his bones like ants. He didn't like this helplessness. The last time he'd felt this way was when Teresa had been sick. And he'd been truly helpless then.

That couldn't happen again.

David scooped up his cell phone from his desk and dialed Jim Barron, his best friend and once a top D.A. for Fulton County. Jim now sat on the City Council and schmoozed regularly with his old friends in law enforcement. If anyone could find something out under the radar, it would be Jim. David just wasn't sure how to explain why he wanted it under the radar.

David didn't give him much of a chance for small talk once he answered. "Jim, I need a favor."

"Sure. Shoot." It sounded like Jim was working late, from the *tap-tap-tap* of computer keys.

"I haven't heard from Mecca all day. We were supposed to get breakfast this morning, and she never came by. All of my calls went to voicemail."

The tapping stopped. "Do you want me to send someone by her dorm?"

"I've already called her roommate and several of her friends. She's not in her room, and no one's seen her."

"I can get a couple guys to look into it. We can't file a missing person report until tomorrow, but we can get them on it now."

David hesitated. Above all, he needed to keep Mecca's secret. But there was no way he would turn down help finding her, especially when he didn't even know how to begin searching. "Yeah. That would be good, if you don't mind."

"God, Dave, of course I don't mind. Let me make a few calls. When was the last time you talked to her?"

"Last night." David weighed out his options and decided to see if he could get any extra information. "The other night someone attacked her outside a coffee shop near campus."

"Shit. Did she report it?"

"No. She came straight here. She wasn't hurt, just shaken up. But she's a bit wary right now, so we've been talking a lot more often." The panic he'd been holding at bay ramped up for a moment — that feeling of uselessness and lack of control. He shoved it back into the little hole he'd banished it to earlier in the day.

"She's probably fine," Jim said, his tone even. "Maybe spending time with a guy or putting in some extra hours on a paper or something."

"Don't try to placate me, Jim. I'm worried. This isn't like her."

"I know."

"Are there other reports of attacks near campus lately?"

"I'll ask when I make my phone calls. Is there anything else you can think of that I can pass on to them?"

"I need her home."

"We'll find her. I'll call you back with an update as soon as I can."

"Thanks." David disconnected the call. He'd hoped talking to Jim would have eased some of his anxiety, but he still felt just as edgy as before. The lighter's flame surged as he lit a cigarette, and then he paced for a while longer. Four different times, he picked up his phone but didn't know who to call, so he put it down again each time. He considered going out and looking for Mecca — again — but still had nowhere to begin the search.

Finally, he booted up the computer on his desk. It, along with every other piece of electronics in his house, was state of the art. Computers had become an obsession for him after his wife died. Too much time creeping around his days, most likely. As a result, he'd wired his home with the latest gadgetry, including controls for all his lights, heating and air conditioning, and locks on the doors. Definitely an early adopter of the smart home tech.

He hadn't even opened a web browser when a message came through.

Solaris: My taser finally came in!

Solaris — Sara — had taught him most of what he learned about computer security. And hacking. David smiled at her excitement and then typed in his response, letting the cigarette dangle from his lips.

Nereus: Congrats. Didn't you order it a month ago?
Solaris: Yeah. Had to call and give them some shit. When are we getting together? I've been here for a few months now and I still haven't even gotten to meet you.

David didn't have the energy to deal with this right now. When Sara had contacted him out of the blue last year, with her mom's blessing, he'd been apprehensive. When she'd enrolled in Atlanta State — Mecca's school — at the beginning of the term, he'd all but   panicked. He'd been begging off any chance of meeting for weeks. He knew he wouldn't be able to put her off forever. After all, he was still her grandmother's widower. But he couldn't just walk away. He couldn't ignore her. In that respect, age — and perhaps having fallen in love — had changed him.

Solaris: Hello?

Nereus: Sorry. Can't meet this week. I've got a crisis going on.
Solaris: Can I help?
Nereus: Don't think so, but thanks.

Knee-jerk, but David wondered whether she could help. If he just had some place to start…

The phone startled him. He grabbed it on the second ring. "David Trenow."

"Hey, it's Jim. I've got some guys talking to Mecca's friends and checking out the coffee shops around the school. Give them a couple hours and hopefully we'll have something. Want to come around for a drink? You don't have to wait alone."

David wasn't sure he wanted company at all. He was already champing at the bit.

"I did learn that there have been some weird assaults in the area lately. I can fill you in."

Well, that decided it.

"I'll be there in fifteen minutes." He hung up.

Nereus: Need to run. Talk later.
Solaris: Yeah. Right.

David signed off, unwilling to placate her. He hadn't asked her into his life, after all. He put the computer into sleep mode, stubbed out his smoke, and went to find his shoes. Feeling guilty about Sara wasn't on his to do list.

—➤➤◄◄◄—

Thirty minutes later — damned Atlanta traffic — David turned onto the long driveway that led to the Georgian colonial nestled among towering pines, surrounded by a rich, green, manicured lawn. He parked in front of the garage and hadn't even gotten up the porch steps when the thick wooden door opened.

Looking comfortable in old jeans and a midnight blue turtleneck, Jim stepped back to let him enter. "How are you doing?"

"I haven't lost it or anything. You know I don't jump to conclusions, but I've got a bad feeling. Thanks for helping out."

"Not a problem." Jim closed the door and led him through the grey granite-floored foyer into the warm coziness of the living room. They turned right and passed through a set of double doors into his office. "It's Carolyn's bridge night, so the place is ours. Scotch and soda?"

"That's fine, thanks." David wandered the room, glancing at the bookshelves he'd seen hundreds of times. Most titles were related to law. He listened to the clink of ice in the glass and the soft cracking as Jim poured scotch over it.

A walnut desk, along with several large, leather armchairs converged in the center of the room. Three Patrick Nagel prints hung on the walls, looking out of place with their art deco style and bright colors. A massive bay window on the south wall offered a stunning view of the cabana and pool, lit by colored floodlights. The light flickered across the surface of the water, winking at him.

"Here you go." Jim held the drink out to him and motioned the chairs. "I spoke to someone at the Little Five precinct. They're investigating rumors of a cult on the ASU campus. It's a small group led by an outsider who's conned some of the college kids into going along."

"So, what, they've been going after people?" The scotch, though exceptionally smooth on the way down, had an after bite. "Do you think that's who might have attacked Mecca?"

Jim raised a hand. "I have no way of knowing. She'll need to give them a statement. Details of what happened, a description. That sort of thing. But we've had someone inside, undercover, for a couple weeks." Jim leaned forward, elbows on knees and his scotch glass dangling from his fingers. "It sounds pretty gruesome. They think they're vampires."

David sat up straighter. "Vampires?"

"Yeah. They practice bloodletting together and they seem to be interested in expanding their circle. The undercover guy says they're gathering drugs — roofies and GHB. He witnessed an attack on a homeless man out near the rail yard where one of them — a kid who's quite invested in this group, according to our guy — almost killed the man, trying to drink his blood."

David sat speechless for a moment. Was this for real? Mecca said the man who attacked her had been older and alone — except for the watcher. Not young, and certainly not a member of a pack. That didn't mean the asshole hadn't been part of whatever Jim was talking about. But it seemed... Strange. Well, stranger than he had even already accepted. David studied his friend. Could Jim be lying? He didn't want to think so. But this made little sense. "They're drugging people and biting them?" Could Mecca *have* been drugged? It could explain her loss of control over her Gift.

An abrupt movement in the bay window caught David's attention. He stood. "There's something outside."

Jim glanced over his shoulder, craning his body toward the window. "Out there? Probably just Mojo, our lab. She hangs out around the pool, especially at night. She chases frogs. Nothing to worry about."

David lowered himself back to the chair, head swimming. Must have stood up too quickly. He peered at his glass, half-drained, and set it on the table between them.

"Not to your taste?"

"Driving. Don't want to overdo it." David concentrated on forming his words. They sounded garbled in his ears. He felt strange. Prickly. "Is there more? To the vampire group?"

"The one kid who attacked the homeless guy apparently bought custom fangs and has started dressing like the vampires in that TV show. The one set in Louisiana, you know? He's been 'hunting' around the Little Five area. So it's definitely possible he was the person who attacked Mecca."

David's gut twisted. Jim was lying. David had known him a long time. And he was lying.

A shadow crossed the window. This time, David was sure. He jumped from his seat. The room lurched like a ship in a windstorm. He stumbled against the coffee table, knocking his knee. A dull pain registered.

"Dave?" Jim stood. "Are you okay?"

"There's —" Confusion and fear coursed through him. His words wouldn't string together properly. He couldn't get his mouth around them. "Outside. Someone — outside." He fell back into the chair with a heavy head. He let his eyes close because they really wanted to be closed. His belly lurched and part of him recognized that he might puke.

An unfamiliar voice came from behind him, one with a thick Irish brogue. "Good job, capt'n."

"I'm never going to do something like this again." Jim's tone was dark and low. "Tell her."

The Irishman laughed. "You'll do as bidden."

"What do you want with him?"

"Not your business, capt'n."

"She said he wouldn't be hurt."

David heard a snort before burly hands grabbed him beneath the arms. They hauled him to his feet. A fleeting vision of Mecca flashed behind his closed eyelids. She looked cornered in a cave. No. A tunnel. Surrounded. And one of those surrounding her owned the eyes through which he saw her.

The scene faded; he tried to move his limbs, but they weighed a million pounds each. He couldn't hold on to consciousness and everything went black.

He rose through the darkness, his body rocking as he slowly came to recognize a sledgehammer's insistent pounding between his ears. Fuzzy-headed, he tried to open his eyes. He couldn't.

He squinted, contracting his muscles, and felt the tape, hard and thick on his skin. Another piece covered his mouth, leaving only his nostrils open. He lay on his side on a hard metal floor. He jostled in time with the vehicle's fast clip. No carpet under him. Probably a van.

A voice, incoherent, slipped into his fogged senses. He shifted very slowly, testing the mobility of his limbs. His forearms arms were together and secured at the wrists; coarse fabric rubbed his knuckles. It was like they'd put cloth over his hands and bound the whole with tape.

He tried to spread his legs, but resistance pulled at his ankles and thighs. Voices slipped into his hearing, the fuzz still heavy on his brain, but lifting.

"What time is it?" a deep male voice asked.

"Ten past. We've got time. Emilia wants him at the compound before midnight." Again the brogue he'd heard at Jim's.

Jim.

Jim's call, the talk of cults, the drink. His mind began to function again, and he pieced together what must have happened. With the thought of each step leading to his capture, David's anger rose. *Betrayed.*

"This is twice in a row we've done for her."

"Aye," Irish replied.

"Why do you think she's wanting these two?"

David strained to hear.

"Don't know."

"There's been talk that the girl's the one who killed Hayden. And, you know, as much as he drove Emilia and the Elders nuts, he wasn't stupid. I knew him, and I can tell you, that wasn't a stupid man, there. How'd you think she did it? She's not very big. I heard he just dried up and died. Think that's true?" The edge of excitement in the man's voice grated on David's nerves.

"Don't know."

"Think that has anything to do with covering his hands and stuff? This guy's, I mean. No skin contact. Same with her the other night."

"You'd prolly do well to shut your gab hole. She don't like gossips."

"All right. All right."

The van rumbled along for several more minutes, rocking David against a wheel well. He'd have a bruise on his hip from that alone. He replayed the evening in his mind, trying to figure out why Jim would drug him and hand him over to two thugs.

He must be in bed with this Emilia woman.

That was the only explanation. Jim had always been honest and honorable; he'd never been the type to take bribes or accept favors. How many times over a beer in the backyard had Jim complained of all the people and organizations that wanted him in their pockets? So what the hell was this?

And now they had Mecca. He'd gotten a brief memory-flash of her in the tunnel. The university? Probably. The Irishman had definitely watched her there, been a part of her abduction. David pushed back fear for her that threatened to grip his heart in a vise. He couldn't panic.

God, his head hurt. The pain suppressed his urge to jump up and kill the two men in the front of the van. It would do him no good to let them know he was awake. Blinded and bound, he would be relying on nothing but luck to keep him alive. He preferred better odds.

"You think I should give him a shot of the stuff we used on the girl?"

"Aye. He didn't drink much, so he'll be waking soon, I reckon. Shoot 'im up."

Shit. He'd wanted to keep quiet until they stopped the van, and he could go after the men separately. This changed things.

He didn't have time to try to free himself. So he lay still on the floor of the van and listened. The road noise was still very loud, but after a few moments, the sound of the passenger getting out of his seat made it to David's ears. David kept his breathing regular, but his heart beat like a heavy metal drummer.

"All right, big man. Time to dope you up some more."

Hold. Quiet. Wait for it.

It only took the man a few steps to reach him. As soon as David felt him crouch down, he grabbed in the man's direction. He opened his hands like a clam and snapped them shut around an ankle.

"Ah fuck!" The man kicked at David's forearm with his free foot. The van shook as the guy fell onto his ass. Pain radiated up David's arm. He couldn't keep his hold on the ankle, and the man tore away.

"What the bloody hell?" Irish's shout from the front came coupled with the van jostling to the right and then the left.

The tinkling of plastic on metal barely registered over the rumbling of the van.

Another kick landed in the same spot on David's arm, and he shouted, his voice muffled by the tape.

"I got him! I got him!"

David pushed himself onto his knees, blind, bound, but with adrenaline singing in his veins. A rustle to his right, very close. Then an explosion of fireworks as something hard and heavy connected with the side of his head. On instinct, he tried to brace as he toppled to his left but landed hard on his elbow. His shoulder connected with the wheel well with a crunch and a riotous flash of fire.

For just a moment, David couldn't move. He lay there, his breath hard in his chest, spirals of pain echoing from his shoulder down his arm. The scent of burnt oil prickled his nose.

But he couldn't stay down. Couldn't stay still. He couldn't let them knock him out. If they did, he wouldn't be able to help Mecca.

He rolled away from the wall of the van with all the momentum he could and slammed into the thug's ankles. The guy landed on top of him with a heavy crash and a string of swear words. His weight nearly blew David's breath out of him.

"Goddammit," came Irish's voice from the front as the van slowed dramatically. "Can't do a fucking thing right."

David hooked his bound hands over the man's head and held him in a tight bear hug. His captive thrashed and jerked. David heaved and rolled himself over, pinning the man beneath him.

He sent out his energy and the Cavern unfolded itself within his mind.

The van shook and they both slid into the wheel well.

With his eyes blinded, the sensations he felt with his energy increased and the Cavern's details crystallized in clear detail.

Mecca had been right. He'd never felt anything like this cold cave, this strange creature's energy center. Dark, desolate, it contained nothing but a stolen soul. The small thing glowed a pale yellow gold, tethered to the Cavern wall with thick, grey, rope-like tendrils. The edges of the soul had no tint at all.

Remembering how Mecca had done it, David reached his own energy out and encompassed it with all the strength he could muster. His own gold, with dark silver edging, held the little pale ball tight. He pulled.

"What the fuck!" Terror colored the man's words, making his voice high and squeaky.

A knee connected with David's thigh, but the impact barely measured for David. A stunted bloom of pain welled, but it didn't matter. He held on tight with his body as he tore the life force from the thing. The muted, golden energy began to stretch beneath the dark vines and, after a moment, finally broke away.

David fought blind, could only see the Cavern; that ugly, ugly cave. But he knew it was almost over. The body below lost its bulk; the muscles atrophied beneath his touch. The creature writhed beneath as the van shook again. And then it stopped moving.

The stolen life flew out of the cavern and slammed into him, a bolt of energy striking David's core like lightning. He shuddered and groaned. Every nerve in his body fired. The charge washed over him like the ocean over a beach in a hurricane — violent, chaotic, stunning. It electrified every cell.

And then he couldn't breathe. Something had clamped around his neck, hauling him off the dead thing. The feather-light body fell from between his bound hands.

David kicked, his feet wedging on the van floor, and he pushed backward against his assailant. They both slammed into the side of the van. The whoosh of Irish's breath being pushed out of him gave David some satisfaction. The hold on David's neck loosened for a moment, but then Irish got his grip again and the edges of David's vision speckled black.

Push. Get to his Cavern.

David sent his energy out, frantically, and the Cavern rose in his mind. It looked almost identical to the other, except this one's stolen ball was much bigger and trimmed in pale blue. It almost lit the entire Cavern; and what looked like *hundreds* of tendrils held it fast to the wall. David wasn't sure he could do this again.

The tightening, hot feeling of having held a breath too long came over him. Rockets launched behind his eyelids and flashing black specks swam along the edges. He couldn't pass out. Not now.

He encircled the stolen soul with his own energy and set to work on the tendrils.

"The hell?" Irish yelled into his ear.

And then David flew. He slammed into the van wall. Irish's panting breath came loud and stationary, but David knew the thing would come after him any second.

He grabbed the tape over his eyes with his mitted hands, took a deep breath, and pulled with his cloth-covered fingers. Fire tore through his face as the tape took ripped most of his eyelashes right out of the lids. He bellowed a muffled cry. It took most of his eyebrows too and left behind the most searing pain. His face felt as if it had been traced with lighter fluid and set on fire.

It took effort to open his eyes; glue left behind made it painful and slow — slower than he wanted it to be. Through sticky lids, the first thing he saw was Irish — huge, barrel-chested, and pissed —pulling back his meaty fist. David couldn't move fast enough.

The fist crunched against his jaw, and his head slammed against the wall behind him. Stars erupted in

David's vision, and his teeth rattled with the impact. Blood filled his mouth. In that second, though, David saw Mecca in the tunnel again, surrounded, looking for a way out. His vision wavered, undulating like a crazy cartoon for a moment before reality snapped back into focus.

Irish pulled his fist back again, and David grabbed his forearm. He pulled the creature to him.

All his anger and fear for Mecca flooded out. He blasted it into the Irishman. David closed his eyes. His life force — stronger from the energy of his first attack — blazed a trail toward the stolen energy.

Another vision of Mecca — still in the tunnel, but scuffling with her abductors.

The tape over his mouth muffled his cry of rage, and he jerked his eyes open. Irish struggled against him, but David's anger fueled his strength. He pushed forward, moved his bound hands over Irish's head, and they both careered into the other wall.

David battered the grey tentacles with his wrath. The bulky man yelled, but weakened under the violent onslaught. David's raw emotion made him hold Irish tighter, squeeze him harder. He jerked them both to the floor, trapping Irish beneath him right beside the remains of the other creature.

Irish's fighting redoubled, but David hit the struggling thug with every molecule of energy he could. He wanted to make it hurt. Make those last moments soaked through with pain. He wanted to *torture* this monster who stole his daughter.

The Cavern layered itself over his vision again. The tentacles didn't even matter anymore. He tore the ball of life from its abductor.

Irish screamed, high-pitched and wailing. He tried to roll away, pushed at David's chest, but David held on. He was not letting go. When the tendrils finally ripped away, energy rushed into him again. His body quaked with the strength of it. He couldn't control it, so he rode it, wave after wave.

Irish's movements slowed and finally stopped.

He'd never felt anything like this. It was monumental. Nothing like the slow, gentle drain of a human being. This chaotic energy took forever to finally crest, but when it did, it began to settle — the human life energy returned to a human, merged.

He rolled over, panting. "Christ," he whispered.

He laid there for several minutes, listening to his heart race and feeling the energy. It roiled inside him, uneasy, almost overpowering. David forced himself to breath slowly and deeply. He concentrated on the air filling his lungs, expanding his chest. He imagined the oxygen replenishing his blood and the cells in his body.

The energy he willed to become a part of him, to be welcomed home.

He stood. Sweat dripped from his forehead, stinging the skin pulled raw by the tape. He winced and pulled the tape from his lips. Fiery pinpricks assaulted him as some of his stubble came out. His whole face felt hot.

With his teeth, he went after the tape around his wrists that kept his hands covered with the canvas sack. The fabric fell to the ground next to what was left of Irish.

The corpse looked like a mummy. David staggered, his head pounding, his shoulder aching. All of the damage he'd sustained in the fight started to register. Knee, side, face. He bent double and leaned his hands on his knees. His belly roiled and for a second, he thought he would puke.

Deep breaths. Just take deep breaths. Okay, heart, slow down. We need to survive the night so we can find Mecca.

A surprisingly robust version of "Bat Out of Hell" broke the silence in the van and David jumped. The song came from Irish's pants. David rifled the pockets, without looking at the corpse, until he found the cell phone, thirty bucks, and the van's keys.

The display on the phone read *Salas*. David decided against answering, swiped Decline, and pocketed the phone instead. Whoever was at their intended destination would probably miss them soon, and he wanted to have a head start. He needed to come down from the energy drains, and he needed to get something for the pounding between his ears, the aches in his joints, and the fire on his face. And probably food.

More importantly, though, he needed to have a very serious talk with an old friend.

Chapter Six: Mecca

She sits on a cushioned chair in the hallway. The hospital corridor, wide and brightly lit, makes her feel very small. A man in blue pants and shirt gives her a smile as he hurries past. She tries to smile back, but it doesn't work very well. Her face feels like a statue's, and her heart is a great big stone in the middle of her chest. She's been sitting here forever, waiting for her dad to come get her.

The door to the room creaks open and he finally peeks out, giving her a gentle smile that doesn't overtake the sadness in his eyes. "Come on, Sweets. Mommy wants to see you." He holds his hand out, and she slides hers into it, grateful.

She tries not to drag her feet as he leads her into the room. Her belly is in knots, and her knees feel wobbly. She hates the hospital, but mostly she hates that her mom is here. The medicine-y smell itches at her nose.

"Hi, honey." Mom's scratchy voice almost makes her burst into tears.

She struggles with all her twelve-year-old strength to hold it back, but she can't stop the hitch in her voice. "Hi, Mom."

She takes in the bed and bites her lip. Machines surround her mom. One holds a tube attached to her arm. An air tube sits under her nose, like the ones on TV. Her mother is so, so thin. A bandanna replaces the thick dark hair she remembers.

Mecca wants to cry again, just looking at the dark skin under Mom's bloodshot eyes. "Are you okay?" Mecca's voice is tiny, and she hates that.

"Oh, sweetie." Mom holds out an arm and pats the bed. "Come sit down."

She doesn't want to sit there, so close, and guilt sweeps over her. She takes several tiny steps and perches on the very edge of the bed, leaning back into the curve of her mother's arm. She's careful that her skin doesn't touch her mom's.

Even sitting this way, she can feel the weakness and thinness of Mom's limbs.

Her mother squeezes her and kisses the top of her head. She watches her dad take a seat in the corner. She can read his sorrow, even though he gives her a courageous smile.

"Honey, you know I love you more than chocolate, right?" her mom says. Their love has always been better than chocolate.

She turns on the bed and looks at her mom, who sits there with her fading spirit, but with lips curled up in a small smile and eyes filled with love. The bright red of the bandanna makes Mecca think of a bloody head wound, and she twists her body around to bury her face in her mother's bony shoulder.

The weight of everything crashes down onto her head.

"Momma, I want you to come home! I don't want you to be sick anymore!" Sobs wrack her body, and her tears soak the dressing gown. Her mother's hand caresses her head, the finger tracing the little braids along Mecca's scalp.

"Baby…" She hears her mom give a heaving breath and knows that she's crying too. "I don't think — I don't think I'm going to be coming home, sugar."

Fear jets through her, and Mecca pulls away. "What do you mean? You're going to live here?" Her voice is panicked and high-pitched, but she doesn't care. Why would her mom not want to come home?

She watches her parents exchange a glance, and then her mom looks at her. She can see all the love in those eyes, even with the tears escaping and leaving wet paths down her Mom's cheeks. "No, sweetie, I'm not going to live here. I'm very, very sick."

"But you came here so the doctors could make you better. They'll make you better!" She holds the sleeves of her mom's gown, her knuckles pale with her grip.

She wants to scream, to push her mom away, to hold onto her and never let her go.

"You have to come home." She sucks in a ragged breath, and the tears pour down her cheeks. She looks at her dad in his chair, his elbows on the armrest, head bowed, his forehead in his palm. "Daddy, tell her she has to come home. Tell her!" He looks up and she sees the tears on his face too. She lets out another desperate sob.

Her daddy never cries.

--->>><<<---

Mecca clawed herself up from her memory-dream, hot tears burning down her cheeks. Memories of her kidnapping piled back into her mind, and dark despair flitted around the edge of her consciousness like a moth against the glass of a streetlight.

She opened her eyes. A young man sat in the chair nearest her bed, watching her. When she looked at him, her belly flip-flopped. In her ears, the drumming of her heartbeat played a thick beat.

What the hell? He barely looked fifteen and a skinny fifteen at that. But in a few years, with his fine blond curls and deep brown eyes, he would be hot. No doubt.

The classical beauty of his features drew her. Concentrating on him let the terror of her memories fade. She was glad to embrace whatever the electricity was — it made the memory dream go away faster. She pushed the awfulness to the back of her mind and concentrated on the beautiful boy in front of her. She didn't usually go for pretty boys, but he seemed to be an exception.

Yet, if it had been a taste in her mouth, his energy, it would have tasted sweet and savory at once, but with a terrible bitterness below the surface. Strange and unbalanced. Like Hayden's had been. But she couldn't help staring at him. He drew her. Just like Hayden had. *Strange.*

Mecca flushed and looked down. She pushed away the warm feeling that gathered in her. It scared her almost as much as the restraints around her legs.

Her wrists were still cuffed, but the cuffs were no longer fastened to the side rails directly. Several inches of chain on either cuff gave her a much wider range of motion than earlier. She could move her hands nearer each other, but they remained about five inches shy of touching.

As she tested the movement, he spoke. "It's only so you can read through the papers she left for you." His delicate, almost feminine voice had an oddly formal air. It sent tingles over her skin, which she didn't understand.

He rose from his chair, his movements graceful; he reminded her of a dancer — beautiful, fluid. She couldn't take her gaze from him. After retrieving several folders from the table, he brought them to her bedside and laid them on her lap.

"Emilia felt you might find these of interest."

She couldn't place his slight accent. He moved back to his chair and settled down into it, his dark eyes still watching her, making her self-conscious. She finally tore her gaze away and looked down at the papers and folders on her lap.

Aside from her strange attraction to this man, her head felt more clear than before. She thought about her run-in with Hayden. She had rescued the last remnants of someone's soul from him and, in the process, killed him. They wanted to know how in a real bad way.

She shuffled through the papers as she considered her situation. For the first time, they wanted her to stay awake for more than a few moments. She planned to use it to her advantage. She had to get out of here.

She looked again at her restrained arms. What if I could get him over here to touch him? Could I kill him the same way? Or at least put him down for a while. Worth a try. She looked at the boy with his ivory skin.

"Could you fix these cuffs? They're cutting into my wrists."

He regarded her for perhaps two seconds. "No."

"Why not?"

"Because they don't need to be adjusted. You should read the papers Emilia left."

"Well, I have to go to the bathroom."

"You'll have to wait."

"For what?"

"For William. Or I can put you back to sleep." He looked pointedly at a medical cabinet across the room.

She wouldn't beg him. She turned to the papers.

What if he *wasn't* one of those creatures?

The question struck her out of the blue. Maybe she had to wait for Will because they didn't trust this guy could handle her. Didn't trust that he couldn't keep her under control. He was so young, so small. Maybe they thought she could overpower him. She easily had about forty pounds on him. She couldn't help peeking at him sidelong.

"If you're not going to look through those, there's no reason to keep you awake, Ms. Trenow."

A jolt jerked through her belly when he said her name.

What the actual hell was going on? She tried to read his face but met only a bland expression. He pointed to her lap, and she felt drawn to the papers there. She closed her eyes and took a deep breath, confused by the last few minutes. *What is it about him?*

She decided to ignore it. If she couldn't figure him out, she'd pretend he didn't exist. She turned her attention to the folders she'd only shuffled around before. Emilia had said that the website mentioned only three women, but that they'd found more.

Dread settled in her belly when she thought about what that seemed to mean. She still couldn't believe it. She wouldn't.

Mecca opened the first folder. It was like rubber-necking on the highway. She didn't want to see it, but she couldn't help herself. On top rested a photocopy of a marriage license between David Brynn, age 19, and Adele Cooper, age 31, married in Orange County, California. Nested beneath, she found copies of the newspaper wedding announcement — there were his eyes again, an article about the new Cooper Exhibition Room added to a museum and other articles extolling the new Mrs. Brynn's generous nature.

The final article, dated two years after the wedding announcement, concerned the woman's untimely death. Mr. and Mrs. Brynn returned from a two month long holiday in South America, cutting their trip short by a month, when Mrs. Brynn caught some illness while in Brazil. She died within a week.

Her distraught husband became a hermit, never leaving the house and taking no outside calls. He eventually moved away from California, citing his inability to cope with his loss. Doctors never isolated the cause of death.

A handwritten note on the bottom said that no further activity under the name David Brynn could be found a year after her death.

Mecca fought tears as she closed that folder and laid it aside. She opened the next: a marriage license for David Marsden, age 23, and Carol Dodson, age 45, married in Pima County, Arizona. Underneath the marriage license laid a death certificate for Carol Marsden. Cause of death: Undetermined.

Mecca's heart ached and her mind whirled. When she'd printed out that web page, she'd hoped that it wasn't her dad. Maybe her eyes had played tricks. But if all of this was true, her dad was a murderer. A murderer. He'd used the Gift to kill those women. How else could they have died?

And that meant that he'd been lying to Mecca since the beginning. The Gift hadn't skipped him. Not at all.

Her heart broke. She had never suspected he would lie about that — or anything. Growing up, she'd always trusted his word. Now, she didn't know whether she could. Her belly felt leaden. She wouldn't be able to move right now even if she weren't attached to the bed. Her entire body seemed frozen.

He'd *always* said the Gift skipped over him, that it had gone to his brother, Ken. When he'd trained her in how to control it so she wouldn't accidentally drain someone, he'd always said he knew how it worked because his father trained him along with Uncle Ken, not because he had it.

She couldn't see any other explanation for those women's deaths though. For someone who didn't know about the family Gift, the women's deaths would always be a mystery.

But she knew.

She thought about all the things he'd taught her: how to control her power, how to be careful and only use it in large groups, so that no one person would bear all the drain. He taught her how to take only a little and only when she needed it.

Bitterness washed over her. She sighed.

"Not particularly light reading, is it?"

She'd forgotten about the man-boy sitting the chair, and his words startled her. Had he been watching her the entire time? She didn't respond, only looked at him.

"I imagine he did it for the money, wouldn't you say?"

The lilt in his voice edged into Mecca's mind. Her belly did another flip. "What interest do you have in my dad? Why did you do all this?" She hoped the anger in her voice would hide the fear in her heart. She wasn't sure it had.

He stood and smiled, his lips curling back, exposing small, square teeth. She'd half expected fangs to protrude from his jaw. Again. The idea of vampires had crept into the back of her mind again when she hadn't been paying attention.

Even without fangs, though, the smile looked feral. She suddenly realized that he looked ancient, as if thousands of years hid behind his eyes.

"Come now, Mecca." Honey-voiced now as he stepped to within a foot of her bed rail. "We can't give away all the answers." He chuckled, dry and deep in his throat. "How was that for a movie villain? Was I convincing?"

A terrible thought struck her. Emilia may be her enemy and might be the more immediate threat, but this man… She could *taste* the danger around this man. Though he looked like a boy, he wasn't. It would be naive to think he would be easy to overpower. She'd begun a dance with a tiger.

"What's your name?" she asked. She heard another soft, rumbling chuckle as he crossed his arms over his narrow chest. The gesture made him seem bigger. Or perhaps it was her shift in perspective. When he didn't answer, she added, "You know my name. It's only fair."

"I suppose that's true. Though nothing is fair in this life, of course." He raised both brows and offered that smile again. "My name is Claude Kassinzi."

"Okay, Claude." The name slipped along her tongue sweetly. She ignored that sweetness as much as she could. Dipping into her reserve of bravado, she put aside the betrayal she felt about her father. "So one of your guys died. Emilia told me. He a friend of yours? Is that why you're here?"

"No. I didn't know him."

"Then what's the big deal? People die all the time."

Claude sauntered around her bed. Predatory. "Yes. *People* do die all the time."

She narrowed her eyes. How much could she get from him? "But not your kind of people." She paused, her fingertip playing with the edge of a folder. "So your friend didn't make the regular meeting of the fanged folk, and you want to know what the little black chick had to do with it?"

Amusement flickered in his eyes, and he laughed, loud and throaty. She would have expected his laugh to be more like a twitter. Another deception.

"You could say that," he said. "We do not die easily."

"Who is we?"

He didn't respond right away and when he did, it wasn't to answer her question. "You must understand, Emilia will find out what she wishes to know." He glided back to his chair and settled into it. "It is only a matter of time. And that is something we have in abundance."

"I guess that's true, if the stories are right."

"Stories?" He looked openly puzzled.

"Vampire tales."

He laughed once again, this one closer to the twitter she'd originally expected. "Yes, well, you wouldn't want to assume to know everything about us based on those."

"So you're vampires?" What a surreal conversation. She just asked a fifteen year old boy if he was a vampire.

"Don't be ridiculous. Everyone knows vampires don't exist. How could they? They're dead."

"But you're not human. Or not people?"

The calculated gaze he laid on her felt like a heavy blanket. After he'd studied her face for a moment, he responded, "Not as such, no." He smiled at her and her belly wriggled again, but then he shifted his gaze to the door.

Mecca wasn't surprised when it opened. Emilia entered, dressed in a silver ball gown with a light, sheer wrap. Will followed, still in scrubs, and closed the door behind her. Rectangular glasses sat on the bridge of his nose.

"Claude," Emilia said, "you will be attending, yes?"

He shot Mecca an enigmatic smile, and then stood. He bowed at the waist and extended a hand, palm up, to Emilia. She slid her own into it, her olive skin dark against Claude's porcelain white.

"You look stunning, as always," Claude said. "And yes, I shall attend." His lips brushed her knuckles before he straightened and released her hand.

"Will is staying with our guest tonight, so you may leave to prepare, if you wish."

"Very well." Claude turned to Mecca and inclined his head. "Good evening." When she made no reply, he gave an amused snort, and then slid past Emilia and Will.

"He seems very theatrical," Mecca said, when Claude left the room. Now that he was gone, she felt like punching him.

Emilia chuckled as she took a clipboard from the table. She glanced over it, before handing it to Will. "Give her another hour to read. Then she sleeps."

Will nodded.

"What is it you're afraid I'm going to do?" Mecca lifted her cuffed wrists to the extent of the attached chains and shook them. She pulled against them with all her strength. Adrenaline pulsed through her. "You've got me shackled to the damned bed! Why do you feel the need to drug me too?"

Emilia barely glanced at her before she returned her attention to Will. "Let me know if anything changes."

Will nodded again.

Emilia strode to the bed, sparing a brief glance at the folders lying on Mecca's lap. "And what do you think of the results from our little information gathering spree?"

"All very interesting, though I don't see what use it is to you."

"I know you're not that stupid." Emilia's jaw tightened. She crossed her hands over her chest; Will seemed to fade into the background. It was a startling effect, but not quite to the level of Claude's. Mecca wondered if they drugged her more than just to make her sleep.

"I've handled you with kid gloves so far, but that courtesy is coming to an end soon. When you've finished reading those, you and I will have a very long talk. It will be in your best interest to be honest with me. And then I will ask you a very important question." Emilia gave her a pointed look, and then turned and left the room with a clacking of heels.

Mecca wanted to come off the bed at her. *What a bitch.*

Will checked Mecca's I.V. bag. "You should tell her what she wants to know."

"Why would I do that?" Mecca drew in a long, quiet breath and worked on stilling her anger.

"Because she'll have the information whether you want her to or not. It will just be easier on you if you offer it." Now he checked the rubber tubing, following it down to the butterfly portal on the top of her left hand. His fingertips grazed along her skin, and he smiled at her.

Mecca grabbed Will's wrist with lightning speed. She shot her energy out, ready to rip away the stolen human life.

His Cavern slid on top of the reality her eyes showed her. There were no tendrils holding the golden light. The light suffused the entire area. The warmth of his Cavern startled her.

She gasped and jerked her hand away. "You're human!"

"Yes." Will stepped away and marked something on the clipboard. He didn't look surprised, but the downturn of his mouth told her she disappointed him.

"You can help me. We can escape together!" Hope burned in her. "Get me out of these cuffs, and we can go. Quick, while they're at their party."

Will sat in the chair and settled an ankle on the knee of the other leg. He pushed his glasses up the bridge of his nose. "Where would we go?"

"Anywhere. Once the sun comes up, they won't be able to look for us. We'll find a safe place." She shook her shackled wrists. "Come on!" She could find her dad. As much as his past made her sick, he would know what to do now.

"What does the sun have to do with it?"

"They can't go out in the daylight."

Confusion slid across his face. Then he laughed. "You think they're vampires?"

Now Mecca felt stupid. Of course vampires in real life sounded ridiculous. She knew that. But it also seemed like the only plausible — "plausible" being relative — idea, even with Claude's warning not to believe what she'd heard about them.

She didn't say anything. All the excitement about possible escape had drained from her.

Will leaned forward and touched her forearm with his fingertips and then withdrew. When he spoke, his tone was gentle. "I can understand why you might think that. I thought it at first too. Much of what became vampire legends came from us trying to understand what we saw them doing, being. That's my idea, anyway. They're not dead humans. They're like us, but different. They're called Visci."

Visci. At least now she had a name for them.

Will watched her and his grey eyes had gone tight, his jawline rigid.

"I'm not releasing you. There would be no place to go. Nowhere to hide. We would both be back here by tomorrow."

Mecca shook her head. There had to be a way.

"You don't understand them. I do. We wouldn't win."

"You don't know that."

"Of course I know that. I've been with them a very long time. I know their relentlessness. We wouldn't be gone twenty-four hours before they'd have us back in here. And then I'd be chained right next to you." He leaned back in the chair. "If they even let me live."

"You can't have been with them that long. You can't be more than a few years older than me."

Will looked at her over the glasses perched on his narrow nose. "You ask too many questions. You have less than an hour. You should use it wisely." He turned his attention to the clipboard on the table. Dismissed.

"Why do you stay?" Being dismissed didn't mean she had to *accept* being dismissed.

The muscles in Will's jaw tightened. "Where would I go? I wouldn't survive a year without them."

"Why?"

"Why does it matter? Read your papers. Consider your conversation with Emilia tomorrow, and think about your own situation. Mine is none of your concern."

Mecca opened her mouth and then sighed. Will's posture told her he wouldn't answer anything more. Not yet, anyway. She thought he wanted to. Maybe the questions she asked hit too close to home. Maybe she hadn't found the right question yet.

Will might be persuaded to help her escape, but it would take time. But how much time she had, Mecca didn't have any way of knowing. She shuffled through the papers on her lap without really seeing any of it. She had to find a way out.

Escape wouldn't be easy. She had no idea where she was being held. Was she even still in Atlanta? Only one door into or out of her windowless room. And Will had used a keycard to unlock that door. She couldn't even see a way to get out of her bonds by herself, and none of those guarding her seemed easily out-smarted. They — the Visci? — had left only her hands and her head bare and they avoided getting too near, either. They feared her, but not tons. At least they remained wary of her touch.

"Will?"

"Yes?"

"Why did they kidnap me?"

Will cocked an eyebrow. The sharpness his voice held earlier was gone. "Because you killed a full blood. I would have thought you knew."

"But how did *they* know? Do they have some weird telepathic thing where they can see what happens to each other?"

Will laughed. "No, no. Don't be silly."

"That's sillier than the existence of blood-sucking...whatever they are?"

"Point taken." He studied Mecca for a long moment. His gaze made her flush. Not the tingly feeling that confused her when Emilia or Claude spoke to her. This seemed more normal. Like she was crushing on him. *Come on, Mecca. No time for Stockholm Syndrome.*

Will shrugged. "Hayden Anderson became something of a black sheep in these last few years. He didn't attend councils. He didn't show up when summoned. He would come when he wanted to come, never when required." He paused and noted something on the clipboard. "He started killing people he shouldn't have been killing."

Mecca reined in most of her questions, settling on only one, in case he didn't continue to feel forthcoming. "They can only kill certain people?"

"Not so much. More precisely, there are certain people they are forbidden to kill. And as I said, Hayden rarely obeyed orders. He began feeding on, then killing, the children of people in high places."

"And Emilia was afraid it would call attention to them."

The corner of his mouth quirked up. "No, not at all. Haven't you yet wondered why in all the time you've lived here, you've never noticed them before? Why you've never heard in the news of any bodies found mysteriously drained of blood?"

Vampires, but not vampires. They don't fear exposure, yet certain people remain off limits. Why? "It's not the

Visci" —the name sounded strange on her lips— "being protected," Mecca thought out loud. "It's the humans. But the powerful ones."

"Well, the families of the powerful ones."

"Because they could be sure of cooperation if the powerful people knew their families would be spared. Or the opposite is likely too. Their families would *not* be spared unless they cooperated."

Will inclined his head. "Just so."

Mecca paused again, still thinking aloud. "Because it's easier to control a city if you control the most powerful within it."

"Hayden killed two college kids. One, the son of a city councilman, the other, the daughter of a state Congresswoman. Emilia and the Elders ordered Hayden be monitored."

Mecca tried not to gasp. The man by the Dumpster. She's totally forgotten about him! It all clicked.

He saw everything. He saw her discover what Hayden was — or, rather, what he wasn't: human — and he saw Hayden wither away to a skeleton. He must have cleaned up the remains. That's why she and Dad didn't find any body or even traces of a crime scene.

"Why didn't they stop me?"

"Why would they? You took care of a difficulty that would have been very sticky for them. When you intervened, they no longer had to worry about convening the council nor about passing judgment on him. You became a very convenient wrinkle at that moment. Now, you're not quite as convenient."

"So they want to know how I did it. Why? To use against each other?"

"Perhaps. They sometimes have problems with rogues like Hayden. And there are other factions, so a power like yours might prove useful."

"Factions? Like political." They had an entire society set up, just underneath the human one. Crazy.

"Somewhat."

"Why are you sharing with me like this?"

"Because in the end, it doesn't matter." Will smiled again, showing straight but lightly stained teeth. "When you meet with her, either you'll agree to whatever it is that Emilia wants, or you won't. If you do, you'll learn all this on your own anyway. If you don't, you won't be in a position to do anything about it."

The timer beeped and startled her. Dread crept along her skin. Will moved to the locked medicine cabinet in the corner.

"Don't put me to sleep yet, Will. Please. You don't have to." Her pleas did earn a pause, but only momentarily before Will began filling the syringe.

"Sorry. You heard Emilia. An hour to read, then to sleep. It's your own fault you didn't read. Though you may wish to jump to the end and read the seventh report."

"Seventh? Emilia said there were six previous women."

"There were."

Mecca flipped the first six folders onto the floor beside her bed and looked at the last one on her lap. She didn't want to open it, but already Will was putting things away in the drug cabinet.

Like the others, a marriage license sat on top of the pile. David Trenow, age 39, and Teresa Stone, age 25. Her mother. Mecca stared for a moment and then turned that sheet over. The next page contained a simple typed report on her parents' marriage, including her own birth and her mother's cancer.

It concluded that "although Teresa Trenow's illness cannot be directly attributed to David Trenow, neither can the woman's death be positively attributed to the cancer itself."

Mecca squeezed her eyes shut.

Tears threatened to tumble as she leaned back against the pillow. Ringing clanged through her head, shaking her brain. She barely heard Will approach the bed. It only took a moment for Mecca to feel the weight of her eyelids. This time, instead of fighting it, she ran to it, embraced it and fell, grateful, into the darkness.

Chapter Seven: David

David passed the old stadium along I-75/85, the highway always busy, even at midnight. They'd taken him south of the city, almost to the country. He didn't realize he'd been passed out as long as he must have been.

He kept the speedometer at seventy, and an old burgundy Ford with chrome spinner rims blew past him. The van swayed, and he tightened his grip on the wheel to keep control. A Volvo on the other side of him changed lanes.

Going back to Jim's might prove to be the stupidest thing he could do. But he only had this one lead in finding Mecca. If he could have left Irish alive, he might have gotten more information. But that hadn't felt like an option at the time. It was also possible that he wouldn't have seen it if it had been an option.

When the interstate split, he took 85 north straight on to Buckhead.

He'd managed to remove all the tape, but his face still burned, like patches of smoldering undergrowth after a forest fire had been mostly contained. The memories he'd leeched from the Irishman told him they had Mecca. Whoever "they" were. If he could get Jim to talk — and he would — he could at least find a starting point. Once he started, he wouldn't stop until he found her.

No matter who he had to kill.

They seemed to think he had the same limitations on his power that Mecca did. Like any other skill, though, their Gift could be refined and honed. After Teresa died, Mecca let him train her only long enough to control it. She refused to learn anything further. She'd originally wanted to stop training altogether. He'd had to convince her to go on, for the safety of others, at the very least. So she had no idea what she could do with her Gift.

Mecca needed skin-to-skin contact for a direct energy pull, but he had no such constraints. Any sort of contact would work for him. Clothing optional. This was a misconception he could use.

Since dumping the husks out of the van, he found that he'd begun distancing himself from his emotions, particularly compassion — the one that had taken him so long to learn. He wasn't happy to return to this state. He'd spent enough of his life there.

Still, Jim's betrayal bothered him more than he wanted to admit. He couldn't understand why Jim would be in league with these people — creatures. It couldn't be for the money. He came from an old Boston family and certainly didn't need the extra padding from monetary gifts. Perhaps they'd found him sticking it to his secretary. Blackmail creates incentive. That didn't sound much like Jim either, but every man has his vice.

David turned off the highway, watching his rear view mirror. No headlights followed as he came off the exit. The drive had given his anger time to dissipate, which was probably good for Jim in the long run. David no longer planned to simply kill him outright. That had been his knee-jerk.

Turning into the tree-lined subdivision, he cut the headlights and eased down the narrow roads. He edged the van to the curb around the corner from the Barron place. The wooded part of the property backed up to the road here. On foot, David cut through the trees and circled around behind the house.

The pool lights still twinkled in the water, but the patio itself remained dark. Lucky break. He crept along the tiled deck of the pool and peered into Jim's office. Only a green-shaded bank light on the desk glowed, leaving most of the room shadowed. Jim sat forward in the leather desk chair, talking on the phone, his back to the window. He gestured widely, his raised voice audible but unclear through the glass. David watched for a moment longer and then slipped into the pool cabana.

In the darkness, he crouched and felt beneath the bench until he found the small box fastened to the underside. David had an identical one beneath the cedar steps of the deck in his own backyard. He and Jim had bought them at the hardware store over a decade before.

With a flip of his finger, the box popped open and the key fell onto his palm. A delicate pressure brushed against his jacket sleeve, and he jerked his arm away, adrenaline spiking. A yellow lab stood just over his shoulder, watching him.

"Oh, Christ, Mojo. You scared the shit out of me."

At the sound of his familiar voice, she bounced forward and licked his hand. He scratched her behind one ear with his free hand, then patted her neck. "Okay, be a good girl and go on." Mojo only watched him, her tail swishing back and forth so hard it made her back end sway. He patted the side of her neck as he stood, and then he pushed past her, out of the cabana.

Within moments, he'd made his way to the back door and let himself in, his adrenaline still spiked and pumping. He moved through the immaculate kitchen and into the living room. Then he stood outside Jim's office, listening. Jim's voice alternately rose and dropped, but David couldn't make out the words. David wrapped his hand around the knob and opened the door.

When he entered the room, Jim, seated at his desk, his shoulder propping the phone against his ear, raised both brows. He stood. "Carolyn, I have to go. We'll talk later. Yes, everything is fine. I love you too."

David pictured ripping Jim's head from his neck and throwing it into the pool. That would be gratifying. But not very practical and probably not possible without a large, well-sharpened object. David leashed his impulse and regarded Jim with what he hoped was an impassive look that didn't match any emotion in him just then.

"Give me one good reason why I shouldn't kill you right now."

"Dave — I didn't have a choice. I didn't want to do it, but — You have to understand." Jim rose and took three steps around the desk.

"What is it I have to understand? I understand that you set me up. I understand that you *drugged* me." David approached the desk. "I understand that you handed me over to two men who would have killed me. Two men who kidnapped Mecca." The words hung in the air.

"Kidnapped Mecca?"

"You still haven't given me a reason not to kill you."

"They said they would hurt Jenny and Carolyn if I didn't cooperate. They mean business. You remember when Tom Drury's boy got killed in that car accident a few years ago?" He didn't wait for an answer. "It wasn't a wreck that killed him."

"Drury. That guy on the council with you?"

Jim nodded.

"Who are they?"

"I don't know," Jim said, everything about his voice and posture overwhelmed.

David closed the distance between them in seconds. He hit the desk lamp as he passed. It clattered to the floor and made crazy shadows as David slammed Jim against the wall. David pinned him with a forearm to the chest.

"*Don't* fucking lie to me, Jim. Who are they?"

"They'll kill my family!"

"Right now, you should be more afraid of me than them." David searched his friend's face. Jim looked more and more defeated as the seconds ticked by. "Tell you what. I already know what they are. How about you just tell me where they are?"

"I don't know where they are. If I did, I swear — *I swear* — I would tell you." Fear and desperation tainted Jim's breath, giving it a sour smell. "You think I wanted to do that to you?" His voice raised with each word until he was almost yelling. "Do you think I want to even be *involved* with them?"

David moved a step back, letting Jim away from the wall.

"I'm resigning my position on the council this week. I won't be manipulated any longer. If they kill me, they kill me. At least my family will be safe."

This was the Jim he knew. This was the man he'd expected to have a drink with earlier. He didn't want to feel this compassion.

The shrill chatter of a cell phone's electronic ring startled both of them. David shot a warning look at Jim, who simply raised a hand and then stepped to the desk and picked up his cell phone.

"Hello? No." He looked over at David as he spoke. "What do you mean he escaped? No, I haven't seen him." A vein in Jim's forehead pulsed visibly as an edge crept into his voice. "Absolutely not. You lost him, you find him. I'm not your lapdog, Ms. Laos, and I'm not one of your foot soldiers." He listened for several moments, then said, "Fair enough. Yes, I have the number. Goodbye." He swiped to disconnect, dropped the phone onto the desk, and ran his fingers through his thick, dark hair. "They're looking for you. If I hear from you, I'm to call them."

"And who was that?"

"Her name is Emilia Laos. As far as I know, she is their leader. I don't know how organized they are, but their setup reminds me of the mob. One head and lots of little soldiers."

"You have their number. Give it to me."

"I only have a cell number, but you're welcome to it."

David stood in silence as Jim took a business card from his Rolodex and handed it over. David read the card out loud. "Emilia Laos. Import export." He didn't recognize the address.

"What are you going to do?"

"Find Mecca."

They watched each other for a moment before Jim said, "You're going to need money. They'll be monitoring your bank account. You have no idea how far their hold goes in this city."

Jim walked around to the front of the desk and retrieved the green-shaded lamp from the floor. He switched the light off and then flipped it upside down. He turned a small wing nut set in the underside of the heavy brass base. When he removed the nut, the bottom of the lamp slipped out and a small bundle of money, folded in half and rubber-banded, fell onto the desk. He replaced the false bottom and tossed the wad of cash to David.

"There's a little over a grand there. It's all I have liquid at the moment. You're welcome to it."

David regarded him with a steady gaze as he pocketed the money without looking at it. He turned and walked away without another word. When he reached the doorway, Jim cleared his throat.

"Dave."

He looked back. Jim still looked like his old friend, but he no longer felt any trust in the man. It had been replaced by bitterness.

"I'm sorry for tonight," Jim said. "And for Mecca. If I can do anything…"

"You've done enough." He left the grand house through the back and headed to the parked van.

He spent a tense and nervous night, his jacket pulled tight around him, beneath the highway overpass in a questionable part of town he didn't recognize. Jim's words had made him hesitant about wanting to go home.

He'd tried to sleep, off and on, but the expectation of crashing glass and the gleam of fangs at any moment kept any meaningful sleep away. Why he kept seeing fangs, he didn't know. He hadn't seen fangs on either of his kidnappers. When the first morning rays penetrated the van's gloom, he breathed a long sigh.

He didn't dare use the GPS on his phone — he kept his phone off altogether — so he stopped at a gas station and bought a paper map. It'd taken him ten minutes to find the rack in the back corner of the store. He plotted his route to the address printed on the business card.

The warehouse district encompassed at least twenty-five city blocks, but he'd had no trouble locating the building belonging to Emilia Laos among eight warehouses of varying sizes.

He parked the van several bays away from the one he wanted. It seemed to be the only warehouse on the street with no activity. As he walked by its neighbor, he stopped one of the gruff-looking men working there.

"Hey, why's that one dark?"

The worker, who looked well into his fifties, narrowed his eyes. A scar on his cheek twitched as he took David's measure.

"I'm looking for new space for my auto parts," David said. "If that one's vacant, I just might move my business over here."

The other man brushed his hands over dirty jeans and eyed him. His suspicions were not allayed, David knew, but the man replied anyway. "Nah, it ain't vacant. Whoever's there don't get stuff in often. We see some guys working out there every couple a weeks."

"Huh. Any idea what they're bringing in? I can't tell from here how much space they've got. If they're just bringing in little shit, I don't think that space will be big enough for me."

The man shrugged and waved a callused hand in that direction. "They bring in a lot, they just don't bring it often. They always got big shipments. Big boxes. Lots of men."

"Thanks, brother. Ever see the owner? He look like a reasonable guy?"

"Seen an old guy come in and out of the office a lot at the end of my shift. And a young broad. Chinese. She ain't here as often. Guess she only comes in for under the desk work, hey?" He cackled, blowing stale, garlic-laced breath.

Who eats garlic for breakfast?

"Thanks again. Maybe I'll go over and check it out. At least look in the windows to see how much space is there. If no one's around to let me have a look-see." He got a nod in return and let the man get back to his work.

David's boots crunched on the gravel of the yard as he approached. The building didn't look very sinister by light of day. All the same, a knot of anxiety and perhaps a small bit of fear gathered in his belly. Leftover from last night, he guessed. His nerves tingled as he got closer.

The area looked abandoned, save for some tire tracks along the drive. Trash gathered against the walls: beer bottles, old rags, a rusted crowbar, and an ancient Coca Cola sign. That was probably worth something somewhere. Old newspapers in various states of decay lay scattered at the bases of the straggly bushes in front. David circled around to the side and found blacked out windows.

Locked. *Damn.* Not surprising though.

The morning sunlight glinted off the glass door as he came around to the front. Tint made the interior look gloomy and desolate. Inside, file cabinets leaned against walls and computers perched on desks. Beneath the inky-black windows on the east wall sat a number of short file cabinets, along with a printer on a stand. Rather sparse, the office contained only the bare bones necessary to run a business.

He checked the door on the off chance it might be unlocked. It wasn't. What next? He had no moves beyond this office. The only clues that might lead him to Mecca hid in there.

He returned to the side of the building and looked at the windows. Could he break one of them without drawing too much attention to himself? He glanced at the small hedge shading this side of the building from its neighbor a good three hundred yards away. Maybe the sound wouldn't carry.

He pulled off his jacket, goose bumps creeping up on his skin in the cool morning air. He wrapped the fleece around his fist and forearm. Breaking the window shouldn't be too hard. Then he'd be able to pull himself in through the window, onto the file cabinets, and down to the floor. He stood beside the window and slammed his forearm against it with controlled strength.

Electric pain shot up his forearm as it bounced off the window with a loud thump. The glass rattled, but didn't move otherwise.

"Goddammit!" He held his arm to his belly, grinding his teeth until the pain faded to a low thrum. *That's the last time I do shit like they do in the movies.*

He needed something harder than his arm to break that window. He circled the building as he pulled the jacket back on, taking care not to jostle his arm too much. Trash against the side of the building caught his eye.

The crowbar.

He snatched the rusty piece of metal from a pile of debris against the wall. The sign beside it told him to have a Coke and a smile. And that sounded good to him right now. The Coke anyway. He wasn't much in a smiling mood.

David stalked over to the window. "Fuck subtle." He swung and the crowbar crashed against the corner of the glass. It shattered. Some pieces fell to the ground, but most clung to wire embedded in the window. He stared at it for a second.

Fucking mesh in the window.

He swore under his breath and looked around, sure that someone must be calling the cops by now. The men in the yard next door continued to haul crates off a trailer. The thudding in his chest slowed.

He smashed the window again and more glass skittered to the ground. He'd cleared the lower left corner now, except for the wire. The rest of the pane was shattered but glass held fast like a gossamer web of crystal.

The mesh remained tucked into the window frame. David hooked the crowbar into the wire and heaved. The metal pulled free of the frame with a grinding sound. More glass sprinkled to the ground.

When he'd pulled up enough of the corner to slip inside, he tossed the crow bar to the ground. He eased himself through the opening and skidded across the top of a file cabinet, head first. Too late, he realized that the inside floor was at least a foot lower than the outside ground. He landed on his head with a grunt.

After he got his feet back under him, David brushed himself off and scanned the office. A tall counter with a Formica top bisected the room, separating the work space from a small waiting area in the front. A computer monitor, keyboard and mouse, as well as a small hanging file system sat on top of the counter. Two desks crowded the work area, both with their own computers and phones. A small stand with a combination fax and printer took up one corner at the end of the file cabinets.

No decorations brightened the desks. No personal pictures, no silly office toys. Nothing suggested that people with personalities worked here.

A door stood ajar on the far side of the room, and David found a large office behind it. Spartan, like the outer area, it contained only a desk, chair, computer, phone and a row of grey, metal file cabinets against the wall. They obviously hadn't converted to cloud storage yet.

He flipped the computer on and looked through the cabinet drawers while the machine booted.

Shipping manifests, invoices, customs documentation; had he really expected to find more?

Emilia Laos apparently imported all manner of things from artwork to horticulture. When the computer beeped behind him, he slammed the drawer closed.

The screen prompted him for a password.

Last year, he'd bought cracking software, partly out of boredom and partly out of curiosity. He wished he had it right now. Picking random words didn't seem to work. He knew it wouldn't. He found nothing in the desk to clue him in to what the password might be. After fifteen minutes, he growled and turned the computer off.

How to find Mecca now? Everything led to a dead end. Maybe he should go back and lean on Jim some more. Just how deep did his friend's involvement go? His loyalty didn't seem to lie with Emilia Laos or her group. David considered the phone call Jim received while he was still there and his own gaze wandered to the phone in front of him. He sat up straight.

The phone had an LCD display along the top. The receiver felt heavy in his hand, though he knew it was made of the same plastic as other office phones. His nerves tingled again as he touched the *redial* button. Numbers appeared on the display. The line rang in his ear as he grabbed a pen and wrote the number across the top of his hand.

"Hello?" A male voice. His mind raced.

"Is Ms. Laos available?" The long pause made him jumpy. "She has something that I want."

"Who's calling, please?"

"My name is David Trenow."

No response came, but he still heard sound on the other side. The line remained open.

A female voice in the background said, "I need to use the bathroom."

David's heart jumped.

The man's voice finally answered. "Hold the line please."

The other voice had been Mecca's.

David waited, listening to the open line, hoping to hear her again. A knot grew in his stomach.

Mecca was alive.

He heard murmuring on the other end of the phone, then a cultured, female voice spoke. "Mr. Trenow?"

"Is this Emilia Laos?" Everything in him wanted to go through the phone at her.

"Yes, it is. It's a pleasure to speak with you." She spoke with a faint accent he couldn't place, though it sounded Asian.

"I can't say the same. You have my daughter." He stood from the leather chair and paced as far as the corded phone would allow.

"I understand your position. Mecca has not been harmed, nor will she be, so please try not to fear for her safety."

"I want her back."

"That isn't possible at this time. However, I welcome a chance to speak with you about the current situation."

What the hell? She was talking like she was conducting a business deal, not about the freedom of his daughter. "How much do you want?"

"Excuse me?"

"What's your price? Let's get this all on the table."

"There is no price, Mr. Trenow. I am not ransoming her."

"Then what do you want?"

"Are you free tomorrow? I have engagements for the rest of today, but am free in the morning. Perhaps breakfast?"

"I want my daughter."

She let a quiet pause sit in the air. "Then meet with me."

Anger sent little pinpricks of heat along his cheeks. "All right, but on my terms," he said. "Tomorrow morning. I will call you at this number. Be ready."

The line went silent for a very long moment.

"Very well," she finally said. "I will wait for your call." The line clicked and she'd gone.

Chapter Eight: Mecca

Someone had removed the leg belts while she'd been drugged this time.

Mecca remained attached to the bed, but they'd left the chains on her cuffs, so she felt as close to free as she had been since she'd gotten here. The added mobility also allowed her to eat the food they'd brought earlier.

For a long time, she'd refused, until Will told her — the last time she was awake — that if she didn't eat, they'd feed her intravenously and put a catheter in her. Mecca decided the turkey sandwich didn't look half bad. She'd eaten the whole thing, faster than she'd expected.

Will had been moving toward the door when she told him she needed to use the bathroom. He didn't reply to her, but as he left, she saw the cell phone pressed to his ear. He must have had it on vibrate. *Damn. If I'd know he was on the phone I could have screamed or something. Instead, I told him I had to pee.*

This might be the only time they left her alone and awake at once. She didn't want to waste any of it.

Mecca shoved the plate off her lap and onto the bed beside her legs. She examined the thick leather cuffs on her wrists. They didn't seem to have any sort of locking mechanism, only a belt-like fastener.

The chain rattled against the bed rail as she frantically worked with her mouth to unfasten the cuff encircling her left wrist. It took a moment, more awkward than difficult. As the handcuff came free, she kicked the covers off of her legs.

At the foot of the bed, the plate with her uneaten chips on it began a slow slide. Mecca noticed too late. She scrambled to catch it. Everything slowed down as the plate fell sideways and smashed to the floor, sending ceramic shards and wavy potato chips in all directions, in spite of the thick oriental rug.

Mecca froze, certain Emilia must have heard the heavy thud from wherever she might be in the building. For those moments, Mecca's head throbbed along with her heartbeat. She fiddled with the cuff on her right hand, but slowly, quietly.

When no one broke through the door, Mecca swung her legs over the edge of the bed. She pulled the chain free of the bed rail and held it and the free cuff in the crook of her elbow as she worked more diligently on the one still on her right wrist. The IV tube stretched and the taped needle tugged on the skin of her hand. She got to her feet.

The room tilted and then wobbled. Someone had turned it on its corner. Then it spun like a top. Mecca eased back against the bed and closed her eyes. *Please don't let me puke.* The turkey sandwich felt alive in her belly. Like it wanted to crawl back up her throat. *Ugh.*

Her stomach twisted. Saliva flooded her mouth. She retched and gagged and then clapped her hand over her mouth. Bile burned the back of her throat.

No. I have to get out of here. I don't have time for this.

She drew a long breath in through her nose that made a tight, wispy sound, but it slowed her hammering pulse. Her belly tightened again and she took another deep breath. *In. Out. In. Out.* She willed her body to relax and concentrated on breathing.

The turkey sandwich settled down and Mecca opened her eyes cautiously. The room remained intact in the proper position and did not seem inclined to move this time. She lowered her hand.

Blood smeared, dark and wet, across the top of her hand. The needle, tape still adhered to it, lay off the edge of the bed. A single drop of fluid hung from its tip, pink with a mix of the clear liquid in the tube and her own blood. Mecca shook her head and started again on the other cuff.

How much time had passed? It felt like an hour, but she knew it couldn't have been. The cuff finally fell away, and she left both of them and the chain in a serpentine pile on the bed.

She pushed to her feet again. The room didn't swim this time so she took two steps along the thick carpet beneath her feet, testing her balance. Though still queasy, her belly had stopped rocking, and the turkey sandwich seemed restful.

She went to the door. The smooth knob turned a quarter of an inch, then stopped, locked. She ran her fingers along the seam, where the door met the frame. Mecca stepped back and looked at it.

It was a simple wooden door, stained to match the chair rails, with a modern, brushed silver knob on the left. No keyhole anywhere. The black electronic pad on the door had no buttons. She ran her fingers over the cool surface. The metal card reader. She didn't think she had any way of overriding it. Mecca took a step back and studied the door.

The hinges. They were on the right side of the door. But more importantly, they were inside the room.

It can't be that simple, can it?

But they obviously didn't expect her to ever be mobile.

Mecca dragged the chair over from the writing desk, positioned it behind the hinges and stepped up with care. The pin in the top hinge turned readily, but when she tried to lift it up and out of its metal casing, it wouldn't budge. She slid her thumbnails between the head of the pin and the top of the hinge. She wiggled it and tried to lever it up. Her nails bent backward and desperation welled up with the burn in her fingertips.

"Come on," she whispered. *Please.*

She tried again, this time with one thumb and two fingers on the same hand. The hall seemed silent. A soft click came from the doorknob. Before she could react, the door opened and slammed into one of the wooden chair legs. The chair shook. Mecca, reflexively, took a step back. Her heel missed the chair altogether. She had just a moment to see Claude's surprised face peek around the door before she fell.

Her right shoulder connected with the wall with a thud. It twisted her body and she slid. She ended up folded between the chair and the wall, her backside almost on the floor. Her left leg remained on the chair and her right leg lay pinned beneath her. She didn't think she was seriously hurt, but her window of opportunity closed as she and Claude stared at each other.

She scrambled to get her feet beneath her and pulled herself upright by the back of the chair.

Claude's surprise had dwindled, and now he watched her, his face drawn in a tight, wary mask. Mecca thought of a snake, tensed to strike. That was how he looked.

Her skin tingled as she watched him. That weird feeling again. Claude closed the door with two fingers. It latched shut, then locked with an electronic *whirr* and *click* that sounded final. She couldn't let it be.

If she could get him down, she'd probably find a plastic key on him. Then she could escape. They watched each other like gunfighters at high noon.

Claude wasn't dressed like a gunfighter though. He wore tight black jeans and black boots along with a navy blue, short-sleeved polo shirt. The outfit made him look more like a porcelain doll than ever.

"You should get back in the bed, Ms. Trenow," Claude said, his voice flat. "Emilia won't be pleased that you're up."

Mecca lunged forward, both arms in front of her. He blocked her right hand, but the fingers of her left hand wrapped around his upper arm, just above the elbow.

Mecca couldn't waste a moment. She sent her energy out into him, searching for the Cavern, for the captured soul she knew he must have.

His Cavern, dark and grey, superimposed itself on reality. Claude's face was clear to her and only inches away from her own, but her soul's vision overlaid his face like a translucent layer, showing her the Cavern as her own energy moved through it.

In the span of a moment, Mecca felt the enormity of his soul's Cavern, empty and crumbling, like the inside of a long-forgotten cave. Fuzz covered the floor, thick and inky black. It reminded Mecca of the wooly surface of mold on cheese, and she was glad she didn't have to walk there.

A faint glow came from a tiny alcove inside the far wall. Behind the vision of the Cavern, Claude's face reddened and his blue eyes flashed with dark anger and knowledge. More than knowledge — understanding.

His grip tightened on her shoulders as her spirit slipped into the alcove. A bound bundle of energy glowed with bright golden light, though it *seemed* dim because hundreds of grey tendrils covered it, maybe thousands, anchored it to the black mossy floor.

How would she ever free it? She circled the energy, trying to find a weakness in his hold on it.

The connection broke. Mecca's life force slammed back into her.

She realized, with sudden surprise, that she was airborne, sailing across the room. The wall stopped her with a crash, and sharp pain knifed down her spine like a plant taking root.

As she hit the floor, her head cracked against the chair rail. The room dimmed. Air hissed out of her lungs, and she gulped to refill them, trying not to panic.

She didn't pass out, but the room wouldn't come quite into focus. It shuddered and wobbled. She couldn't stop sucking in large swallows of air; it was the only sound in the room. Claude stood over her, but as she tried to center her vision, she found that she kept seeing two of him. She closed her eyes. She opened them again and blinked several times. A hammer thrummed at the back of her head.

He squatted beside her and brushed the tip of his finger against her chin, light as a moth's wings. The shiver that traveled along her spine wasn't unpleasant. She didn't like that. She looked into his sea-blue eyes.

"I'm going to take you to the bed." He spoke slowly, gently. "I don't want to have to knock you out to do it, but I will if I have to. Do you understand me, Mecca?"

She nodded once. Still groggy but coming around, she doubted whether his small frame could support her weight. She could still try to get him down and get his key while he struggled to lift her. When he slid his arms under her and she was close enough to reach out and touch his face, however, she didn't have the will to send her energy into him.

And he lifted her without a second of hesitation or difficulty.

———»»««—

Later, Will had returned and replaced the needle in her hand before stepping out for a moment. When he came back this time, he had a small brush and dustpan, along with a hand-held vacuum. He began cleaning up the broken remains of the lunch plate without asking what had happened. Claude had left without telling him anything and Mecca hadn't spoken a single word to Claude since he'd returned her to her bondage on the bed.

She lay there under the crushing weight of her captivity. Of her failure.

"Why are they keeping me here?" Mecca asked, now that they were alone.

"I think you know the answer to that."

"They want to know how Hayden died."

"Yes."

"But why keep me here, drugged? Why all the reading?" Mecca hated the soft whine that crept into her voice. "Why not just get everything over with?"

Will dumped the contents of the dustpan into a small trash can. The ceramic clacked as it tumbled. Moving from his crouched position, he sat back on the floor and looked up at her. A small crease developed between his eyebrows as he watched her. When he finally spoke, his voice was gentle and quiet.

"I can't pretend to know what Emilia is thinking. I have been with her for a long time though, and I do know that everything she does, she does for a reason. She always has a plan of action. She is keeping you here, giving you the research on your father—"

"Those are not about my father!" Mecca's face burned, both with her anger, but also with embarrassment and inevitability. She didn't want the papers to be about her dad.

Will lowered his head, his eyes hidden by a wave of his nut-brown hair. Then he looked up at her again. "Very well. She is keeping you here, giving you those papers to read, because she believes it will give her the results she wants."

"What results?"

"That, I don't know." He moved forward, into a crouch again, and picked up the brush and dustpan. He swept the smaller pieces and dumped them into the trash can.

"So why are they drugging me? It's not like I can even get away from this damn bed." She pulled hard on her cuffs. The chains rattled against the metal side rails.

"Well, obviously *that's* not true." He gave her a pointed look and held up the dustpan. Then he said, "It's the easiest way to keep you quiet." A wry smile lit his face. "Emilia will be in later. You may wish to ask your questions then."

Mecca leaned back against her pillow and closed her eyes. The motorized suction of the vacuum turned on, and she listened to its whirring as Will ran it over the carpet near the foot of her bed.

As far as she could tell, all their research came as a result of the original information she'd printed out at the library but never read. They had much more information. The articles were so damning. It was like someone had wrapped a hand around her heart and squeezed the life out.

Growing up, he'd always told her the Gift had passed him over. His father and brother both had it. Sometimes it didn't manifest in every child, he'd said, but every child could be a carrier. That's how Mecca got the Gift. So he said.

She'd never doubted his word. Not ever. But now... There was no other explanation for the deaths of his wives. The doctors would never know. Neither would the families.

But *she* knew.

He'd lied to her. Her heart broke again with the betrayal.

And her belly roiled. Mecca didn't want to believe the awful stories. But those photos — she couldn't discount them. His face. He'd been married to those women who'd died.

Been murdered.

She shuddered.

Even worse was having the crushing truth handed to her by these people — these things. Will had called them Visci, but Mecca didn't know what that meant. Not really.

The idea that they witness her betrayal made Mecca's skin crawl. It made her angry and that anger mingled with the pain of her father's deceit. The whole mess was like a bubbling, rotten stew threatening to spill over the edges.

In her mind, she pushed around the haunting sentence from her mother's file. *Although Teresa Trenow's illness cannot be directly attributed to David Trenow, nor can the woman's death be positively attributed to the cancer itself.* A tear squeezed from her closed eye and slipped down her cheek.

But it wasn't him, was it? They couldn't know that.

Mecca wanted to shove the whole thing from her head and forget she'd ever read any of it, ever even entertained what she knew felt more and more true yet didn't want to be true. But the faces of six murdered women weighed in on the other side, and their deaths could not be brushed away.

Was everything he'd ever told her a lie? Perhaps her mom had never been sick at all. Maybe that was how he started it every time. Perhaps, if it hadn't been for her father, Mom would have gotten to see Mecca go on her first date, to her first prom. Perhaps Mom would have been around to see her graduate.

Maybe I wouldn't have fallen asleep that afternoon. Maybe it wouldn't have mattered if I had.

Mecca couldn't really shift gears away from herself. Her own guilt held strong, even though her rational mind understood the evidence she was looking at.

A sob crashed through her, but she strangled it behind pursed lips. Pressing her eyes tightly shut, she resolved not to let any of her fear and betrayal show. She had no idea how she would get out of here, but she wouldn't be doing it by letting them see her hurt any more.

She sucked in a soft, ragged breath and released it quietly through her mouth. She opened her eyes. Will sat in the chair nearby, the brush, dustpan and vacuum in a small pile near the door.

"Will Emilia be here when I wake up?"

Will looked up from the clipboard on his lap and nodded. "She may not actually be right here, but she'll be down soon after."

"They're afraid of me, aren't they? They've got me chained up, and they're afraid to let me stay awake for any extended amount of time."

"I don't think they're so much afraid of you as they're not sure what to do with you. You're an unknown, and so carry a certain amount of risk. I don't think caution should be equated to fear."

"Have you done this before?"

"Done what?"

"Guarded someone they kidnapped."

"No," Will said. "They don't often take the trouble to kidnap people."

"They're not worried that I'm going to attack you and escape?

"Well, you had your hand on me once, yes? There was your chance, and you didn't take it. She guessed you wouldn't." He watched Mecca for a moment, but she couldn't read his eyes. Then he said, "Once upon a time, I was a medic. Emilia's made sure I kept up with the times. I'm probably the best qualified to deal with a medical emergency, should one arise."

"A medic? Like a paramedic?"

The metallic ring of the timer sounded, and Will stood, setting aside the clipboard. "Not the sort you think of today."

She didn't understand what he meant. She watched him fill a syringe with liquid. She didn't say anything as he slid the needle into the butterfly portal and depressed the plunger.

As the weight of sleep crept into the edges of Mecca's consciousness, she said, "I'd like to know more sometime."

His voice, sounding thick in her ears, replied, "Perhaps sometime."

Chapter Nine: David

David stared at the phone in his hand. Relief coursed through him like a tidal wave. She was alive, at least, and she sounded okay. He had no idea where she was or what they were doing with her, but she was alive.

The reality of the situation hit him full force. The old urge to cut and run pinged him.

I'm not that man anymore.

When he had Mecca safely home, he'd worry about whether to run. He could take her with him if he needed to.

The silence of the office seemed to push on him now, oppressive and stifling. He pulled in a long breath, filling his lungs until his chest burned fire. As he let the air out, he looked around to see whether he'd missed anything. It occurred to him that Emilia Laos probably knew where he'd phoned from. He shouldn't stay much longer.

The computer under the desk interested him. He reached down and pulled the case onto the top of the desk. When he tugged, the cords and cables came away like some fantastic sea creature, all tentacles. He tossed them aside and popped the case open. In the mishmash of electronics that made up the gut of the thing, he found what he was looking for. David disconnected the hard drive with care and then closed the case and shoved the computer under the desk again.

One last look around and he took off, slipping out the broken window. He kept his eyes peeled and made his way back to the van with the hard drive tucked under his jacket. Though it looked safe enough, he circled the van completely and peered inside each window. It looked as empty as he'd left it. When he was finally inside with the doors locked, he laid the hard drive on the seat beside him and headed to the public library.

He found a twenty minute wait for the computers with net access. A long twenty minutes. Finally, a machine in the back came available. He signed on as Guest and found the website he wanted right away. He logged onto the site as Nereus and waited for an anxious five minutes before she logged on at their usual time.

Nereus: You busy?
Solaris: Nah. What's up?
Nereus: Things have been crazy. I need a favor.
Solaris: Shoot.
Nereus: I have something I need to get into, but I don't have access to my equipment.
Solaris: Why don't you have your stuff?
Nereus: I can't go home right now.
Solaris: Why not?
Nereus: I just can't. Will you help me?

David's stomach knotted as he waited for the reply. He hated bringing Sara into this. They'd never even met face to face, but he didn't know where else to turn. He wished he could just get back to his house; he had what he needed there. But they must have his house under surveillance. That's what David would do.

Solaris: Okay. There's a coffee shop down in Little Five. Brew-haha. It's right next to the pizza place on Moreland.
 Nereus: I'll find it.
 Solaris: Give me about an hour.

Little Five Points was more crowded at mid-morning than he'd expected. He parked behind the plaza shops in the back lot pocked with holes. The bumps made the van creak and shake.

This is where Mecca was attacked.

He pushed the thought away. He didn't want to waste energy on it now. He parked, tucked the hard drive into his waistband, locked the van and slid the key into his pocket.

Sunshine warmed him as he made his way toward the tiny hole in the wall shop. Street sellers and musicians had already begun setting up in the small cobblestone plaza. A tall, whippet-thin man with deeply ebony skin and thick Rasta braids gave him a white-toothed smile and a nod. David inclined his head in return. His weariness weighed on him, and he realized how little sleep he'd gotten. There probably wasn't a drop of adrenaline anywhere in his system.

He sidestepped into the shadowy entrance of the apartments above the shops. He closed his eyes, leaned back, and let his spirit reach out into the air above the moving crowds.

The energy crackled as people ambled and rushed, talked and laughed, or simply sat and watched others in their daily meanderings. When he opened his energy, his soul, to it, the familiar tapestry super-imposed itself on reality, the buildings across the street playing a backdrop behind the gorgeous layer.

Colorful and vibrant, like the greatest masterpiece, that collective life energy woven into a work of art. David had always found the swirl of colors mesmerizing. Blues, reds, oranges, every color of the rainbow and more, all infused through with the richest golden light.

He picked at the tapestry above, snagging a thread and pulling it to him. When he embraced the thread with his own life's fabric, it funneled energy down to him, filling him, making his entire body prickle. Faint pain mixed with the energy, like the bristly feel of a sharp metal brush against skin. He released that thread and chose another.

When he knew he couldn't take more, he slit the thread and sent it back to the invisible cover above. The breath he took in the next moment filled his lungs in an electrifying rush, and the hairs on his body rose, his limbs tingling. When he exhaled, muscles that he didn't know were tense unknotted and relaxed.

His stomach growled.

The rich smell of brewed coffee enveloped him as he stepped back into the sunlight. In front of the cafe, people sat at rickety metal tables, but they didn't seem to mind. Many looked to be on the tail end of an all-nighter, bringing cups to pierced lips and drinking deeply.

Inside, ceiling fans whirled overhead to combat the heat of the coffee machines and steamers. Behind the counter were two women who looked to be complete opposites. The younger, a teenager, had black hair tipped in electric blue, dark black eyeliner, and silver pierced through lobes, nostrils, brows, lips, and one dimpled cheek. Her colleague wore her graying auburn hair pulled back in a loose ponytail, curly wisps framing a face dotted with pale brown freckles. The goth and the earth mother, working side by side.

"What can I get for you?" the earth mother asked.

"Large black coffee." He pointed to the glass display case between them. The cloudy windows showed their age, but on the inside, muffins, doughnuts, and pastries teetered in high piles on clean stoneware plates. "Those cheese Danish look good. Give me one of them as well, please."

She hummed along with the flute music being piped through the place as she placed the Danish on a brightly decorated ceramic plate and then filled a large paper cup with steaming coffee. She rang him up on an old fashioned register. It clanged in an oddly comforting way.

"Four twenty five, please."

He handed over a twenty from the roll Jim had given him. "You've got pretty low prices."

She smiled indulgently as she counted his change back. "Just holler if you need a refill."

He nodded his thanks, took his coffee and Danish and turned to find a place to sit. Small round tables with mismatched chairs packed the tiny dining area, and a beautiful mural graced the back wall. Fashioned in the shape of a giant window, it looked out over a bright green meadow edged with majestic oak trees. The painted sun was perpetually setting, throwing rays of ocher and deep lavender across the sky.

"Hey." A quiet female voice spoke from behind him. "Grab the back corner table and I'll be there in a second." David looked over his shoulder at a young woman of about twenty who carried a worn nylon satchel over one shoulder. The girl went to the counter and spoke with the earth mother. "Hey, Maggie! How's the brew today?"

David made his way to the corner and dropped into a chair, turning so he could observe the room. And the girl. The energy from his tapestry pull still tingled along his nerves, like adrenaline in his blood. It made him a little edgy, but it was better than the bone-tired exhaustion that he knew was waiting in the wings to overtake him. He looked toward the counter.

Sara stood just over five feet with short, tightly curled black hair, a pale complexion and freckles along her nose. She approached, a large ceramic cup in her hand. She blew on the foam riding the surface and gave him a small smile.

She looked *exactly* like her grandmother, Susan Harrington. No doubt at all. A pang of regret echoed through him.

She settled in the chair to his right.

"How did you know who I was?" he asked.

"I was outside watching you. You look just like the picture on Mom's dresser. A little more grey, maybe, but...." She waggled fingers at the top of his head and then shrugged with a grin.

"Your mom has a picture of me on her dresser?" He hadn't expected that. At all. Some weird mix of happiness at that, guilt, and the ever-present regret coursed through him.

Sara nodded and slipped the satchel from her shoulder. "Yep, in a double frame. Your pic on one side. Gran's on the other. You don't look grandfather-aged though."

"Yes, well, I was young when we got married. Your mom was about thirteen." David's face grew hot. *This is a bad idea.*

"My mom, a teenager." Sara laughed, then took a sip of her coffee and licked the foam off her upper lip. On an older woman, it would have been seductive. On Sara, it simply looked practical. "Okay, so what is it you need?"

David looked around and then pulled the hard drive from beneath his jacket. He set it on the tabletop. "It's a Windows OS, but I couldn't get in manually. And I have no idea what security I'll find once I get inside."

"We'll have to go to my place. We can hook it up to my machine there."

David's mind spun. *Too close.* He was getting her too involved. "Can't we use your laptop?"

"No, what I need is at the house. Come on." She slid the hard drive into her bag.

"All right. But we have to hurry."

She nodded and stood, grabbed her coffee, and then slung her satchel over her shoulder. "Let's go then." She zigzagged around chairs toward the door, raising a hand to Maggie, who smiled at her as a mother would. "Be back later, Mags!" She hefted her mug. "I'll bring this back."

"Careful out there, Sara," Maggie said.

Sara laughed. "I will, *Mom*."

David watched her without moving, uncertain whether to follow. Finally, he stood and took his coffee too, which was in a paper cup. He'd left his Danish untouched. He wasn't really hungry anymore.

"It's only a couple blocks away," she said when he joined her outside.

David nodded and scanned the crowd as they walked. He didn't want to go back to her place. He didn't want to get that close to her. Not only for her sake, but for his. He didn't want her personalized any more than she already was.

But he had no choice.

"So who are you looking for?" she asked.

"What do you mean?" Did she know about the vampires, if that's what they were? About Mecca being kidnapped? Surely not. Surely his paranoia was knocking him in the head and scrambling his brains.

"Well, you keep checking everyone out. Thought you were looking for someone."

"Oh. No, I'm not. Just keeping an eye out."

"Okay, if you say so." They walked half a block. "What is it you think is on this thing?"

David hesitated. He hadn't wanted to bring her into things, but he did anyway. Because he was selfish. So now, didn't he owe her some of the truth? *Maybe.* "I'm hoping something on it will lead to where my daughter is."

The rhythm of her step faltered, but she recovered quickly. "What happened to her?"

"I don't know. Someone has her."

"You didn't call the cops."

"It's complicated."

"Yeah. Okay." She quieted for a moment. "Mom never mentioned that you have a daughter."

"She doesn't know."

"Why not?"

"She just doesn't." She tensed beside him, but he didn't elaborate. He felt a little crazy just then. His worlds were on a slow-motion collision course. And he couldn't stop it.

Sara quickened her pace and turned a corner to the right. After several minutes, she pointed to an old, but well-maintained, wood frame home. Painted a robin's egg blue with white trim, it fit in well with the other pastel homes on the street. She took the steps up and unlocked the door. The door on the right. He hadn't realized it was a duplex when he'd first looked at it.

"How does a college student afford this?"

She held the door open. "Mom bought it with the money you gave her after Gran died. She saved every check in an account for my education. She used that savings to pay for my college, and she bought this. She rents the other side out to some nursing students." Sadness tickled at the corners of her eyes as she added, "She comes here sometimes."

Susan's only daughter, Grace — Sara's mom — had been thirteen when David married Susan. Grace had just graduated from high school when her mother died, and Grace had gone over the edge, plunging into silence and refusing to speak to anyone for months.

One evening about two months after Susan died, David had returned home early from work and found her passed out in the bathtub with an unlabeled prescription bottle, empty, on the floor.

It had been a turning point for him. He'd tried to make amends. Was still trying. He continued to send Grace a check every month, though he hadn't spoken to her in decades. She'd gone through emotional hell to make a life for herself, he knew. That she was funding Sara's college life with the money didn't surprise him.

Serious second thoughts — who the hell was he kidding? Third and fourth thoughts — flitted through his mind about whether he could handle this situation. He could just leave, find some other way to crack the hard drive. Or maybe Jim could give him more information on how to find Laos. Even as he thought of each of his options, he knew none of them were valid. Sara was his best hope. But, God, he hated it.

The house looked larger on the inside than it looked from the outside. He came into the main area from the foyer to find a stairway leading up along the left wall. The living room opened to the right.

A comfortable-looking blue sofa and rust-colored love seat crowded around an oak coffee table. Nothing matched. Goodwill decor at its finest. A battered armoire that probably housed a television leaned against the front wall. The living room faded into the dining area toward the far wall and ended in a swinging door which he assumed led to the kitchen.

Sara locked the front door and came into the room, unloading the satchel onto the floor near a silver umbrella stand. She bent and retrieved the hard drive. "The setup is downstairs." She pointed to a door set into the paneling beneath the stairway to the second floor. "You want more coffee?"

"No thanks. Any more caffeine and I'll start jitterbugging."

She laughed as she slid a key into the lock on the basement door.

"You keep it locked?"

"Yep. Lots of expensive and secret stuff down there. Shh." She winked at him and led the way, turning left after entering the doorway. She led him down a flight of wooden steps.

The air cooled the lower they went, and David took a deep breath. He realized he was starting to relax. He didn't think they'd been followed, but he was still surprised at the safety he felt. His muscles began to unknot themselves.

"Light," Sara said. Brightness illuminated the room and the hum of computers filled the air.

The basement spanned the entire length of the house. The concrete floor should have made it like a cell, but the cherry red paint covering the floor offset that impression a lot. Furniture and equipment took up much of the space. Each wall had been painted a different, bright color, a lot like a kid's playroom. David suspected Sara spent most of her time down here.

A microwave and sink huddled in the back corner, near a brown dorm fridge covered in stickers. A coffee maker on top of it held about an inch of dark sludge. The light for the hot plate was off.

Two desks dominated the room: one was large and L-shaped, pushed up against the wall where four flat-screen monitors had been mounted. The smaller desk stood almost in the middle of the room with another desktop computer with two more monitors along with several docking stations with multiple ports on each. Homemade cinder-block bookshelves stuffed with books lined the front wall, where the door would be upstairs.

"Welcome to Headquarters." Sara smirked.

"Interesting place." He walked around as she plopped into the chair in front of the wall-mounted monitors. They each had different things on them. One a Windows desktop, two with Linux desktops, and the fourth held lines and lines of code, green on black background.

"Yeah, it's home." She took the hard drive and hooked it up to a tangle of cords jumbled together at the back of the desk.

The bookcase caught David's attention. He found an interesting range of subjects from black holes to computer books. And there was *Ender's Game,* snuggled in between Stephen Hawking and .NET architecture. David smiled, though his heart ached with regret. Again.

"Sara."

She looked up, startled. "I didn't think you even knew my real name."

"Of course I know your name." It startled *him* that she would think he wouldn't. He wandered over to her desk. "How's Grace — sorry, your mom?"

Sara shrugged and went back to installing the drive as she spoke. "Okay, I guess. Slightly boozy, but that's normal for her. It's been worse." She typed her password in to the computer.

"Hello, Sara." A deep, masculine voice tinged with a Scottish brogue, boomed through the room. Sara grinned. "A little megalomaniacal indulgence there."

David couldn't keep from laughing. It felt good. "We all have our vices."

Her eyes twinkled. She leaned back in the chair and waved a hand at the monitor in front, which had changed from the original Windows desktop to the password screen that David had seen in the warehouse office. A small black square was now in the lower right corner.

Sara tapped some keys and word combinations began flashing through the box. "There won't be a whole lot to see until the program cracks the password. It'll just go through the dictionary first, then it will add special characters and numbers and stuff. Finally it will start a methodical testing of random groups of characters and numbers until it eventually finds the right combination."

They watched it for a few moments, and David asked, "How long will this take?"

"It could take five minutes. It could take three days."

"Three days? How do we speed it up?"

"We don't. It's going as fast as its little processor can go. And actually, that's pretty fast. You hungry?"

His belly growled, and he remembered his uneaten Danish at Brew-haha. "Well, yes, I suppose that means I am."

She laughed. "Come on upstairs, and we'll see what I've got in the fridge. Don't expect a gourmet meal or anything. I'm not my mom." She stood and made her way up the stairs, leaving him to follow.

--→»«←--

"I considered going into the military and getting into cryptography," Sara said, between bites of scrambled eggs. "But I'm pretty sure I couldn't handle the whole authority hierarchy thing. I'm more of a loner. And then there's all the fighting. And the guns."

"Not a big gun fan?"

"Not at all."

David nodded, munching on a slice of buttered toast. His belly finally felt comfortably full. He couldn't remember the last time he'd eaten. "I can understand your decision about the service. So you want to go into computer security then?"

"Yeah, I think that would be cool. And it's something I'm good at. I'd also like to expand into AI. That's an amazing field right now, along with VR. Man. Love that shit." She raised her shoulders in a shrug. "I guess it's a gift, but computers have always been really, really easy for me. I built my first one from spare parts when I was ten or eleven. It's just a knack."

"I'm glad your mom gave you my e-mail address when you came out here for school. I'll admit, it was a surprise to find that out too. A strange coincidence."

Sara finished her last slice of bacon and downed her milk. "Well, the university has an outstanding prof who's doing some amazing stuff with AI. That's the real reason I chose to come here. I had a full-on scholarship to Brown, but decided I'd rather hang out with the really big geeks." Her smile lit her face, and it reminded David again of her grandmother.

He pushed back his chair and stood. "Let me clean up?"

"Sure. I hate doing dishes. Anyway, I'll go check on the computer. Maybe we got lucky."

"Is that likely?"

"Nope, but I'm going to check anyway."

David gathered the dishes and tried to keep his guilt in check. He'd tried to do his best by Grace. It had been her slow, painful descent into alcoholism and self-sabotage that burrowed into him. He didn't know why he'd kept in contact with her. He suspected that a bit of remorse had set in after years of coldness; he felt responsible for her breakdown.

He hadn't remarried after Susan. Not until he met Teresa. And Teresa had changed everything. She'd made him a better man. A much better man.

David finished washing the dishes and set about drying, leaving them stacked on the counter top to be put away. After, he left the kitchen and went down to the basement. Sara was leaned back in the chair, her feet perched on the edge of the desk. Her gaze fixed on the screen, watching the characters fly by. A thick trade paperback lay open on her lap.

"Any luck?"

"No." She looked up at him. "Man, you look beat. I think your jitterbugging days are done. You wanna nap for a while? There's a spare room upstairs."

David hadn't thought about it in a while, but when she mentioned sleeping, he realized he was fast coming to the end of his line. The energy pull and the coffee had lasted a while, but with a full belly, he found himself droopy. His only other option would be to take from Sara, and he wasn't willing to do that.

"Yes, that's a good idea. You'll call me if the program cracks the hard drive?"

"You bet. I wouldn't know what you're looking for anyway. Bedroom's the second door on the right at the top of the stairs. Bathroom's just across the hall. Towels under the sink."

He smiled as he mounted the stairs to the living room. "Thanks."

Chapter Ten: Claude

"What is it?" Salas asked. He'd been laying out Claude's attire for the day and had included a set of cuff links which housed stones of a bright blue — lapis lazuli. Set in silver, the beautiful stone tapped something inside Claude's mind. It had been his mother's stone. She had worn it for wisdom in leading the Visci.

"I've finally remembered."

Salas stared at him for a moment, a shirt in hand, and then realization dawned in his eyes. "Mecca Trenow?"

"Yes." Claude turned and slid his arms into the silky sleeves of the garment Salas held out for him.

The memories had come to the forefront in pieces, chunks. The wild flurry within the throne room, the hushed whispers. Flashes of a mummified corpse being carried in.

"We had one of her kind invade our kingdom when I was very young." He began fastening the ivory buttons, his mind only half in the present. "I'd forgotten."

"What happened?" Salas continued holding garments out for him in the manner he preferred — pants Claude stepped into himself, a jacket offered.

"I was never told the actual details. I was still a child. But what I pieced together from eavesdropping and listening to the servants gossip was frightening. A man had come from the east — I don't think I ever learned where — and he had been traveling with a family heading for Spain."

Salas paused in his attendance and watched Claude as he listened.

"I had an uncle who made a habit of preying on travelers, though my mother had done many things to try to break him of this habit. It had been his body — a husk, really — that I'd seen them bring in. It was as if he'd been dug up from a grave after having been long dead." The wispy, thin scattering of hair on the corpse's head was what had stuck with Claude. His uncle had had a full, thick crop of midnight black hair. What was left on the corpse had been fragile, white, and nothing like what Claude had known of him.

"Did they discover what happened?"

Claude tried to remember details, but they were slow in coming. Four hundred years of memory was a lot to sift through. "I think they did, but I don't recall anything specific. As I said, I was young. I do remember a word though." He had been hiding under the great table, listening to the discussion when his mother had said it, almost in a whisper. "*Jivaja.*"

"I do not think I know what the word means."

"It means 'mover of essence.' Of life force." He looked Silas in the eyes. "I believe that is what our Ms. Trenow is."

Salas gave nod. "I will see what I might find on these Jivaja. Perhaps there is more information out there."

"Very good. Now, here. My shoes and then the blood. I have things to do."

The switch only took moments. Claude suspended the plastic IV bag, dark red and bloated with his blood, above Mecca's bed. Like a swollen corpse on a gallows, it hung from the metal stand while Mecca slumbered through her drug-induced nap.

He clamped the plastic tube, so he wouldn't spill any of Emilia's blood onto the sleeping girl when he unhooked the bag. He reattached the clear tube to his own bag and less than a minute later, with Emilia's blood hidden inside the satchel at his hip, Claude stepped out of Mecca's room into the empty hallway. The door lock whirred as the latch caught.

When he reached his own quarters, he found Salas waiting for him in the sitting room, as he expected. Claude drew the satchel off and held it out to his manservant.

"Dispose of this."

Salas wound the strap around his burly hand. "Did you have any trouble?"

"None at all. Will had already stepped out for his own rest. Emilia is limiting access to that floor so as not garner any extra attention."

"She's keeping the girl a secret."

"Of course," Claude said. "Mecca has the potential to be a very powerful weapon, if handled properly."

"You'll have to control Emilia in order to control the girl." Salas lifted the satchel for a moment. "Your blood will only help a little bit if Emilia is the one Mecca chooses to be bound to."

Claude had thought of that. It would be complicated. He'd replaced Emilia's blood with his own twice now. He had to ensure that most of what Mecca received was his. Otherwise, Emilia's hold over the girl would be stronger or, worse, if the levels remained equal, Mecca would choose, albeit subconsciously.

He didn't think Mecca knew her own ancestry, and he didn't know much about the Jivaja. He couldn't even be sure the blood would affect her as it did humans.

But Claude wanted her. And he would have her.

Emilia could be manipulated, if he were careful about it. She'd changed much since she'd last been with him. The past hundred and a half years, she'd come into her own strengths and found for herself that part of her he'd always seen as destined for leadership.

Despite her independence, he felt confident that he could still bring her under his control. But he wasn't sure he would be able to direct Mecca in the way he wanted if he had to do it through Emilia. He would contemplate that bridge crossing a bit later.

"I don't think Mecca will choose to be bound at all," Claude said. "I believe she will fight. And she will have to be taken. It's the way with her kind."

Though the look on Salas's face showed his curiosity, Claude was glad his servant controlled himself. It had taken decades to train the man to keep his tongue, to hold his curiosity.

"Go and get rid of that," Claude said, waving a hand at the satchel in Salas's grip.

"As you wish." Salas took four long strides and placed his hand on the doorknob. "Emilia asked for you to stop by her suite when you have a moment."

"Thank you."

Claude strode down the long hall approaching Emilia's quarters. At the door, a young woman perched on a sturdy, wooden stool. She had a faint smell of apples about her. Claude tried to recall her name, but her face, though pretty, was just one of dozens of young ones who'd come to Atlanta. Claude had lost patience in trying to keep track of them all.

She ducked her head as he approached, brown hair obscuring her angular face for a moment.

Respectful, at least. A half-breed? When she raised her head and met his gaze, Claude found her deep-set eyes compelling with their cornflower blue pools.

"She's expecting you." The young woman flicked the door handle with her fingers and gave it a push and it swung open without a sound.

"Thank you," Claude said. She would make something of herself in this life. Later, though, when she'd learned the ways. "Your name?"

"Victoria Thornton."

"Well met, Miss Thornton. And good evening." He inclined his head, which brought a smile to the young one's lips.

"Good evening to you, as well."

He went through the entryway and into the sitting room. It looked exactly as it had the last time he'd come here, with Emilia at her computer again. He approached the desk. "The girl at your door, Victoria Thornton, she's promising."

"Yes. She'd been working the streets for a few months before she was brought in."

"She will accept responsibility well, I think."

"I agree. I was pleasantly surprised," she said, her voice melodic as it had always been. "I'm glad you could come by. Tonight, I'll be dining with Mecca on the music room balcony."

Claude kept his face expressionless as he listened and leaned against one of the chairs facing Emilia's desk.

"I'd appreciate it if you would bring her up for me."

A glorified nurse, pushing a wheelchair. "Of course." Claude paused, then decided to take a calculated risk. "She is a willful girl, you realize."

"Yes, she is. But I think I can persuade her."

"Do you? Is there leverage you might use?"

"Have you seen the reports on her father?"

"Briefly. I didn't look very close, I admit." Claude had read each report on David's former wives with care. "But I believe I caught the overall meaning. You will pursue him as well?"

"Yes. Having two in the fold will be a great advantage at this time." She leaned back in the desk chair and the scent of cinnamon and cloves drifted over Claude again.

He waited a moment before nodding. "Yes, the power they have would prove very useful in the coming conflict."

She turned her almond eyes on him. "I don't want the war to come to Atlanta, but I am afraid it's too late to stop it."

"I believe that's true," he said. "In a previous age, you might have been able to fortify and keep the zealots out. Today, everything is immediate and it only takes moments to make something distant local."

"Mecca's power, along with her father's, will tip the scales, I think."

"Do you have a theory about this power?"

Emilia fixed him with an intent gaze. "Do you think we've had it wrong about the Blood?"

He didn't answer right away. He wasn't sure where she was going.

"Do you think it's possible," she said, "that the Blood isn't what sustains us?"

"What do you mean?" He ground his teeth, frustrated at himself for not yet understanding, but feeling an enormity behind what she was getting at.

"What if the Blood is only a carrier?"

Everything became surreal as his thinking shifted to accommodate the shake-up of all the long-accepted tenets of their existence. Just contemplating it made his world tilt, yet in a way that made him feel the need to embrace it. Because it felt true. "It's an intriguing idea. Tell me what you're thinking."

"I'm not sure yet. The way she killed Hayden—she drained him of life, but not blood. Yet he wasted away. Does it not follow that there is something other than the Blood?"

"Yes," he said. It made sense. "What about sharing blood with humans? How does that fit in?"

Emilia leaned back in her chair. Her nostrils twitched almost imperceptibly as they always did when she concentrated. "I don't know yet. Perhaps whatever we take with the Blood fuses with us in some way? When we share it with them, it gives us some measure of control over them?" She shook her head, her brow creased. "I don't know."

"I believe it's something we should consider seriously."

"Yes. If all of the beliefs we have about the Blood are wrong…"

Claude remained silent for a time as they both considered the shift in reality such a discovery would entail. He did not want to abandon his original question, however.

"So how do you hope to use the father to get the daughter?" He knew Emilia would not deny answers outright, their entwined past would ensure that, though she might hedge.

Emilia's eyes narrowed for only a moment and Claude knew her defenses had raised. He walked a fine line between acceptable curiosity and prying interrogation.

"I hope that his previous crimes," she said, "will alienate Mecca and make her open to other possibilities. Wouldn't a murdering father cause a daughter—even a loving one—to pull away?" The question was rhetorical.

"Do we know for certain that he killed his wives?"

Emilia shrugged, her petite shoulders barely moving. "Do I know without a doubt? No. But I think it's probable. And, more importantly, I think Mecca won't be able to come to a different conclusion, as much as she may want to. I'm counting on it to make her distance herself from him. Make her more vulnerable." She watched him with fire in her eyes. "If not, we'll eventually get him as well. He won't be able to stay away forever."

"And if he tries to rescue his daughter?"

"Him coming to us would make it that much easier. I suspect he's the more powerful of the two."

"Perhaps so," Claude said, though he believed it to be exactly so. David Trenow had made short work of the two who'd been sent to fetch him. Claude wanted to ask more of her plans, but it wouldn't be welcome. He shifted topics. "Are things ready for the Maze Gathering?"

"Almost. We have the offerings, and we've received most of the invitation responses. We have dozens arriving from outside the city. It will be a full house. We haven't had a Gathering here in several years."

"The diversion will be welcome."

"Yes."

"Have you chosen who will play?"

"Not as yet. You're welcome, if you wish. We'll only have five spots this time, as we did last Gathering. I believe having fewer players makes the competition that much keener."

"I may play. I haven't participated in a Maze in quite a long time." At least eighty years, he thought.

"Oh, very good." Emilia's smile radiated sincerity. "I may send Victoria in as well. What do you think of that?"

"Do you think she has the constitution to gather the hearts?"

Emilia inclined her head, a smile curving her lips and a twinkle in her eye. "That's the question I'm hoping to answer."

"So you *do* have plans for her." Claude found himself a little bit enchanted, as he sometimes did with Emilia.

"Perhaps I do." She looked back at the computer monitor and then said, "You will bring Mecca to me at ten o'clock tonight?"

Recognizing the dismissal, Claude executed a small reverence to her as he spoke. "Of course. I would be honored."

"Very good. I will see you then."

"As you wish." He stepped back and then turned away.

He had plans to make.

Chapter Eleven: David

"But how do you know how to do this if you don't have the Gift?" Mecca looked at him with her big, chestnut eyes. Teresa's eyes. Sorrow stabbed him in the gut. Theresa had been gone almost two years. He didn't think he'd ever be used to not having her around.

"I helped my dad when he trained Ken, remember? I spent so much time letting him suck the energy out of me, I started feeling like a gas pump!" He grinned and was rewarded with Mecca's ringing laugh. A fleeting feeling of *deja vu* slid over him.

Her hand rested on his arm. They were doing what his dad had always called Aura Exercises. It didn't have anything to do with visual aura. It referred to the energy aura he knew Mecca could feel around him. He kept himself tightly shielded so he wouldn't seem different from any other person. Difficult, but he'd been accomplishing it well, he thought.

"Okay, now draw just a little from me. Not much. Just like a sip of water." He opened a tiny hole in his mental defenses so she would have something to draw from. He felt the tug of her energy, pulling his own out like liquid through a funnel.

"Is that right? I can feel it. Wow." The small voice she used reminded him of what she'd sounded like as a very young girl, not a girl who'd just entered her teens.

"That's it. You're doing it exactly right. Now, slow down. Feel it almost stop. Just a trickle. Good girl. Now stop altogether. Excellent. You're getting better. Now tell me what you felt."

Mecca leaned back in her chair, breaking contact with him. Her chest rose and fell quickly, from the energy rush. He knew from experience that it took a while to learn how to integrate the energy so it didn't feel like she'd just touched a live wire. She'd get the hang of it.

"I could feel you. Like you know how clothes can feel static-y when you take them out of the dryer? All sticking together and stuff? I could feel that around your skin when I first touched you."

David nodded.

"Then I just imagined myself pulling at that." She grinned at him, her smile wide and beautiful. "I could feel your energy coming into me. And now I'm really hyper."

He laughed. "Okay, go on outside and run it off. It'll be good practice for the track tryouts. Just be home before dark."

"Okay."

From the bay window in the kitchen, David watched her head toward the trees. The back of the house bordered on a small, wooded area with running trails. Mecca, sprinting in that direction, looked back and waved. Foreboding gathered in David's gut like a stone. Something wasn't right.

The day darkened, but Mecca ran on, her dark ponytail bouncing side to side. The sun disappeared.

Too fast. It shouldn't be dark yet.

The sense of familiarity that had persisted suddenly broke. The yard's floodlights flashed on, illuminating the backyard. But light never touched the entrance to the woods. Sick panic snaked through his veins.

"Mecca!" He raised his hand to the window.

She kept jogging until she reached the mouth of the trail that led into the blackness. He saw the vivid green of her jogging suit in the bright lights. Without warning, three shadows tore out from the woods and enveloped her. She screamed—screamed for him.

David crashed through the window and ran toward her. The trail at her back warped and shifted and became a tunnel. His legs felt heavy and slow, like he moved through water. He watched, horrified, as she struggled beneath the shadow-forms.

Her wiry legs kicked out, but she never made contact with any of them. One pulled her ponytail backward, arching her back and exposing her neck. Wheeled around, she faced the house, and he could see the caramel color of her soft skin before the largest of the figures smashed his teeth into her neck.

Her scream rang out and then withered into a sharp gurgle. The shadow-monster ripped upward. Where there had been the beauty of his daughter's neck, now was only bloody gore punctuated by wet, choking sounds.

Something yanked at his ankle. Or maybe he just stumbled. He skidded on the grass. His chin hit the ground with a brain-rattling snap of his jaw. He wanted to pull himself up, but his limbs wouldn't cooperate. It was like the earth held him tight and wouldn't let him go. He couldn't get to her. He could only lie there and listen to Mecca's watery, sucking breaths.

It took only moments for the sounds to peter away, leaving the gentle chirrup of crickets. He lay his forehead on the ground. Sobs raged from his throat, rumbling out of him like a bullet train.

When he quieted, many tears later, he realized he'd been hearing a rustling up ahead for some time. The soft scrape of something dragged through grass. He thought about just lying there. Staying and letting whatever it was have him. He had no idea where the vampires were—certainly they were vampires—but he no longer cared.

Mecca was gone. Nothing mattered.

That rustling again. Irregular, but constant.

His head felt heavy, but he lifted it, raised his gaze to see what made the sounds. The world had settled dark and hazy, but he made out her shape, moving along, close to the ground.

Bile rose in his throat.

She dragged her torso along. He saw the grisly wound in her neck. Blood glinted scarlet in the dim light from the house. It covered her lips and chin, dripped from her mouth, from her neck. The grass below her became stained with it as she moved.

He looked into her eyes and saw nothing he recognized. She was no longer the thirteen year old girl he'd been teaching just minutes ago. Fully grown, her shirt had been ripped open, exposing her small breasts as she pulled herself along the ground toward him. Her eyes twinkled with animal need, her lips upturned in an utterly grotesque smile. Her canine teeth had grown long and pointy.

He backed away on his hands and knees. Fear pricked through his veins, and his belly jumped in protest. He barely turned his head in time—vomit spewed from him with such violence, it seared his throat. He wiped the back of his hand across his mouth.

She still came toward him. "Daddy—I need you, Daddy. Come, let me touch you." That voice, low and guttural, carried a promise that made him want to puke again.

Within four feet of him now, the thing that could not be Mecca scrambled closer.

David's limbs wouldn't work. Panic brushed the edges of his mind. Losing control—even insanity—seemed almost welcome. He held it all at bay as he pulled his knees under him and crawled backward.

The world shifted, and he was on his feet with Mecca standing before him. Her hand extended toward him, and he recoiled. He backed away until a solid wall blocked his path. How did he get so close to the house?

She pressed her body against his. The coppery smell of her blood engulfed him. He convulsed with a dry heave.

"Mecca," he whispered. "Please."

She smiled and flicked her tongue over one of her teeth. "I love you, Daddy," she said in a lilty, quiet voice, wholly unlike the one he loved.

She turned his head to the side. Her sharp teeth pressed against his skin. His mind tripped, and his heart broke. A strange mix of sadness, dread, and inevitability whirled through him.

She'd set the path. He could only follow.

As her fangs broke his skin, he shot his energy out, straight into her and zeroed in on what remained of her life essence. He clamped his arms around her and drew her tight as she embraced him.

Without hesitation or second thought—he couldn't allow himself that—he ripped it from her. He pulled her energy toward him as if he reeled in a marlin. Her head jerked away from his neck. She screamed, pain and terror in the sound. She stared at him with huge dark eyes, stained with agony.

Her skin pulled taut against her bones. She tried to yank away from him, but he clutched her tight. He wouldn't let go. He couldn't.

Her muscles weakened beneath his grip. She whimpered as her knees buckled, and she slid down. He went with her, still pulling, feeling the energy break away from her like a popped rubber band. Her face grew leathery and the gaping hole in her neck had browned and shrunken.

"Daddy." The words came in a dry croak. "Please, don't. Please..."

Grief and regret stabbed him. Tears coursed down his face, and he squeezed his eyes shut, no longer able to watch as he destroyed his own daughter.

She cried beneath him, her body frail in his grasp. He willed himself not to listen as her energy finally tore free and slammed into him.

He staggered and fought for control as it rocked his soul. He rode it, and when it finally finished with him, he'd fallen to his hands and knees beside the withered husk of his daughter-turned-monster. He forced himself to look at her once beautiful face.

As he did, he realized it wasn't Mecca's face at all.

It was Sara's.

-->>><<--

David jerked awake and bolted straight up, a scream on his lips.

At the edge of the bed, Sara jumped a step back and put her hand on her chest. "Jesus Christ! Are you okay?"

David barely had the presence of mind to nod as he fought the panic that brought an acid taste up from his belly. Adrenaline pumped through him. "I'm sorry."

"No, it's cool. You just scared the shit out of me, is all. You okay? That must have been one bad-ass nightmare."

He nodded as he fought to get his breathing and heart rate under control. He pushed aside the details of the dream. He didn't want to analyze it.

"Well," she continued, "I came to wake you up because the prog came through. You're in."

"Thanks." The panic began to recede, but he couldn't concentrate on the good news Sara brought. "I'll be down in a couple of minutes."

"Okay. I went out to the Brew and got some muffins while you were asleep. I had a taste for something sweet and they've got the best orange cranberry muffins. I'll be in the basement when you're ready."

He sat on the bed for several minutes after she left, breathing deeply as he regained some control. When he felt he could walk, he went across the hall to the bathroom. He immersed himself in the mundane tasks of relieving himself and cleaning up.

In the mirror, dull, washed-out blue eyes looked back at him. If he could just find Mecca, they could disappear and become different people. David had the paperwork hidden away in a safe deposit box. It would only be a matter of signing a few bank accounts over to a holding company before transferring them to a different identity and then updating the paperwork with current photos.

He splashed water on his face. In the movies, that always seemed the thing to do in a bathroom, but it really only made a mess. He reached for the towel on the rack, but drew back. The red of the towel brought the horror of his dream. David pushed the memory aside, snatched the towel and wiped up the spilled water. Ignoring his haggard reflection now, he left the bathroom.

The living room was quiet when he trudged down the stairs. The basement door stood ajar, warm light seeping around the edges. He thought about the cracked hard drive waiting for him down there, and the dark cloud of his mood lifted enough to let him hope.

Sara sat at the second, smaller, desk, typing on the keyboard. She looked up when he entered and treated him to a smile.

"Feeling any better?"

When he shrugged, she motioned to the counter along the back wall. The black sludge in the coffee pot had been cleaned out and a fresh pot steamed on the hot plate. A mug about the size of a soup bowl sat beside a small plate with three muffins.

"Coffee will help. At least it always helps me when I have nightmares." She brushed a hand through her short, dark hair. "I didn't start looking through the drive, by the way. I figured you'd want to do it yourself."

"Thanks." David poured the steaming, black liquid into the mug and thanked fate that Sara had grown up to be so resourceful. He held the cup with both hands and let the warmth settle into his fingers, glad to see that his hands didn't shake. The hickory-tinged aroma settled his nerves. He moved to the unoccupied chair and swiveled so he could face her. "Sorry I scared you."

"It happens. At least you know it's a nightmare and not real. That's the plus side of waking up screaming."

Theoretically. But he said, "I suppose there is that, yes." He spent a moment wondering why she would wake up screaming.

Sara nodded at one of the monitors on the wall over the larger desk. It held a Windows environment with shortcuts for typical business and internet programs. "There it is. Just go through it like you would a normal desktop. E-mail's there. Files are there. Let me know if you need help, yeah?"

David found himself struck by her goodness and couldn't speak for a moment. He coughed, to clear the frog from his throat, as he rolled his chair over. "Thank you."

She only smiled and turned back to her own monitor. The smooth voice of Nat King Cole crept into the room from unseen speakers. A surprising choice of music given her age, he thought, but he found himself glad of the soft sounds. He sipped the rich, black coffee and took a deep breath before tackling the computer.

The time on the screen read 5:48 p.m.

-→➤➤◄◄◄-

Two hours later, David had looked through the files and programs on the hard drive and found them to all be business related, from a common accounting program, down to interoffice memos. They all pertained to the running of the import-export business.

Nothing about kidnappings, college girls, or death in a parking lot. He wanted to put his fist through the damned monitor. Any of them.

He did find several e-mails from Emilia Laos to someone named Thomas, who seemed to be the person in charge of running the business. All her communications were directives about how to deal with the customs officials, where a particular delivery should be made, when to acquire specific pieces of artwork. He could find nothing that hinted at where Mecca might be.

David leaned back in the chair and closed his eyes, rubbing the bridge of his nose with two fingers. It didn't help. There had to be something to discover, some way to find Emilia Laos. When he opened his eyes, the e-mail on the desktop caught his attention again. He found the text itself trivial, but he looked at the e-mail address associated with Emilia Laos.

"Sara?"

"Hmm?" She'd spent the entire time tacking on her own keyboard, sometimes humming along with the music in the background.

"The header of e-mails can tell us where they came from, right?"

"Yeah, usually. It's got the originating Internet address unless the sender sets it as something else."

"Can you find a geographic location based on that?"

She turned her chair around to face him. "Not directly. And it really depends on whether the e-mail comes from their Internet service provider or whether it's from an e-mail service, like Yahoo! or Gmail."

"I doubt she would use a service. I think she's too much of a control freak for that. Besides, the e-mail address looks like it's from her business."

"Maybe she has her own mail server then. That could make things easier." She rolled over to him and looked at the screen, then reached for his mouse. "May I?"

When he withdrew his hand, she took over, clicking here and scrolling there until she had the full header of the e-mail. She pointed to a group of numbers sandwiched in among symbols and letters.

"That's the sender's IP address. The same way longitude and latitude can find you an exact place on a map, an IP address can find an exact machine on the Internet. Every computer connected to the net is assigned an IP address, either permanently or temporarily. If she's got her own server, it's could be a static IP."

She opened a web browser and pulled up a search page. Watching her sure-handedness, he realized that, though he liked to play with technology and computer security, he didn't really know anything. He could buy all the password breaking programs he wanted; he could play his little hacking games, but he'd never be as adept at the Internet and computer security as Sara.

She keyed in the IP address and several lines of information came up, including the name and contact information of a company called Speedy DSL.

"And there's the ISP," Sara said, leaning back. "They'll have a record of who has what IP address."

"How do we get a location?"

"This is where it gets fun." She shot him a lopsided grin. "Well, fun for me. It may not really be fun for other people." And with that, she clicked and tapped at a speed that David could barely follow.

"What's your daughter's name?" she asked.

David looked from the screen to Sara. "You need that to find the location?"

Sara stopped and looked at him like he was an idiot. "No. I'm curious."

"Oh." And now he felt like an idiot. "Her name is Mecca."

"That's pretty." Sara went back to typing.

"Thank you."

An awkward almost-silence settled over them, the only sound the clacking of her keys. David tried to follow what she was doing, but had been lost within a minute. He finished off his cold coffee. He still hated involving Sara, but he'd been honest when he'd said he was glad he went to her. She'd proved even more resourceful than he'd thought.

"Can I ask you a question?" she said, still looking at the monitor.

"Shoot."

"Who's got your daughter?"

David couldn't answer right away. He found a hitch in his throat that he had to swallow down. He couldn't tell her the complete truth anyway, but he owed her some measure of it.

"There are people who think she did something, and they kidnapped her. I don't know exactly why. She's still alive—or she was this morning—but also I don't know what they plan to do with her."

"And you don't want the cops involved."

"No."

Sara nodded and though she didn't say anything more, he knew she must have had a million questions.

"I don't want to tell you too much. I've already put you in danger just being here."

Disappointment flashed across her features for a moment, and she shrugged this time.

A wall went up between them. "Play it how you like."

By 9:30, David had been pacing the floor for half an hour. Sara came up from the basement.

"Well? Do you have the address?" As soon as it came out of his mouth, David realized how it sounded. Selfish. Like he was using her.

She watched him for a moment and then asked, "What are you going to do when you get it?"

"Go over there. I'm going to see what the situation is." He ran a hand over his short hair.

"You going to go in like the Terminator or something?" The corner of her mouth tilted up.

"I doubt it. What I do will depend on what the place is like, how many people are there, if it's guarded."

"What if she's not there?"

David frowned. He hadn't considered the possibility that Mecca might be held elsewhere. That had never occurred to him at all. "She'll be there. She has to be."

"I'm sure she is." Silence settled for a few minutes. Then Sara offered a folded square of paper to him, held between two fingers.

He looked from her to the paper and back again, before he finally reached out and took it from her.

"I have a pair of binoculars, if you think those would help." She went to a door tucked away in the corner and rummaged around in the closet. She brought out a small, black case. "It's got a tiny digital camera built into it, between the lenses. I don't know if you'll need to take pictures, but the binoculars might come in handy anyway. Just don't leave them hanging from some tree limb, okay?"

She grinned, and he couldn't help but smile as he took the case and hiked the strap onto his shoulder.

Her personality was so much like Mecca's. A stab of guilt twisted his gut. He fished into his pocket and came out with the wad of bills. Sara raised a brow as he split it, put half back into his pocket and held the other half out. "Here."

"Thanks, no. I don't need it."

"Consider it my contribution to Headquarters. It's the least I can do."

She hesitated, but then finally took the money. She nodded at the paper he still held. "You know where that is? I think it's east of Stone Mountain."

"I'll look it up." David put a hand on her shoulder, feeling a pride he had no right to feel. "Sara, your grandmother would think the world of you. You're amazing."

She blushed and looked at her toes. "Thank you. Are you leaving right now?"

"Yeah. I need to get out there."

"I want to come with you."

"No. Absolutely not."

"Why not?"

Hadn't they already gone over this? "I'm not going to put you in any more danger. You can't imagine what these people are like. I could never have imagined until I met them. Please trust me on this."

She frowned, her lower lip stuck out just a little. "There's a spare key around back, underneath the garden robot, in case you need to come back."

"Garden robot?" What the hell was that?

"I'm a geek. Gnomes aren't my thing." She gave him that grin again. "Promise you won't be a stranger?"

If I get out of this alive. "I promise."

Chapter Twelve: Mecca

She is sobbing. The bedspread beneath her is soaked with her tears. The voices of the people downstairs waft up to her, with their condolences and apologies, their handshakes and hugs. She'd had to escape from them. What do they know about it anyway, with their sad eyes and pity in their voices? Patting her shoulder and hugging her tight.

It only made Mom's death more final. More painful.

She knows she can't stay up here much longer. Dad will wonder where she's gone. Everyone will wonder. Then will come another round of *tsk-tsk* and "the poor child."

She pulls herself up and sits on the edge of her bed, clutching on to Katybun. The floppy-eared, stuffed bunny—her first gift from her parents as a baby—is as stained with her tears as the bedspread.

She runs a hand across her face, using the sleeve of her black dress to dry her cheek. She wanders out of her room and sits on the top step of the staircase, settling Katybun on her lap and wrapping her arms around him. The fuzzy head tickles as she rests her chin on it.

Downstairs, people roam around, speaking with her grandparents and talking to each other. Soft music plays in the background, and she recognizes the voice of Billie Holiday, Mom's favorite blues singer. Fresh tears spring to her eyes, but she snatches them away with the back of her hand.

From the hallway behind her comes muffled voices. She didn't know anyone else was up here. She stands, still holding Katybun close, and walks down the hall. The voices come from the door of her father's office. If she leans in, she can just make out most of the words. Dad and Gramps are having an argument.

"You need to tell her, Dave," her grandfather says in his husky voice.

"She doesn't need to know. It's not necessary."

"Of course it's necessary. She'll find out."

Mecca's heart skips a beat. *It's true. It's my fault.* She bites her lower lip, trying to keep the tears from tumbling down. Her heart sinks in her chest.

"Is that a threat?"

"Relax, Dave." Uncle Ken is in there too. He's younger than Dad, but is always the middle man between Dad and Gramps. "I don't think he means it that way. But for what it's worth, I agree. You should tell her."

"I have one question for you." Gramps again, accusation in his voice. That confuses Mecca. "Did Teresa die naturally?"

She stifles a sob and leans so close to the door that her ear is touching the cool wood. The silence spirals out. Finally, her father speaks.

"That's not your business, Dad."

Mecca can't stand there any longer without bawling. Dad must be protecting her. He must know that her falling asleep with her mom is what... what made Mom have to go to the hospital. He doesn't want to tell Gramps and Uncle Ken because he doesn't want them to blame her.

She shuffles down the hall and pushes open the door to her parents' room. The king size bed is taller than her own twin size, but Mecca scales it, Katybun clutched under her arm. Not until she is curled up in a tiny ball with her head on her mom's pillow does she let her sorrow loose again. Her body shakes with her weeping.

When all her tears are spent, she lies there, motionless. Everything is just too heavy. She listens as the sounds from below eventually die away, and she stays there. Her only movement is to snuggle with her father when she wakes in the night to the sound of him sobbing beside her.

Mecca drifted up into consciousness and had an odd sensation of being both in her dream and in reality at once. She remained still, waiting for the strange feeling to pass. Thoughts of her father moved through her mind and though love welled in her heart, bitterness and confusion tinged it.

If she could wish anything right now, she wished to never have known about Susan Harrington or the other women. She wished to be back in her dorm room, making plans for dinner with her dad over the phone. It was Sunday, she thought, and that's what she should be doing. She pursed her lips and fought to reign in her emotions.

"Welcome back." The voice was male, soft, familiar. Mecca opened her eyes to see Claude reclined in the chair nearby. He wore a dapper black suit with a cream colored shirt, a single button open at the collar. One slim leg draped over the other, showing off well-polished black shoes. "You slept much longer than expected."

Mecca realized she wasn't lying down any longer, but sitting in a wheelchair. Her hands were free, covered with thin gloves, but she found her legs bound with leather straps. Her feet had been cuffed to the leg rests of the chair.

"What's going on?" When Claude seemed disinclined to stop her, she touched the wheels of the chair and then gave them a push. She rolled across to the far wall, then maneuvered around to turn and face him. His gaze met hers and her heart thudded.

"Emilia thought you might like some fresh air, so she will be seeing you out on one of the balconies. She has arranged for dinner to be served there." He rose and approached her and then slipped behind.

"Aren't you afraid I'll jump out and do something terrible?"

He laughed.

Why did her belly quiver?

"I doubt you will be much of a threat this evening. You are bolted in that chair too tightly for you to even consider getting free." He turned her around and opened the door with his keycard before pushing her through and closing it behind them.

Small sconces threw soft light along the wood-paneled hallway, giving it warmth. Mecca blinked quickly, trying to get her eyes to adjust faster.

The chair's wheels made no sound as he pushed her along, the bottoms almost engulfed by the thick carpet beneath them. He didn't seem to have any trouble pushing her. The hall wasn't long, but half a dozen dark wooden doors lined either side.

"What are behind those?" She inclined her head toward one as they passed.

"Various things: research rooms, conference rooms and the like. I believe there's a room full of computers behind one of the doors as well, though that may well be a rumor." He laughed again, softer and more gentle.

"So where are we going?"

"Upstairs."

At the end of the hall, Mecca spied a recessed elevator door done in dark wood to match the others. When they approached, Claude produced his plastic card from his pants pocket and waved it over the metal pad to the right of the elevator. The doors slid open as he pocketed the card. He wheeled her inside.

Mecca looked at the panel on the wall as Claude turned her around to face the door. A dozen buttons from the number four at the top to B1 through B3 and S1 down to S4 at the bottom. The S1 button glowed white. Claude moved beside her and tapped the button for the third floor with a pale finger.

"How old are you?"

Claude looked down at her and quirked a brow. "That is quite the thing to ask."

"I've never been good with segues. Older than Will, I suppose."

"That's a very good guess."

"Are you Emilia's boss?" Mecca wanted to take advantage of his candid mood. Let him play the ostentatious host.

"Me? No. I'm just an old friend who's visiting for a while."

"Where are you visiting from?"

"You are full of questions tonight, young Ms. Trenow."

She watched him for a span of two floors. She wasn't going to let him off that easily.

Finally, he chuckled and said, "I was born in what is now the Ukraine."

Well, that explained the accent. "You're Russian."

He inclined his head. "As you wish."

The elevator chimed a low note, and the doors slid open with a quiet pneumatic sound. Claude got behind her and wheeled her down another, longer hallway with hardwood floors. Electric sconces lined the walls here also, but the wood was of a lighter grain than below, giving the hall a brighter appearance.

"Think there's any way I could get a shower? I feel disgusting."

"Perhaps. I'll see what I can do about that."

"Thanks."

The hallway ended in a set of French doors. Images of lily pads and reeds were etched into the glass and tinted with subtle color. As much as Mecca didn't want to see beauty here, the doors were lovely. It pissed her off a little bit.

Beyond, Mecca saw a great room with posh and expensive furnishings. Claude opened the door and pushed Mecca through, the wheels of her chair again sinking into rich carpet.

A black baby grand piano stood along one side, the top propped up, finish gleaming as if had just been polished. Nearby, a cello leaned against its stand. A thick oriental rug covered the hard wood floor, leaving only a foot between its edges and the walls. She didn't have an eye for art, but the paintings looked museum quality, framed in intricately carved wood. Everything in the room looked old, antique, exquisite.

Claude turned her away from the instruments and moved her through a sitting area flanked with tall bookcases, on which stood small musical items. Beyond a pair of Queen Anne chairs, they came to a set of smaller French doors with the same lily pad motif carved into them.

On the other side of the tinted glass, Mecca saw a large stone balcony with a thick pillar rail; a bistro table had been laid with a bright, white tablecloth. It seemed luminescent in the darkness.

The slim and striking figure of Emilia sat in one dainty chair. Set a few feet behind the empty space at the table where the second chair would be, a fire burned inside a square metal fire pit. When Emilia saw their approach, she rose and opened the glass door.

"Good evening, Mecca, Claude."

Claude wheeled her through the threshold and onto the balcony. He pushed her chair up to the table and then excused himself and slipped back into the music room. A cool breeze brought the scent of gardenias on the night air.

Mecca remained silent, but studied Emilia closely. She hated to admit it, but the woman was stunning. Emilia wore a long sleeve linen blouse in a flax color along with loose-fitting black, silk slacks. Her dark hair, swept back on top, left only the pageboy curl at the base of her neck, near her collar. She wore very little make-up, enough to accent her almond-shaped eyes and her high cheekbones. The woman moved with efficiency, yet each move was fluid and graceful.

"I thought a breath of fresh night air might do you good. I hope you don't mind dining with me." Emilia sank back into the seat opposite Mecca's wheelchair.

"In truth, I hope I'll be eating alone." Mecca's bravado overcame her.

Emilia's forehead wrinkled. "Pardon?"

"Are you going to have a bowl of blood? Maybe a freshly killed squirrel?"

Emilia laughed, a light, genuine sound. "You're serious, aren't you?"

Mecca pursed her lips.

"No," Emilia said as the French doors opened. "Tonight we'll be having salmon, not squirrel."

An old man wearing a well-tailored butler's suit complete with snow-white gloves came out onto the balcony, pushing a silver cart, like those found in fancy hotels. He bent into a deep, formal bow for Emilia, then offered a smaller one to Mecca before putting two dome-covered dishes before each of them.

When the old man removed the first dome from in front of Mecca, a white cloud of steam escaped and the rich smell of potato soup wafted to her nose. Her belly rumbled. She wished she wasn't hungry.

He lifted the second dome and revealed a white plate stacked with fresh greens, cherry tomatoes, carrots and cucumbers. A small dish of vinaigrette perched on the edge of the plate. The man set the domes on his cart, then took a step back, putting his hands behind his back.

"Is that satisfactory so far?" Emilia asked.

The potato soup looked thick and smelled like heaven. Mecca nodded.

Emilia waved a hand at the servant, who promptly disappeared through the French doors, taking the cart with him. Mecca watched him close the doors, then turned to look at Emilia, who gave her an encouraging nod.

"Go ahead." When Mecca hesitated, Emilia continued. "If we'd wanted to do something as simple as poison you, don't you think you'd be dead by now?"

Mecca didn't fear poison. She simply found herself uncomfortable eating in front of Emilia. Since she'd be wheeled up to the table, Emilia had been watching her with a strange look. Predatory. It made Mecca self-conscious. Not to mention the inability to leave — to even stand.

But her stomach growled its protest at the delay. She gave in and lifted the spoon to her lips. The hot soup warmed her mouth and tasted as good as the smell had promised. The earthy potato taste comforted her on some level she didn't understand. She ate spoonful after spoonful, unmindful of Emilia, who'd begun to eat her salad.

Finally, the woman spoke again. "I think you understand what it is I want to know." Emilia's voice was soft, but held the strength of steel behind it. "My end goal isn't to hurt you, though you should know that I will if I must. That is entirely up to you. But in an effort to show you that I'm not your enemy, I will answer some questions you might have. There are things I will not answer, but you may ask what you wish and will speak as truthfully as I can."

Mecca couldn't keep the look of surprise from crossing her face. "Why would you do that? You've kept me here for who knows how long, drugged, against my will. How can you say you're not my enemy?"

"I'm not. Have you been hurt while you've been here? Has anyone done you any sort of harm whatsoever? You've been very well cared for. You've been fed. You're getting fresh air."

"I make a nice pet then."

Emilia's pert nose wrinkled. "If I truly were the demon you seem to think I am, then I would have gotten the information out of you, ripped your throat out and gorged myself on your life."

Mecca blanched. It was probably true. She looked out over the rail into the darkness and watched the shadows on the lawn below. Just past the light being thrown from the balcony, Mecca made out a very straight and square hedge. The apparent enormity of the estate intimidated her.

"All right," she said. "Questions, then. What is it you have against my father?"

"Against him? Nothing. Nothing at all. The research that you'd done — the print outs from your bag — we only expanded upon that. It wasn't difficult making the connections, once we knew what to look for." Emilia took a sip of her own soup and made a satisfied murmur beneath her breath. "I do find him very interesting, in the same way I find you very interesting. Is that so surprising?"

"I suppose not." She reminded herself again that she and her father shared the Gift. After a lifetime of being separate, different, she found it hard to remember that she and her dad were not as different as she'd always thought. It surprised her every time she recalled. A sad bitterness enveloped her. She set aside her soup bowl and began picking at her salad. "What do you want with us?"

"We'll get to that in a bit."

"Fine. I saw your guy. That night." She watched for a reaction, but Emilia seemed to have none. "I know you were spying on Hayden. Why?"

Emilia leaned back in the little bistro chair and folded her hands on her waist, her elbows resting on the chair's arms. Her gaze traced Mecca up and down. The appraisal made Mecca uncomfortable, but she continued to toy with her salad and tried to seem oblivious.

"Hayden," Emilia said, with a hint of reluctance, "had been under surveillance for quite some time. He was a bit of a rogue in our little family and had caused some trouble. We kept an eye on him, especially when he paid visits to that part of town. He got into trouble there on more than one occasion."

"What sort of trouble?"

"We have rules, you know. Unfortunately, Hayden was not one to follow rules unless he made them."

Just as Mecca pushed her salad plate away, the French doors opened and the older man returned with his cart. He swept away the bowls and salad plates, tucking them onto a shelf beneath the main tray.

A large, covered plate appeared before Mecca and another before Emilia. He lifted the domes with an economy of movement that impressed her. The full plate came into view. It held rice, steamed broccoli, squash and cauliflower, and a grilled salmon fillet. The aroma alone made her mouth water.

The man refilled her water goblet and filled the other glass with iced tea. Emilia waved her hand away when he tried to do the same for her. His ministrations complete, he took a single step back and waited, hands behind his back. Emilia gave him a small nod, and he wheeled his cart through the doors and closed them behind him.

Mecca took a sip of the tea, then looked across the table at her hostess. Hundreds of questions flew through her mind, but only a few really stuck out. She didn't want to think about her father for a while. "What is Will? He's not one of you, and I get the impression he's not exactly one of me, either."

A wry smile played across Emilia's lips. "You're asking all the hard ones, aren't you?"

"And what would you ask, in my position?"

"Point taken." Emilia sipped her water and looked out over the darkened yard.

Mecca took a small bite of her rice. As time drew out, she wondered whether Emilia would answer her question. It seemed like a very long time before the other woman looked back at her, her jaw set.

"First, you need to know about the Visci," Emilia said. "My people."

Mecca said nothing about Will mentioning the Visci to her already. He'd been kind, and she didn't want to get him into trouble if he shouldn't have told her. "Is that something like the Native Americans?" Mecca asked. Maybe if she played *really* dumb, she'd get more information.

"No, nothing at all. We are not human, as you may have guessed, yet we are just as natural as humans. We are a different species."

"So you're not vampires?"

The smile that crossed Emilia's face wasn't arrogant but amused. "Not as you would think of them. There are many of us who believe your vampire legends come from mistaken assumptions about our kind."

Though Mecca had tasted the salmon and found it delicious, Emilia's story became her main focus, her appetite gone. She hated that the story intrigued her so much, but she couldn't deny it.

"We do feed on blood, that is true. Our lives are much, much longer than a human's, though we can die of old age. We are difficult to kill by the normal methods. There are a few differences between us and humans, but more similarities, really. And when we share our blood with a human, some of our traits are transferred to him on a temporary basis."

"Like a longer life?" That would explain Will's cryptic comments about being so old.

"Yes."

Mecca realized she'd been leaning forward, and she forced herself to relax and settle back. Heat from the fire pit had warmed the vinyl supports of the wheelchair, and it felt good against her back. "This sounds crazy, you realize?"

Emilia extended her hands in an open gesture. "And what you do wouldn't sound crazy?"

Mecca groused beneath her breath, but said nothing out loud. She didn't want to talk about herself or her Gift.

"So, to answer your original question, Will is my companion. He is human."

"And you've extended his life with your blood?" The thought of Will drinking blood made her shudder. Did he drink it from her neck? From a cup? How did that work? She couldn't bring herself to ask.

"Yes, I've extended his life."

"What will happen if he stops?"

"If he doesn't have access to Visci blood? He's already outlived his natural life. He will die."

Her matter-of-fact tone startled Mecca. She'd assumed that companion meant lover. Or at least someone very close. Emilia seemed disconnected from the feelings her words should have brought up. At least, to Mecca's way of thinking. And that made Emilia cold-hearted.

"I've given you some very important information," her host said, when Mecca didn't respond. "Information that is not generally shared with humans. Now, I would ask for something in return."

The hair on the back of Mecca's neck rose. "What something?"

"I would like details of yourself and your…talent. You've exhibited some abilities which intrigue me."

"Like killing Hayden."

"Just so. I am particularly interested in that. I'm prepared to offer you a certain amount of freedom in return for your cooperation."

Now, the tiny hairs on Mecca's arms stood at attention too. "What are you talking about?"

"Unfortunately, it would cause problems if we were to let you roam free without any sort of supervision or guidance."

The salmon had grown cold in the night air, and Mecca dropped her fork to the plate. She was going to be kept a prisoner. "You know," Mecca said, her voice flat, "I understand every word that's come out of your mouth, but the way you're stringing them together doesn't make the least bit of sense."

"Don't be insulted." Emilia's voice lilted across the table and embraced Mecca with its tone. "You don't want to kill innocent people, do you? Don't you see what your father did? He has this same talent, and how did he use it? He killed people."

The words stabbed straight to Mecca's heart, sharp and vicious. She couldn't keep the tears from welling in her eyes. The fear and self-doubt smothered her. She clutched at her anger as she tried to pull herself from the darkness.

"He wasn't much older than you when he started killing for profit, Mecca."

How could her voice be resonating so deeply? How could she know those fears Mecca held tightly since she'd first seen the fuzzy photo of her father on that website? After a long moment, Mecca finally raised her gaze, took a big breath, and met Emilia's eyes. "What my father may or may not have done when he was young has no bearing on who I am. What is it, exactly, that you want from me?"

"I've told you. I want to know about you and your power. I want to know who else besides the two of you has this power. And most of all —"

"I don't know who else has it." The words tumbled out before she could stop them.

Emilia raised both brows. Her eyes glinted like ice as she leaned in, elbows resting on the table. She fixed her gaze on Mecca. "Don't lie to me. I will always, always know when you lie to me."

Mecca jerked back, away from that intense stare. She closed her own eyes, shook her head. A coldness crept along the edges of her mind; it was a physical feeling. Something foreign in her thoughts, in her mind.

She opened her eyes again and leaned forward, rage rushing through her. "Get out of my head!"

Chapter Thirteen: Mecca

Mecca glared across the table as the coldness receded from her mind. Emilia watched her, calm and undisturbed, her thin pale lips turned up in a smile that looked more friendly than predatory.

"And most of all," Emilia continued her previous statement, "I want you to agree to a proposal. But first, I do require information."

The urge to answer right away rose, but Mecca fought it down. She flexed her calves. The restraints on her legs tightened as she tried to bring her anger under control. Being upset wouldn't help her situation. Why did she have this compulsion to answer Emilia? It had happened more than once. Instead of responding immediately, she considered what to reveal and what to keep secret.

She had to believe that at some point there would be an opportunity to get away. She must remain clear-headed enough to recognize it when it happened. If she could just give Emilia enough information to satisfy her, then maybe Mecca could find a way to escape.

"I can feel people's energy. I can take it from them and use it for myself. That's the nature of my gift."

"And that's how you killed Hayden, by taking his energy?"

"Hayden had no energy of his own." An angry edge crept into her voice. "What I took from him was not his."

"I see." Emilia studied her for a moment. Mecca saw a question in the woman's eyes and for a moment expected her to ask it. Instead, Emilia said, "What made you choose him?"

"I didn't choose him."

"But you went out with him. Why?"

Mecca looked down at her gloved hands. "He just felt strange to me. I guess I was curious."

"So you didn't plan to kill him?"

A sharp stab of anger flashed through Mecca's belly. "Kill him? He attacked me. I reacted."

"You were just defending yourself? I know he tried to feed from you."

"Yes." She'd killed him trying to free the stolen soul he had inside. But she wasn't going to share that with Emilia. Let her believe what she wished. "You said earlier that you have a proposal to offer me."

"Indeed, I did. I would like for you to join me. I could use someone of your talent and ability. You will be well compensated, of course. And you can complete your studies at university if that's what you wish."

Mecca tried to stifle her shock. Of all the things she'd anticipated, becoming Emilia's "employee" had never entered her thoughts. Her mind spun. "I don't understand."

"For the most part, you will live your life in the same way you have so far. The only difference will be that sometimes I will give you an assignment to rid of us some problems. Like your own society, we have those who continually live outside the bounds of our laws. If they will not correct their behavior, they must be reined in. You are perfect for that sort of thing."

Realization slowly crept into her mind. "Wait a minute. You want me to assassinate people?" How much crazier could this get?

"That is harsh. When people go beyond the law, there must be consequences. Hayden, for instance, couldn't control himself. Or perhaps it's more accurate to say that he *wouldn't* control himself. When there are those who would disrupt our society— any society — with their rebellious ways, then they must either be brought back into the fold or removed permanently."

Now it all made sense. *Emilia didn't kill me because she wants to use me.* "I don't think I'm cut out for that sort of thing."

Emilia waved a hand in the air. "Of course you are. It's what you were made for. You're the perfect killing machine: quiet, unassuming, and deadly. Just like your father. But unlike your father, you would be doing it for the greater good."

"Greater good. Right." Mecca couldn't keep the sarcasm from her voice.

Emilia leaned in, resting her elbows on the arms of her chair. "In order for us — my kind — to survive in this world, we must always remain under cover of darkness, as it were. We must be aware of exactly who is available and who is off limits to us. We must all adhere to certain rules."

"You mean when killing someone."

"Killing isn't necessary." Emilia smiled. "We are not so different, you and I."

Mecca tried to jump to her feet. The restraints bit into her skin. "I am nothing like you! Don't you ever say that!" She jerked against her bonds again, frustration pricking through her veins. She had to find a way to get out of this place.

"All right. I don't want to argue the philosophical points of our existence right now, at any rate. Just know that those of my kind who do not respect our laws become a danger for all of us as a whole. They do not recognize those who should be safe from us. They do not follow the rules. In getting rid of them, we benefit, of course, but humans benefit as well. Those who should always be protected will remain protected."

"Like you would protect anyone."

Emilia leaned back and opened her hands, palms up. "We're not as terrible as you seem to think. There are people who are, or rather, should always be safe from us. Children, for example. It is within our code that children are not to be preyed upon. If a rogue disregards that rule, then your society suffers as innocent children are killed."

"And you care?"

"I won't try to mislead you by saying that the law is not self-serving. Children's deaths tend to be heavily investigated. If we prey on children, the chances of our being discovered increase. In this case, the edict is mutually beneficial." Emilia fixed her with a pointed look, and Mecca's belly did a flip. "And if one of mine does not follow it… well, that is where you would come in."

"To slaughter the monster who is killing the innocents." Mecca's voice played flat.

"You can understand how this arrangement would be for the best, in all regards."

Mecca gave no reply. When did her life go insane? Her father — a killer. Herself — an assassin? *Too much.*

Emilia rose with grace. "I will give you tomorrow to think on it. Will is here to take you back to your room, unless you have further questions? Though it's a shame you didn't finish your salmon."

Through the etched doors, Mecca could see Will across the music room, fingering the keyboard on the piano. His polo shirt, tucked into belted blue jeans, hugged his torso and defined his shoulders.

Half-formed questions bounced around in Mecca's mind. Then the only fully realized question bounced from her lips. "Would I be the way he is, then?" Her gaze swung up to meet Emilia's. "Would you be feeding me your blood?"

Emilia smiled. "Of course. It's been going well thus far."

--→⇥⇤←--

Emilia had left after the old man had cleared the table. Mecca put her head in her hands, closed her eyes and allowed self-pity to wash over her. The soft, smooth gloves covering her hands only reminded her that she was trapped. She resisted the urge to cry, though she had no idea how long she could keep the tears away.

She swallowed back the bile that rose at the thought of Emilia's blood coursing through her own veins. They must have done that while she was asleep. The IV had been taken out for her little date with Emilia, but they must have used that to give her the blood while she slept. She couldn't remember seeing anything but clear liquid in the bags when she was awake.

That bitch.

Mecca had killed Hayden in self-defense. She wasn't a murderer, not really, but if she could get her hands on Emilia…

Mecca took a deep breath. That line of thinking wouldn't help her right now. She fought her anger and the accompanying sense of doom and tried to think rationally.

Emilia's offer was clearly an ultimatum. They would not let her go if she didn't help them. They'd kill her as surely as they drugged her every day.

A vampire assassin. Okay, so they weren't really vampires, but in their own way, they were.

What would life be like? Perhaps she would have ended up here anyway. She'd gone on that research binge with the intention of learning about vampire legends and folklore. Why? Had she planned on going this route? Had she thought she might be like some medieval slayer of the undead? Or Buffy?

The French doors opened, and Will stepped onto the balcony in his polo shirt and faded, well-worn jeans. They watched each other for an appraising moment.

"Are you all right?" he asked.

Tears sprang into Mecca's eyes at the simple question. She blinked several times to keep them from falling and nodded. Will approached and wheeled her into the sitting room.

"She's really not a monster, if that helps you at all."

"How can you say that, knowing what she does?" The chair moved slowly through the thick carpet.

"You don't know what she does or doesn't do, Mecca. She runs this city well and with a minimum of disruption. She doesn't kill indiscriminately, generally, and she doesn't tolerate those who do. You would be hard put to find a lower crime rate in a city of this size or a better economy."

"And in exchange, we sacrifice virgins to the dragon?"

"If you wish to be melodramatic, then yes. With the good always comes the bad. Everything has its price." His tone, though matter-of-fact, was also gentle.

"What if I don't want to be bought?"

They'd reached the elevator and Will stepped around the chair, pulled a plastic card from his jeans pocket and waved it over the card reader. The lift doors whooshed open.

His shirt accented his toned chest and especially his arms. He wasn't chiseled, but she could see the movement of his bicep as he slid the card back into his jeans. She found herself glad he hadn't worn his lab coat.

"If you don't wish to be bought," he said as he wheeled the chair into the elevator, "then you're in the wrong century. Everyone is bought."

"You're cynical."

"Perhaps. I've seen enough to be realistic."

They rode in silence as the elevator descended. Mecca wondered, if she accepted Emilia's proposal, would her attitude be like Will's as time wore on?

"What happens to you if Emilia dies? She told me that you're only alive this long because of her. So when she dies, you'll die too?" Mecca couldn't see Will behind her, but the long pause told her she'd caught him off guard.

"Emilia won't die."

"I thought you've seen enough to be realistic? Everyone dies."

"Very well. Any of them can do for me what Emilia does. Whether they would find me useful enough to do so is debatable."

"And how long would that take? How much time would you have before you died?" The lift stopped on their floor and the chair jerked forward as Will pushed.

"I have no idea. I've not tested it."

As they made their way down the hall, Mecca's thoughts flew. Every step he took brought Mecca closer to that bed, with its restraints and haze-inducing drugs.

She inched her hands closer together and then reached beneath the sleeve of her gown. The glove rose just above her wrist and fit tight to her hand, with an elastic edge. She slipped two fingers under the band and brought her arms in to her belly.

Please let this work.

They stopped at her door and Will again laid his card on the reader. Mecca heard the lock release. She swayed in her chair and groaned.

Will eyed her as he opened the door. "What's wrong?"

"I'm feeling...a bit light-headed. And my stomach hurts."

Will pushed the chair into the room and closed the wooden door behind them. The lock caught with a click. Mecca swayed again as Will set the brake on the chair.

Please let this work. And please don't let me accidentally kill him.

Mecca let out another loud groan and slumped forward, relaxing her whole body. Now, while it was shielded from his sight by her body, she pulled the glove off her hand.

"Shit." Will rushed to her side and slid his arm between Mecca's chest and legs, bracing to pull her up by the shoulders. Mecca let her head loll to the side as he heaved her into an upright position.

As she was moved, Mecca grabbed Will's arm. He tried to lurch backward, his eyes wide with surprise, but Mecca held on.

"I'm sorry," Mecca whispered when the surprise turned to panic.

Will's Cavern superimposed itself on Mecca's vision. His energy filled the place with golden light, making the walls seem to glow. The fringes of the light glinted a very pale green. *Strange.* The edge colors were usually vibrant, almost pulsing with whatever color.

But she couldn't linger to admire. She dipped into the golden luminosity and began siphoning it off quickly, almost the way one would drain off gas from a car.

Behind her vision of the Cavern, Will's eyes widened and his mouth opened. A gasp escaped his lips before the loss of energy began to affect him. He tried to struggle then, but it was too late. Mecca held him easily.

He rocked on his heels, eyelids drooping. Mecca slowed the energy drain just as Will began to slump. As soon as he hit the floor, unconscious, Mecca released his arm. He fell into a heap beside the wheelchair.

Mecca licked her finger and held it under Will's nose. She'd seen that in some movie or other. The wetness cooled with the small exhales coming from his nostrils. Her relief came out in a rushed breath that she hadn't realized she'd been holding.

Energy sang in every cell of her body. She'd never drained anyone to unconsciousness; she felt like running ten miles.

Mecca unbuckled the strap across her lap and then reached down and unfastened the cuffs that held her ankles to the leg braces. She hoisted herself out of the chair and stumbled before getting her feet back under her. It took a minute to steady herself and get used to standing again. She stretched her legs and jogged in place for a moment before she trusted them fully.

Will lay at her feet, in a crumpled heap. But he still breathed. A wavy lock of coppery-brown hair lay across his nose. Mecca crouched and brushed it back, to show his closed eyes. His eyelashes, a deep brown, were so long the bottoms and tops tangled together. She pulled her gaze away from his face, and then checked his pulse. It beat strong enough to convince her that the man wasn't dying.

She didn't want Will dead. The others, maybe. But not Will.

Mecca pawed through his jeans until she found the passkey that would open the doors. Her heart sat thick in her throat and beat a hard tempo in her veins. If they caught her, would they kill her?

Probably.

She couldn't go trying to escape in the white gown they'd put her in. "Oh shit." She didn't even know why they did it. She checked the tiny bathroom, then the closet, but neither had her clothes in them. She looked down at Will. Mecca could probably fit into his clothes, though they would be way too big. Will stood about three inches taller.

She wasted no more time thinking. She stripped Will down to his navy blue briefs, trying not to stare, a ferocious heat in her cheeks the entire time. She turned her back to him, tucked the keycard into the back pocket of the jeans and pulled the clothes on. She rolled the legs up at her ankle twice so they wouldn't drag the floor and tucked the polo shirt in. She cinched the black belt and fastened it on the innermost hole. The jeans still rode low on her hips.

His shoes didn't fit at all. She'd have to go barefoot.

She looked at Will's almost naked body. She took a moment to drape her white gown over his still form." I'm sorry. But I have to get out of here."

She pulled the passkey out of her pocket. The plastic card, cool in her hand, disengaged the lock, and she eased the door open. After a glance in both directions revealed no one else in the corridor, she stepped through and closed the door. It locked with a satisfying *click*.

The elevator looked miles away. Mecca straightened her back and strode toward it. The small metal panel blinked when she put Will's card on it. The doors opened to reveal an empty lift.

So far so good.

She pressed the button for ground level. The elevator rose. Her nerves, already over-worked, tingled from the draw she had from Will; it felt like her entire body of energy resided just below her skin. If anyone touched her, she would flash like a camera. As the elevator rose, she stretched her legs the same way she would before a track meet. If she had to run, she'd better be prepared.

The doors slid open, and she stepped into a hallway that resembled the others with its wood paneling and hardwood floors. This hall had no carpet runner and the wooden floor cooled her feet.

The music room upstairs had opened onto a balcony. Probably the room below it opened onto a patio. She turned in the same direction Claude had taken her upstairs.

The quiet hall unnerved her. She tried to keep her steps measured in case someone saw her.

Most people will accept that you belong somewhere if you act like you belong. Life's all about faking it.

She found the room which she thought corresponded to the music room from upstairs. It also had double doors, but in solid wood, rather than glass. One sat ajar, soft light flickering through the opening. She slipped through and closed the door quietly behind her. She wheeled around, hoping to find patio doors she could sneak out. She stopped mid-spin and stood as still as a lamppost.

Ceiling-high bookcases covered every wall, stuffed with hard covers; dozens of paperbacks crowded the bottom shelves. A rolling ladder leaned motionless in a corner to her left. On the opposite wall, a fireplace entertained a small blaze while a cozy leather seating arrangement clustered around.

Standing beside the fireplace, a tall, dark-haired man looked at her, brows raised, remaining as motionless as she. The dark tang of fear crept up her throat.

On the leather sofa, with a book open on his lap, sat Claude.

Chapter Fourteen: David

David brought the binoculars to his eyes and looked across the road. Balancing in the boughs of an oak tree, he sat, freezing his ass off, and studied the house. Well, studied the *estate*.

David had reconned the perimeter when he'd arrived over an hour ago. The wall surrounded the estate as far as he could see. The back of the property abutted a small side road and from there, a rutted track led to a rust red, pipe gate set into the estate's wall. He'd parked on the main road and doubled-back to check out the gate.

In the darkness, he'd made out a stout man sitting on a folding chair just inside the gate, an assault rifle lying across his knees. The track led into a copse of trees. He couldn't see farther in the darkness, but as he'd returned to the van and driven the rest of the way around the perimeter, he'd thought the back gate might be a way to get in.

The tree branch creaked as he shifted his weight. The last few leaves that had clung to his branch sifted to the ground.

The imposing colonial perched on top of a gentle rise, surrounded by landscaped lawns dappled with dozens of species of trees and bushes. The winding drive passed through the gates of a stacked stone wall.

Coiled on top of the wall wound nasty looking cords of barbed wire. Just inside the gate, he made out a squat guard station.

The house itself sat like a crown on the hill. Majestic was a fitting description. It didn't surprise him to see men patrolling along the wrap-around porch. Although they didn't seem heavily armed, they each wore a hip holster equipped with a pistol. David lowered the binoculars and inched along the branch, toward the trunk. Within a minute, his feet crunched on the fallen leaves around the base of the tree.

He moved farther into the tree line, but kept the gated wall in sight. He'd parked the van a few hundred yards away, off an old service road that looked like it hadn't been used since the Carter administration. Close enough to run to if it became necessary, but out of sight of the two lane blacktop that led to the estate.

With each step into the woods, the faint smell of moldy leaves came up to meet him, sour and damp. He took a cell phone out of his pocket — the one he'd taken off Irish — and found the number he'd keyed into it earlier.

"Hello?" A soft, feminine voice.

"Ms. Laos, this is David Trenow."

He got no response at first. After the pause, she said, "It's almost two a.m., Mr. Trenow."

"Yes. It's time for our meeting."

"You keep very odd business hours."

"Get into your car and drive toward Stone Mountain. I'll call you and give you directions to where we will meet. Come alone."

"Very well," she said. "Understand that I do not often take orders. I make an exception this one time, simply because I am interested in meeting with you."

"Noted." David closed the phone, ending the call.

Less than twenty minutes later, the iron gate opened and a smoke grey Audi rolled through. From his crouch, deep inside the tree line, David looked through the binoculars. Everything came into sharp relief. He stayed low as the car came down the short drive, toward his position. In the still night air, the engine's purr sounded like a rumble. Through the windshield, he saw the murky figure of a woman driving. He couldn't make out anyone else in the car, though it was possible someone could have been hiding in the back seat.

The car turned left onto Route 78, which would lead to Stone Mountain Parkway. The Audi's headlights cut its arc through the woods. David ducked his head. The side windows, tinted so dark they couldn't be legal, didn't even give away the silhouette of the occupant.

When the taillights disappeared over the rise, about half a mile away, David stood. He brushed oak leaves and pine needles off the knees of his jeans and then started toward the road where he'd parked the van.

He hadn't gone ten yards when the noise of a second engine caught his attention. A dark — he couldn't tell whether it was blue or black — SUV pulled down the driveway. Its headlights flicked on. He'd already been out of the line of sight, but he ducked into a crouch anyway. The SUV turned along the same path the Audi had taken, heading toward Stone Mountain.

David redialed the phone.

"Mr. Trenow. I'd expected to be closer before you called."

"I told you to come alone."

"I am alone," she said, her tone calm and all business.

"In your car, perhaps. Tell the SUV to go back to the house. Or our meeting is canceled."

She didn't answer right away. Did he hear tapping in the background?

"All right, Mr. Trenow. You win. They are turning around. You're following me, I assume?"

He ended the call and waited. It didn't take long. Light edged the top of the hill, then crested, two bright eyes in the darkness. David stayed down, but watched until the SUV drove into the estate and the gate closed behind it. Then, he finally made his way back to the van.

It bumped along the old service road until he hit 78, there he turned right. He figured he was about ten, maybe fifteen miles behind her, tops. He drove another ten minutes then rang Emilia again.

"This is beginning to get tedious, Mr. Trenow."

"You'll get over it. Are you in Stone Mountain?"

"Yes," she said.

"Take 285 north to the LaVista exit and go west. Stay on LaVista when Briarcliff breaks off at the mall. About a mile down, at the corner of Montreal, there's a diner. Go inside and wait for me."

Only two cars shared the diner's parking lot: the Audi and an old red Ford pickup truck with a fist-sized dent in the driver's side door. David pulled into a space away from both.

Inside, the brightly lit diner wore its 50's motif like an old, second hand work shirt. The dull chrome reflected barely discernible, fuzzy shapes. The red vinyl bar stool seats showed their age — ripped in some places. Yellow foam padding oozed out the gashes.

A frizzy-haired old man with leathery skin balanced on one of the stools, hovering over a cup of coffee. He didn't look up when the bell above the door twanged twice to announce David's entrance. Neither did the young waitress who thumbed through a magazine at the other end of the bar.

The only other person in the dining room sat in a booth in the far left corner, with her back to the wall. He tried to keep the surprise from his face as he met her eyes. Anxiety settled in his skin. Emilia Laos didn't look older than twenty. She didn't look older than Mecca.

She smiled at him from across the room, her teeth small and straight. She didn't stand. And she didn't extend her hand when he slid into the seat across from her.

"It's a pleasure to finally meet you," she said. "I wish it were under better circumstances."

"I want my daughter back."

"I know." The harsh diner lights glinted along her black hair. "But I need her."

Before he could say anything else, the young waitress bustled over. Emilia ordered hot tea with milk; he asked only for water. The girl poked the pencil behind a pale ear and walked away.

"Need her for what?" He didn't want to waste time, but he had to understand what was going on, exactly.

Emilia looked through the glass to their right and watched a single car pass along the street outside. When she looked back, she met his gaze.

"My people are approaching a civil war. Some of the fringe call it a holy war. It hasn't come to Atlanta, as yet, but the rumblings are there. The signs are clear."

A civil war? Her people? He tried to process this, but it didn't make sense to him. Even so, what did all this have to do with Mecca?

The waitress returned. She pushed a tea cup on a saucer across the table to Emilia, set a small cup of milk beside it and then plunked down a glass of ice water, complete with lemon wedge and straw, before David.

"Anything else?" The girl's voice squeaked and reminded him of a dog's play toy.

"No, thanks," David said. The waitress went back behind the counter and took up her post in front of her magazine. The old man who'd been nursing a cup of coffee had left. David and Emilia were now the only customers in the diner.

"I don't know what you're talking about," David said, continuing the conversation. "And I don't see how it relates to Mecca."

Emilia studied him for a time. The smooth skin of her forehead creased in thought and she made a faint humming sound. When she let out a sigh, the scent of cinnamon traveled across the table to him, sweet and spicy.

"The purists of my kind wish to eliminate those of mixed blood. For a very long time, the full blooded have worked side by side with the mixed, but now suddenly, their blood is too pure and can't be tainted." Her expression soured. "They wish to eliminate anyone who isn't of the full blood." The young-looking woman leaned in a fraction. "I will be plain. I need Mecca to deal with my enemies, with those who would try to kill me, or mine." Her dark honey-colored eyes narrowed for a second, then were open again. "She can kill with a touch. As you well know. And that is an advantage I need."

"What the hell are you talking about?" He wanted to lunge across the table at her, drain every bit of stolen energy out of that small, compact body. "You kidnapped my daughter to make her a killer?"

Emilia looked toward the counter, where the waitress had raised her attention from the magazine. When she looked back at David, her expression had hardened, her jaw set. Her voice came in a tight whisper. "She is already a killer." She tilted her head and regarded him, her eyes unreadable. "She's your daughter, after all."

The weight of her stare pushed against him.

She knows.

Fear tamped out his anger. That old fear that he'd kept hidden for so long. He pulled in a slow, deep breath, and he reminded himself that no matter what this woman knew, she'd kidnapped Mecca. That was what mattered.

"If I thought she would have come willingly," Emilia continued, "I would have approached her that way. I didn't think she would. I now suspect she doesn't have the same mentality as her father. I suspect she will be an even more difficult sell. What do you think?"

He didn't trust himself to speak right away. He took a swig of the cold water, holding the straw away from his face with a finger. The icy path it cut down his throat helped him reinforce his control over himself. He returned the glass to the table, centering it on the wet ring of condensation that had gathered where it sat.

"I think you should release her." His voice came out low and gruff — unintentionally, though he was glad of it. "She is not yours to keep or to use."

"For that, I need an incentive." Emilia, who wore a turquoise blue silk shirt with pearl buttons down the front, reached into a pocket of her jeans and pulled out a few bills. She left a five on the table and stood. "I will take you in her place, if you wish to make a trade. Call when you decide. You obviously know the number." A smirk traced her lips as she turned away from him.

He reached out to grab her, but she moved impossibly fast. Emilia had reached the door before he'd even closed his hand around the air where her arm had been. The bells on the door tinkled as she went into the night.

David jumped from his seat and rushed through the diner. He couldn't let her go. When he made it through the door, the Audi was already pulling out onto LaVista.

Chapter Fifteen: Mecca

Mecca reached back to grab the door knob, not letting Claude or the man beside him out of her line of sight. She waved her hand behind her twice before her fingertips knocked against the round knob. If she could just get out of the room, she might be able to outrun them.

Claude rose and Mecca turned the knob, trying to be quiet. He watched her. She saw his gaze move from her face to her fingers wrapped around the doorknob. He raised one slender hand.

"Go back out and to the end of the hall. Take the last door on your right. You will find your escape route," he said.

He was letting her go? She couldn't hide her surprise.

He smiled. "Stay along the back of the house, going toward the woods. There are guards, so watch carefully. You'll see a small building in the distance: the guest house. Behind that you will find a well. Walk directly away from the well in the direction of the woods. A fire road leads to a small gate and out to the main road. There will be a single guard there."

The door latch gave, and she pulled the door open as she stepped back and toward the hall. The other man in the room hadn't moved an inch from his spot. Claude didn't approach her.

"Why are you helping me?"

"You'd best go now. It won't be long before you're found out." He sat back down on the sofa, sinking into the cushions, and opened his book. The dark-skinned man only watched her.

She slipped through the open doorway and back into the hall, her mind reeling with confusion.

Mecca leaned against the rough bark of a young pine tree. She lifted one foot gingerly and brushed a dead leaf from the bottom. A thin, uneven layer of blood smeared across her heel. Her fingertips skated along the a cut beneath all the blood. An electric spark of pain shot up her calf. She winced. A jagged rock had been buried in a pile of leaves and pine needles. Waiting in ambush, obviously.

The cut burned with each step she took, but she knew she was lucky. She could easily have turned her ankle. That would have made this trek through the woods even more difficult.

She pushed herself away from the tree. Sharp tendrils of pain pulsed up her leg with each step, but she forced herself to move faster. She knew it could only be a matter of time before someone found Will, or Claude reported her disappearance to Emilia. Mecca wasn't even sure whether they'd find Will dead or alive. Sure, he'd been breathing when she'd left him, but who knew how all this worked?

Dad.

Dad knows.

She pushed the thoughts away. Right now, she needed to concentrate on getting away. Plenty of time to freak out about everything later.

Leaves rustled beneath her feet, and she couldn't keep them from getting stuck to the blood every time she took a step. She traveled along the fire road, ten yards into the forest, just in case someone came along.

The way out of the house had been exactly as Claude had told her, right down to the well behind the guest house. Why had he helped her? She didn't think for a minute that he was on her side. If he had, he wouldn't have made her go back to the bed when she'd tried to escape earlier. Why hadn't he just let her go then?

There had to be a benefit to letting her go now. What did he get out of her escape? She tossed it back and forth in her mind, but she just couldn't make sense of it. Her escape had to undermine Emilia's plans. Unless Emilia thought Mecca would let her guard down and trust Claude for his help.

Well, trusting any of them wouldn't happen in this century.

She shoved her way through thorny underbrush and wished again that she had shoes. A sharp twig stabbed her ankle, drawing another trickle of blood. Christ, if she didn't stop bleeding all over the place, they'd just be able to follow the smell.

She froze. What if they *could* track her just by the smell of her blood?

That thought got her moving. And faster than before.

The back gate had to be coming up soon. She didn't know whether the guard would be human or Visci. And, truly, she didn't really know whether the difference would matter.

She wondered how many others there were like Will. What would possess someone to enter into a situation like that? Or maybe she assumed too much about his part in it all. Perhaps he just didn't want to die. Who really did?

Her toe caught, and she staggered forward, into the outskirts of a clearing. She stumbled back into the tree line for cover. Crouched low, she took stock of the situation. She was glad of the moon tonight. It gave her light to see by.

Several feet from the small pipe back gate, a guard leaned against the stacked stone wall, a folding chair nearby. In one hand, he held a gun. She didn't know what kind, but it looked big and ugly. Mecca could outrun a lot of people, but she doubted she could outrun a bullet.

The stone wall rose seven feet high, easily, and barbed wire topped it. Mecca's spirit waned. An armed guard and no way to scale the wall. How was she supposed to get out?

She could try to drain him, but she didn't know how she'd sneak up without him seeing her. The area around the gate was wide open. He'd see her approach from the woods. She strained her ears and heard a rumbling in the distance, coming in fast. She ducked down into the underbrush and listened.

A battered, gunmetal grey Jeep came into sight, bouncing along the rough pathway and kicking up clouds of dirt. Mecca covered her mouth to stifle a surprised gasp. The man behind the wheel of the Jeep looked just like the man who had stood at Claude's side in the library. What the hell was going on?

He scanned the sides of the road as he drove through. Mecca crouched lower. The Jeep passed, leaving a trail of dust like a stunt airplane. She pivoted and watched it approach the gate. Just before reaching the guard, it swerved and parked, its hard top blocking her view. She moved ten feet down the tree line, bringing her a little bit closer, and watched Claude's man swing out of the Jeep.

He took long strides toward the guard, and his height gave him such a strong presence that Mecca could feel it even at her distance. The man at the gate looked him up and down and then swaggered over, closing the distance between them. Claude's man jerked his hand, and the Jeep's keys went flying to the guard. Surprised, the man fumbled the catch and had to stoop to pick them up from out of the dirt. The tall man hooked a thumb in the direction of the house as they exchanged words.

Were they talking about her? Had Claude decided he didn't want her to escape?

Fear and bile gathered in the back of her throat. It was all a game. Claude had let her think she could get away, and now he'd sent this man to bring her back, just so she'd know who was in charge.

The fear turned to anger. She'd made it this far. She'd be damned if they were going to put her back in that room with those tubes and needles! She'd drain anyone who touched her.

She'd worked herself into a good fume by the time she noticed that the guard had climbed into the Jeep and gunned the engine. He cut the wheel and circled around. Mecca scrambled behind a bush just as its headlights swung in her direction. As the vehicle roared down the fire road, Mecca looked back to the gate.

Claude's man stood still, except for the slight movement of his head as he scanned the tree line. As his gaze came to her bush, a grin slid across his lips. He turned and made a show of setting the gate ajar and then he moved several yards away. His gaze swung back around to her bush for a moment before he looked away.

He was sending her a message! Mecca pushed all her questions to the back of her mind. She would figure out why he let her go later. Right now, she just wanted to get through that gate.

Unease prickled at her skin. He knew she was here. No use being subtle. She rose to her full height. Her movement brought his attention to her and that grin lifted the corners of his mouth again. He took another three steps away from the gate. An invitation.

Mecca came forward with quick steps, not looking away for even a moment. The black oxford shirt he wore clung to his chest, stretching across his muscles. She glanced down at his gun, then back at his face as the distance between them shortened. He made no moves, only watched her.

Almost there.

She only needed another twenty feet to get to the gate. Would he spring on her just as the taste of freedom sweetened her tongue? Would she have to kill him?

Ten feet.

He remained motionless. Maybe he really would let her go. Maybe Claude wasn't toying with her, offering her an escape. But she still couldn't figure out why he'd work against Emilia.

Five.

She couldn't keep from speeding up until her hand closed over the cool metal gate and she slid through the tiny opening. She forced herself to pause, muscles taut and ready to flee. She watched Claude's man, waiting for him to spring toward her. He only gave her a slight smile. She pulled the gate shut.

No more fooling around, her mother's voice said in her head. *Get going.*

Mecca turned on her heel, sending a jolt up her leg. She spotted the main road about fifty yards up and broke into a jog. Pain radiated from the cut on her heel, but she embraced it. It meant she was alive.

The pavement curved, taking her out of eyesight of the rutted fire road. She stopped, drawing long, fiery breaths. Her nerves were shot. Blood covered both feet and her arms looked like an old dartboard from the bushes and tree branches she'd run past. She didn't even want to see her face.

The realization that she'd gotten away from that place struck her with a suddenness that made her knees give out. Tears filled her eyes, but she blinked them back. No time for crying. She'd gotten out, but she wasn't safe yet. She wrapped a hand around the small trunk of a young birch and hauled herself to her feet.

She pulled the hem of the shirt up and wiped the sweat and grime from her face. She just wanted to lie down and sleep for about three weeks, but instead, she moved along the shoulder of the road, stepping gingerly with her tender feet.

She passed a green sign that told her Stone Mountain was eight miles ahead. It would be another ten or fifteen miles to the university after that. It was going to be a long night.

—➤➤◄◄◄—

She stopped at the first gas station she found and used the bathroom to clean herself up, glad to get the grunge off her face and the blood off her feet. By then, the first rays of sunlight had peeked over the horizon. Once she no longer looked homeless, she caught a ride from a couple other students commuting in for an early class. That had been a lucky break, especially looking the way she looked.

Ten minutes after they dropped her off, she stood in the student union, talking to Josie on a campus phone. Twenty minutes after that, she sat behind the wheel of her friend's blue Toyota, driving north and away from school, wearing borrowed clothes and shoes.

It had taken a bit of time to convince Josie not to tag along. In the end, Mecca had to promise to call later in the day and check in. At least Josie left her cell phone for Mecca to use. Mecca had tried to call home, but only got voicemail. The same with her dad's cell. That may have been for the best. She wasn't sure what she would have said if he'd picked up.

Sitting at a light, on her way through Little Five to the interstate, she dialed the phone again.

It was answered on the second ring. "Hello?"

"Jim? It's Mecca. Have you talked to my dad recently?"

Silence.

A horn blatted behind her. Mecca jumped and hit the accelerator, propelling the car through the intersection. The guy behind her sped into the other lane and flipped her off as he flew by.

"He was here last night. He's worried. Where are you?"

"I'm near school. Where is he? I called the house and his cell."

"Are you in your car?"

"No, I borrowed a friend's. What's with all the questions?" More silence. The hair on Mecca's skin rose and goose bumps covered her flesh. Her right foot throbbed as she slowed down. "What's wrong? What's happened to him?"

Please don't let them have gotten him. Images of him being restrained in a room just like hers somewhere in that house make her stomach knot.

"Some strange things have been going on. Do you remember the way to our cabin up north? The one we used to go to in the summer? Could you get there?"

"Stop it. You're freaking me out." Dread set up camp in her belly. If she didn't puke right down her front, she'd count today a victory.

"Go up to the cabin," Jim said. "Don't go home. I'll try to get in touch with your dad."

Cars zipped past on her left as she slowed further, not able to concentrate on traffic.

"I swear to God, today is not the day to fuck with me. I haven't been to the cabin since I was twelve. I have no idea how to get there and I'm not going anyway. Where's my dad?" She finally reached the interchange for I-75/I-85 and got on the northbound ramp.

"Look, I'll try to find him, but you need to be somewhere safe."

No shit.

"You obviously know something's going on," she said. At seven in the morning, traffic downtown sat gridlocked. The gas pedal hummed against her ravaged foot. "I'll be at your place in an hour." She disconnected just as he began to protest.

A blue and white taxi crawled in front of her as she wound her way through the streets of the Barrons' neighborhood. It took each turn she needed to take and slowed further just as she spied the bright red and white tulips that surrounded the red brick mailbox. When the taxi turned into the long driveway, Mecca stopped on the street.

Why had he called a cab?

Her curiosity getting the better of her, Mecca pulled the nose of the car into the drive and followed the taxi up. The long driveway meandered and twisted through pine trees for a couple hundred yards before it ended on a small rise. The house stood atop, tall and wide.

Mecca parked on the side of the three car garage. She got out, her feet sore and throbbing, and stood at the corner of the garage, watching the taxi in front of the house.

The front door opened, and Jim hefted two suitcases out to the waiting cabbie, who already had the trunk open. Carolyn, Jenny's mom, came through next, carrying a pumpkin-colored autumn coat. She wore an immaculately tailored, cream Chanel pant suit, her matching purse hanging from her elbow. In contrast, Jim wore a French blue oxford shirt with the first three buttons unfastened. It hung around him, wrinkled and unkempt. His khaki slacks looked slept-in.

Jim came to Carolyn's side and spoke in a low voice. She nodded, her forehead wrinkled in a concerned frown. She let him kiss her on the cheek before she disappeared into the cab. Jim paid the cabbie and watched as the taxi drove out of sight, into the trees.

"Where is she going?" she said from behind him.

"Christ, Mecca, you scared me."

And she still scared him, judging from the expression on his face. She knew she looked like a wreck. Josie had flipped out when she'd seen Mecca's clothes and the condition of her feet. Josie had pulled her shoes off right then and made Mecca put them on.

Now Mecca stood on Jim's porch, in borrowed clothes, her hair — her entire body — a hot mess. He grabbed her arm and pulled her into a fierce hug. "Thank God, you're all right." His breath puffed against the side of her head. He drew back and held her shoulders, looking her up and down. "Okay, we need to get you inside."

He fairly pushed her through the open doorway and into the foyer. He paused on the porch long enough to look around, then came in himself and slammed the door behind him.

"You shouldn't have come here," he said, his voice insistent and sad, at once.

Well that was pretty fucked up. All "I'm so glad you're okay," to "you shouldn't have come."

"What the hell is going on? I know you know something. And if you know how I can find my dad, you need to tell me." She glared.

"Come with me." He led her through the expansive living room and to the kitchen, then started down the stairs to the basement game room. The only windowless room in the house. "I'm going to give you directions to the cabin. The key is in the flowerpot near the back door. You'll need to pull the plant out of the pot in order to get it." He'd already gone halfway down before he realized she hadn't followed him.

Mecca stood in the kitchen, at the doorway, and crossed her arms over her chest. She wanted to pull her hair out. Or maybe she wanted to rip his hair out; she wasn't quite sure.

"I don't have time to goof off in the woods. If you're not going to help me, I'm out of here." She turned away and heard him scramble up the stairs.

"Mecca, wait. I'm trying to help you." He grabbed her arm. "Come down and I'll tell you what I know, but you probably won't like it. You have to promise me, though, that once I tell you, you'll go out to the cabin while I try to get hold of your dad."

Mecca allowed herself to be led down the stairs. "Is he okay?" she asked. "At least tell me that."

"The last time I talked to him, he was fine. Pissed, but fine."

Chapter Sixteen: David

David opened his eyes and a sunbeam nearly blinded him. Light knifed into the room through the partially opened curtains, illuminating dust particles in the air. The Batman clock on the wall told him it was a little after ten. Five hours sleep. Maybe.

He'd found the hidden key to Sara's door and had fumbled his way inside and onto the sofa before passing out. Even with everything he had to think about, he couldn't keep his eyes open once he'd laid down last night.

Grit clung to the edges of his eyelids. He rubbed them, chasing the sleep away. The front door opened with a quiet squeak. He tensed and pulled himself to his feet. Sara peeked around the corner from the front door.

"Oh good, you're up. I wasn't sure whether you would be." She came into the room and tossed a backpack onto the recliner across from the sofa. "I had an early class, and I figured you needed your beauty sleep. You're looking pretty rough around the edges." Her grin, a little lopsided, shone with genuine cheer. "Did you get to see her?"

"Not Mecca, no." David dropped back onto the cushions. "It's a big property. There were guards."

"Oh."

As she watched him, he realized how surreal the conversation was. Then the weird moment was gone.

She flopped down onto the chair across from him. "Well, I think I might have found something for you. I went through some of the e-mails on that drive. I found a separate, hidden folder that I must have missed the first couple times. It took a while to crack, but I came across several e-mails in there pertaining to a kidnapping at the university." She wrinkled her nose. "I didn't hear anything on campus about anyone being kidnapped though."

"You wouldn't have. I doubt it was reported." Weariness made his limbs heavy. Not physical weariness, but the emotional weariness that comes from being on a high wire for days.

"How does that even happen?" She stared at him the entire time he wasn't answering her. She shook her head. "There was another one about a councilman setting up another man to be captured. In both e-mails, she was adamant about the men not touching either person's skin: the woman at the university, or the man drugged by the councilman." She left off with an expectant look.

"Is there more?"

"Yes. The councilman's daughter. The woman sending the e-mail said that he would play much nicer if they had his daughter in hand. I tracked down our guy's reply. He said he had people over there and would make the arrangements."

"When was this?"

"Dated a couple days ago."

A knot formed in David's gut. They planned to pull Jenny into this. Jim thought he'd kept her safe by sending her away. He'd said as much in his office. In truth, he'd only isolated her and made her an easier target.

"Where is she?" Sara asked. "The daughter. I'm guessing you know whose daughter this is."

"England." At that moment especially, David wished Teresa were still alive. He needed help working out what to do. He could always count on her level-headedness, and he needed it right now. She could find her way out of any problem. Mecca had inherited that trait from her mother. "I have to call him. I may not be able to do anything for her, but I can at least warn him."

"Anything you want me to do?"

"Was there more in those e-mails?"

"You can look through them. I don't know what's going on, so I may have missed something you would consider important."

He knew she wanted him to give her some details. The danger he would put her in didn't balance with the benefit he might get by bringing her fully into the situation. He stood. "I'd like to look at them. I need to call Jim right now. I'll be down in about ten minutes."

Sara nodded and took the hint. She stood, slung her backpack over her shoulder, and turned away. Her stiff jaw told him she was angry as she headed downstairs.

He initially tried Jim's office, but his secretary said that he wouldn't be in until after noon. David pinched the bridge of his nose and tried to think. It was probably just as well; they most likely had taps on all Jim's phones. It occurred to him that using a land line might not be a good idea. David headed for the basement.

The room looked deserted.

"Sara?"

"Yeah?" Muffled.

"Where are you?"

"Under here." A hand waved from beneath the big desk. "I'm connecting a new machine. Playing with the new Linux OS."

"Do you have a cell phone?"

Her head popped over the edge of the desk. "Duh."

David laughed. Mecca would have answered the same way.

Sara crawled out. She pulled the phone from a dock on the desk and tossed it to him. "Cool, huh?"

The screen flashed a colorful Celtic knot. "Cool," he said. "Thanks."

He went back up to the kitchen and tapped Jim's cell number into the phone. He counted five rings before it rolled over into voice mail. He didn't leave a message. He redialed. He called a total of four times, until the line clicked before the voice mail kicked in.

"Yes?" Jim barked.

"Are you alone?"

The silence on the other end lasted for a good twenty seconds.

"Yes."

"I need to talk to you about something very important. Meet me where we spent our first Fourth of July, the place Jenny and Mecca got dirty. One hour. Be alone."

Another moment of silence. Finally, "All right."

The line went dead.

David drove the van along the winding road of Wildwoods State Park. He'd made it to the park fifteen minutes early. He wanted to check the area out before meeting with Jim.

Sara had tried to get him to take her car, since he'd stolen the van from the "bad guys." He didn't want to tell her that the bad guys probably had the cops in their pocket. If he got caught here, they'd trace the car back to her. And that was unacceptable risk. So he bounced along in the van, bad shocks and all.

Wildwoods had been named appropriately. Tucked away in the hills north of the city, the park spanned one hundred and twenty acres. A quarter of it had been plowed out and landscaped into a beautiful family park, complete with small lakes, picnic areas and the occasional playground for the kids.

The rest of the park was for hikers and campers of different varieties. RV'ers could find sites to set up their roving homes, and tent campers could choose pre-cleared sites to set up their gear. More adventurous folks could camp out in the woods.

He turned down a narrow dirt roadway that went off into the woods. Every turn brought memories of Teresa, and he missed her with an intensity he had trouble harnessing. This park had been her choice for their first Independence Day with the Barrons.

"No time for that." David shook his head, pushing memories away. "Focus on what's at hand."

The van jolted along the uneven roadway, and David slowed. He took a final turn and pulled over beside a hard-running little creek. He didn't bother locking the van when he got out, but he closed it with care. The less noise he made, the better.

He did a quick walk around the area, staving off memories of better times. His nerves, already frayed, couldn't handle thoughts of a smiling Teresa or a laughing Mecca. It hurt too much.

There didn't seem to be anything unusual around. When he heard an engine approach, he realized that he'd been anticipating seeing Jim again. Not an angry anticipation, but an honest, glad anticipation.

Jim pulled up in his wife's silver Jaguar convertible, top up, windows closed. He cut the engine and stepped out. He approached David with a slow stride.

Jim's usual pressed-and-creased clothes looked as if he'd slept in them. An untucked shirt fell over deeply wrinkled khaki slacks. He sported a day's worth of stubble on his cheeks. His shoes, though, shone with their usual polished sheen.

"You look like hell," David said.

"Yeah, thanks. You're looking like Brad Pitt yourself."

David chuckled, then nodded toward the creek. "Remember when they slid down that embankment? What were they, eight?"

The corner of Jim's mouth lifted. "Seven or eight, yes. God, they came back filthy. I thought Carolyn was going to trounce me for letting Jenny play in the mud."

"Teresa *did* trounce me."

This time they both laughed. The tension between them lightened.

"I'm sorry, Dave. I didn't feel like I had any choice—"

"We've got more important things to worry about. Let's walk."

They started on a tight pathway into the woods. A blanket of pine needles crunched underfoot and shadows hid beneath bushes. David got an odd feeling of *déjà vu*, but shook it off.

"You need to bring Jenny home," David said.

Jim stopped walking and stared at him. Then he shook his head. "No. I won't bring her here and put her in danger."

"You've sent her away and put her in danger. Do you think they can't get to her over there?"

"She'll be safer than if she was here."

"Are you willing to bet her life on that?"

"What are you saying?"

"I found an e-mail from Emilia Laos to whoever your contact was when you set me up."

Jim lowered his eyes for a moment before meeting David's again. David wondered how things would be between them when this was over. If this was ever over.

"Go on," Jim said, brushing his palm over the stubble on his chin.

"She directed him to send someone to get Jenny. They want you more easily controlled. I don't know whether they're actually going to snatch her, or if they'll only keep tabs on her until they need her."

Jim's step faltered and he slowed. "I just sent Carolyn over there."

"Bring them both home."

He shook his head. "I can't protect them here."

"You can't protect them an ocean away, for Christ's sake."

Jim stopped and leaned against a tree. His face had gone grey. When he looked up at David, he said, "Why did you come here to tell me this? You're putting yourself in more danger."

"Because Jenny is Mecca's best friend. At least, she was before college. I don't know what they are now. But either way, it's not her fault you got involved in something completely fucked up. You need to take care of your daughter."

"Like you took care of yours?"

The words smashed David in the gut like an iron mallet. Bitterness coated his tongue. David looked at Jim one last time, then turned, back stiff and straight.

He stalked down the path, toward the parking lot. Jim followed on his heels.

"I'm sorry, Dave. I didn't mean that. It was a shitty thing to say. I know there was nothing you could do, just like there's nothing I can do. Stop. Dave, stop."

David didn't even slow. Fire burned in his veins, and he fought his instinct to turn, grab Jim and drain him of every last bit of energy in his sorry little body.

"Mecca got away," Jim said.

David stopped so quickly that Jim tumbled into him. For one moment, David's spirit rejoiced, then he reined himself in. How could Jim know whether Mecca'd gotten away? Did Jim's involvement go even deeper than he'd suspected?

Jim took a couple steps back. David felt him, even though Jim was behind.

"She escaped," Jim said.

"How do you know that?" he asked, not turning around.

"She came to me this morning. That's why I was so surprised you called. I was trying to figure out how to get in touch with you."

David spun and pointed a finger in Jim's face. The other man took one step back. "If you set her up the way you set me up, I swear on Teresa's grave that I will kill you with no regrets. None."

"I didn't," Jim said. "I wouldn't. I sent her up to my cabin and told her I would find you. That's all."

Adrenaline — and not a little relief — flooded David's system. Mecca was alive. Not only alive, but free. All he had to do was go get her, and they could disappear. They could go anywhere. Be anyone. He would set up assumed names, histories, everything. *But first, deal with this.*

"How can I trust you, after what you did?"

"Dave, if I could go back, I would do everything differently. I made a huge mistake. I don't expect you to forgive me. I have no idea how I'm going to get myself out of this shit, but I will do anything I can to help you help Mecca."

David searched his face and had to reluctantly admit to himself that Jim seemed sincere. "All right."

"She almost wouldn't go to the cabin. I promised her that I'd find you. She said she'd stay up there until tomorrow at noon, and if you hadn't gotten there by then, she was coming back to the city to find you herself. I have no idea how she planned to do that."

David found his paternal instinct overtaking his hard-ass. "How did she look? Was she hurt?"

"She's looked better. I don't think they hurt her physically, but she said she ran through a long stretch of woods and didn't have shoes. Her feet are in pretty bad shape. She'd put them into sneakers, but we took them off to clean her up and they were so swollen, she couldn't get them back into the shoes for a while."

David growled.

"What are you going to do?" Jim asked.

"I'm going to go get her. We'll decide what to do after that." He looked at Jim, hard. "And if you've set us up—"

"Enough with the threats already. I feel shitty as it is."

"You should."

They stood, staring at each other, time drawing out. David felt the presence of the old Jim, the honorable Jim, and he finally spoke. "What are you going to do about Carolyn and Jenny?"

"I don't know."

David started toward the car park again and motioned Jim to come. "I could send my brother out there. I don't know if Ken would agree to go, but I can ask him."

"Is he a cop?"

"No, but he's worth more than a cop in this situation. I'll call him when I get back. Give me your cell number so I can put it in this phone."

They exchanged numbers, writing them on the back of business cards from Jim's wallet.

"You can reach me at that number, but don't you try to trace it, Jim. I swear…"

"I won't." He slid the card back into his wallet.

"I'll let you know the deal after I talk to my brother."

"Dave, I really am sorry." Jim stood in his driver side door with one foot in the car, looking at David over the top of the roof. "If I could take it back..."

"There are a lot of things I wish I could take back. I suppose, in the grand scheme of things, this isn't the worst that could have happened. Go do whatever you need to do. I'll be in touch."

They maintained eye contact for a moment longer, then Jim slid into his car.

—➤➤◄◄◄—

"Hi, it's David."

"Hey!" Sara's bright voice made him smile. "Everything go okay?"

"Better than expected, but things are still pretty rough. I'm not going to be back for a while. Maybe not tonight, maybe not tomorrow. Maybe not for a long while. I wanted to let you know so you won't worry. And I wanted to thank you for your help."

Silence met him for a moment before Sara cleared her throat. "Are you going to keep in touch?"

"Once I'm gone, it's probably best for you if I stay gone." Another long silence. "I left money in your desk. I know you didn't want to take it, but take it anyway."

"I was hoping you'd go see Mom. Maybe talk to her."

Now David took his turn in keeping silent. His emotions churned — a thick mix of regret, sadness, and guilt. Always guilt. How could he speak to her mom? He hadn't seen Grace in years. Decades.

"I don't think that would be a good idea, Sara."

"Why not? She thinks the world of you. Maybe you could say something that would…"

Get her to stop drinking.

"…help her."

David sighed. He knew he couldn't help Grace. She wouldn't have his help. And she certainly wouldn't listen to him. "Once this whole thing blows over," he said, "regardless of where I end up, I'll get in contact with you, and we can talk about it then. Is that fair?"

"Yes. That's fair."

Another silence.

"Sara?"

"Yes?"

"Thank you again."

"You're welcome."

They said their goodbyes, and David leaned his head back against the seat and closed his eyes. That had been much harder than he'd anticipated. He liked Sara a lot. She reminded him so much of Mecca. It was like the two young women were related somehow, though they weren't. Any claims of family he might have with the Harringtons died with Susan.

Of the two calls he had to make, he had thought the one to Sara would have been the easier. If that was true, he was in for a really rough time. He dialed his brother's number.

Ken picked up on the fourth ring and sounded winded. "Hello?"

"Hey, it's David."

"Hey brother. Long time. You must want something. Not money though, yeah?"

David winced. His relationship with Ken had always been touchy. "I do need a favor, but it isn't for me. And it's damn important."

"Oh?" Ken sounded dubious. "What is it?"

Suddenly, David realized he had no idea how to relay the information he needed to without telling the entire story. "Do you have time? You might want to get a couple beers and sit down. This is going to take a while. And it's going to sound crazy."

"Already got the beer, and you usually sound crazy. Shoot."

Chapter Seventeen: Mecca & David

Mecca poured the last black dregs of coffee into her mug, then set up another pot, knowing she should slow down. Any more caffeine and she'd have to be scraped off the ceiling. Knowing that didn't stop her from turning on the machine and watching the dark liquid drip into the carafe though.

She didn't want to sleep. When she'd tried, she was caught in a gruesome, bloody dream. It had started as a rehash of her run-in with Hayden at the Brew, but it kept morphing and changing into other scenes.

The one that woke her, drenched in sweat and screaming, had had her mother in it. Not the laughing, loving mother from her childhood. Not even the gaunt, sick mother of her pre-teen years. In this dream, her mother stood young and beautiful, with sparkling brown eyes and sharp, dainty fangs. The horror only got bloodier as the nightmare wove on, ending with her father's head rolling across the ground at her.

Mecca hobbled back to the round kitchen table. Though she'd changed the bandages on her feet when she'd arrived, she still felt as if she were walking on glass shards. She dropped onto a straight back chair and traced the dapple of early afternoon sunlight on the surface of the table. It warmed the tip of her finger.

What would she do when her dad got here? She wanted to see him in a desperate sort of way, wanted the comfort she'd always felt with him. But his past terrified her.

Maybe a good daughter would assume the best, that the papers she'd read in that room had all been lies. Perhaps Mecca's temptation to believe them made her a traitor. A terrible daughter. She put her head in her hands and willed herself not to weep. She blinked back the sting of tears. She'd cried enough.

It was hard being there alone, with nothing but the awful feelings she carried around. Sitting in the cabin still haunted by memories of happy children, normal dads, and moms who didn't die.

Coming here had been a mistake. She should have just found a hotel and holed up for the day, told Jim to send her dad there. The ghosts of her youth haunted this place.

A car door slammed.

Mecca's breath caught in her throat. Claude's face floated through her mind. She raced to the kitchen window, wincing with each step on the tiled floor that sent electric shocks through her feet. Her heart thrashed against her sternum.

She didn't recognize the dirty white van parked behind the house. She opened a drawer with one hand and felt around until the cool blade of a kitchen knife touched her fingertips. The sun glinted off the windshield, so she couldn't see inside, but she would be prepared.

After a moment, the van door opened and a familiar form slid down from the high seat. Relief washed over her at the sight of her father. She left the knife in the drawer and closed it.

He looked ragged. He hadn't shaved in a couple days at least, and his clothes looked rumpled and slept in. His eyebrows seemed uneven, like some hair had gone missing. She tried to harden her heart against him, but it didn't work. How could she reconcile her dad with the man who'd killed those women?

She pushed the confusion about his past to the back of her mind. That could be dealt with later, after the more immediate threat was handled.

She couldn't keep the smile from her face as she watched him look around the woods which surrounded the cabin. Mecca pushed open the screen door and ran down the three wooden steps. "Dad!" She hurled herself at him, not caring about the stones she stepped on or the twigs that poked into her sore feet.

Mecca poured two cups of coffee and added a spoon of sugar to each. "Sorry, there's no milk."

"That's fine," her dad said.

As she handed a mug to him and his fingers brushed hers, the enormity of everything crashed down on her, like a roof collapsing, trapping her. The weight of her captivity, of being hunted, of fear for her father's safety — and the new fear of her father himself

— all of these things suddenly swarmed in and took her breath away before returning it in a sob.

So much for the resolve not to cry anymore. Tears filled her eyes, clouding the vision of the worried face that she'd loved her whole life. When he took the mugs and set them aside, then opened his arms to her, she could do nothing but fall into them, her cheek against the rough material covering his chest. His hand brushed and petted her hair, and he kissed the top of her head. She felt safe. Safer than she had in days. Her chest ached with her sobs.

"Shh," he said. "It's going to be all right, baby."

But it would never be all right, she knew. Never again. And that knowledge made her heave another breath and weep harder. Emilia and her brood would never let her — or probably them — be. And if not Emilia, then maybe Claude. And if not him, someone else. And if no one ever came after her, she would still always know they were out there, killing people. Stealing innocent life. She only had fear in front of her.

Her dad drew her back by the shoulders and looked down at her. Mecca couldn't help but feel a surge of love for him. Here he was, the man who'd helped her with math, who'd kissed her and bandaged her scrapes, then sent her back out into the world to try again.

"Are you okay?" he asked.

Mecca only nodded, not trusting her voice just yet.

"Here," he said as he turned and retrieved one of the mugs from the counter. He pushed it into her palm. "This will help." He smiled.

She tried to make her lips mimic his, but she could only give him a weaker version as the cup warmed her hand. She beat back the confusion that threatened to take over her mind, her entire being.

"Let's go sit down," he said as he guided her into the cozy living room, his hand steady against her back. They settled on the cushioned sofa with the old lace throw blanket that had always looked out of place in this rustic cabin. "How are your feet? Jim told me you ran barefoot through the woods to get away."

"They're sore. The swelling's gone down though." Her voice came out stronger than she'd expected.

His eyes were darker blue than normal as he scanned her face. "Do you want to talk about it?"

Mecca felt the floodgates open again, but she bit the tears back. "Yes. I need help, Daddy. I don't know what to do." Then the story came pouring out: being snatched from the library, waking up drugged, the Visci, Will, and her dinner with Emilia.

"They want you to kill for them?" he asked, the surprise clear on his face.

"Yes. Because when they have to deal with their own, they can't just kill them outright. I think it's political. They have rules to follow. I don't know."

He stood and paced the room, his footsteps heavy on the wooden floor. "Okay, we'll need to get you a new passport and some cash. I know someone in

Barcelona with a safe house we can stay at for a while, until I work something else out. I'll have to call—"

"What are you talking about?"

"We've got to get out of the country, and I imagine they'll be watching the airport. I would, in their shoes."

Her fear slipped into anger, and she stood so fast, coffee sloshed over the top of the mug and covered her hand in heat. She winced, but it didn't deter her. "You want me to run? Just drop everything, my entire life, and run away?"

"You think we can fight them and win? We don't have any idea how many there are, or even what they can do."

Mecca slammed her mug down on the side table. "I am not running. You can run if that's what you want. Get your passports, your fake identity — whatever it is *you* do — and go, if that makes you feel better."

He grimaced and guilt fluttered along the edges of her bitterness. He turned away from her, reached into his pocket, drew out his phone, and put it to his ears. Its vibrations stopped.

"Hello?" The number was Jim's home phone but the voice David expected to hear in response was not the one he heard.

"Mr. Trenow, have you considered my offer?" Emilia Laos's voice came through flat and unemotional.

"I believe I was to call you."

"Plans have since changed."

David stepped away from Mecca and into the hallway. He didn't want her overhearing, but he also needed to put some distance between them. The anger in her voice had skewered him and scrambled his thoughts.

"Why are you calling from this phone?" he asked. A knot of worry coiled along his spine.

"Mr. Barron and I had some business. I dislike it when someone works against me." The timbre of her voice lowered and something that reminded him of a growl crept in. "I suspect you may wish to speak with him one last time."

Panic burst from the knot of worry.

"Leave him be. He didn't act against you. I did."

"Lying to me doesn't benefit you, Mr. Trenow. And begging doesn't become you. Have you spoken to Mecca yet?"

"What do you mean?" Could he fake her out? If he could make her believe that he didn't know Mecca had escaped, perhaps he could get his daughter out of the country undetected.

"Oh, David, David." Her words bubbled with condescension. "That will cost your friend some pain. Please give Mecca my regards. I'm sure I will see you both very soon. Do let me know when you've made your decision."

The line went dead before he could reply. When he turned around, Mecca's gaze pierced him, and his feet remained rooted to the floor. He read alarm in her eyes, but behind that he saw anger. Anger at him? Or at her captors? He didn't know. Perhaps both.

"What's happened?"

"I have to go to Jim's. You stay here. I'll be back as soon as I can."

"Like hell."

He bristled at her tone. "Mecca, I don't know what I'm going to be walking into. I don't want you there."

"I don't care. At least I have some defense against them. What do you have?" Mecca's left eyebrow cocked up.

"Fine." David pulled the van's keys out of his pocket. "Come along if you want to. But I don't know what we're going to find."

—⇥⇤—

Awkward silence filled the van as they sped toward the city. Mecca couldn't tamp down the hostility she felt for her dad. The man who wanted to run from danger didn't jibe with the man she knew as her father. Anxiety made her palms sweat and her ears ring.

As they merged into city traffic, making their way to the affluent Buckhead neighborhood where her best friend's family lived, Mecca shifted her gaze sideways to look at him.

He seemed like the same man she knew. All right, so the stubble on his face was out of character and his shoulders bent a little from fatigue. And he was definitely missing some eyebrow hair and more than a few eyelashes. But the intense set of his straight jaw line, his short, well-kept flat top haircut, the bright blue of his eyes: these things all comforted Mecca. She recognized them as her dad.

"Why are you staring at me?" he asked, his voice subdued.

"You look tired."

"It's been a long couple days."

The van angled to the right as he took the turn off the interstate, driving faster than normal. She latched on to the door handle.

"I'm sorry I snapped at you before, Dad."

He didn't reply, but his head bobbed with a small nod.

"I'm just on edge, I guess. You know they'll never let me go."

"Maybe."

Her anger flared again, but Mecca pushed it back. He hadn't spoken to Emilia. He didn't know how determined she had been. She wouldn't let either of them just disappear. Mecca knew it. Emilia would always hunt them, like some rare and wild game. And if Emilia couldn't get them to play by her rules, she would just have them killed. She'd never let them get away.

Only the rough rumble of the van's motor sounded as they entered the Barrons' subdivision. The familiarity of it brought tears to her eyes. How could things have gone so wrong? How could these streets no longer be as peaceful as they'd always seemed?

Her dad parked around the corner from the house, and the engine rattled down to silence. He looked over at her. She read resignation in his eyes.

"You're going to insist on coming to the house, aren't you?"

"Yes."

A sigh slipped from his lips. "All right. We're going to go around the back and have a look first. They may not be gone."

She nodded, butterflies twittering around in her belly.

"Don't do anything without letting me know first, okay?"

"Okay."

"Let's go."

The hike through the wooded area behind the house reminded Mecca of her escape from Emilia. It took everything in her not to break into a panicked run toward where she knew the house sat. She let the early evening air fill her lungs as twigs crunched under her sneakers. Little stabs of pain shot up from the soles of her feet. She welcomed them. They kept her focused.

The house loomed up, dark except for a dim light from the office. The pool looked like a murky pit without the soft, colored lights usually left on. A stifling sense of disaster gripped her.

Her dad turned back and put a finger to his lips and then moved like a ghost across the patio. She followed close behind. All her nerves perked up. She strained her ears, trying to pick up any strange sounds, but only the breeze spoke as it slipped through the leaves behind them.

When he reached the big picture window that she knew opened into the office, he held up a hand for her to stop as he peered inside. Heat prickled under her skin and she ignored his gesture. Instead, she stepped up beside him and focused on what she could see on the other side of the window.

The once-elegant office now had streaks of red sprayed across the walls. Dark blood pooled on the corner of the big oak desk and dripped, like a faucet, onto the hardwood floor. She could almost hear it.

Three feet from the desk, Jim Barron lay with his throat ripped open. His chest rose and fell, but the long pauses in between scared her. With each breath, a little spray of red droplets erupted from the chasm in his neck, falling in a fine pattern on his chin.

Mecca's gut wrenched. She doubled over and heaved, spraying the bottom of the brick wall with regurgitated coffee. She had just enough time to pull in a ragged breath and sink to her knees before the muscles of her stomach knotted and she retched again. Brown spittle hung from her lips.

Her father's hand rested on her shoulder. He'd crouched beside her when she went down to the ground.

"He's—he's still alive," she said. The scene inside was more horrible than even the dried husk of Hayden she'd left behind.

It was Jenny's dad.

And the blood. Everywhere.

She dry-heaved again. Bile burned the back of her throat. Her heart knocked around in her chest like it wanted to escape the confines of her rib cage.

"Yes. I need to get inside. Will you be okay out here by yourself? I don't think anyone's around."

She shook her head. "I'm coming in with you. I'm okay. Just let me get up." She struggled to her feet, with his help. *Get it together, girl. Come on.*

"Are you sure? You don't have to see it again. I don't want you to."

Mecca straightened and pushed his hand away. If she planned on fighting Emilia and her crew, she would have to get used to scenes like this. She drew a deep breath of the night air, letting it fill her lungs completely before she released it. Her pulse slowed and she tried to calm down. "I'm okay. Let's go."

Chapter Eighteen: David

Shadowy darkness stretched through the house as they hurried through. The felt heavy, pressing in on him from all sides. A slice of muted light edged from the office door, which stood ajar. David shoved it open and rushed into the room.

He hadn't thought it could, but it looked worse from the inside. Blood littered every surface, even if only a few drops. Spray on the walls, ruby red drops scattered along book bindings, pooled on the desk. The metallic scent hung heavy in the air. That was the worst of it, as if Jim's life could simply evaporate like steam.

David glanced back at Mecca as he made his way to where Jim lay. She had become a statue in the doorway. He wanted her to stay out of the office, but she'd become his shadow once they got inside the house. Now she looked more like a little girl than ever. Her eyes, wide and gleaming, didn't meet his, but rather looked over his shoulder at the room. Her face grew chalky. He wanted to sweep her away, but he couldn't.

"Call 911," he said.

He didn't wait to see whether she did it because Jim's wheezing breath brought David's attention back.

He went to his friend's side and crouched down. Dread skimmed along his spine.

Jim wouldn't make it through this. He couldn't. Not with this kind of damage.

His friend's face sported a jumble of bruises and welts. His left eye, black and swollen, barely opened and the part of his eyeball that should have been white gleamed bright red. A bruise darkened his cheek, blending in with his puffy lips.

"Jim? It's Dave. We're calling an ambulance. Hang on."

Jim's good eye lolled for a moment, then rolled around and focused on him. The wheezing increased and blood droplets sprayed up and out of the hole in Jim's throat, scattering over the top of David's hand. Jim tried to lift his head from the floor, his swollen lips moving in time with the wheezing.

"Shh," David said. "Don't try to talk."

Jim's hand grappled and pushed against the side of David's leg. His fingers waved like the branches of a dead tree in the wind. David leaned in and listened as Jim's shattered voice box allowed a few words to creep out.

"Jenny...Caro...Carolyn. Save.."

"Jenny and Carolyn are fine. They're in London with Ken."

"No!" The exclamation wasn't above a whisper. "She… she is going… to kill…"

"Dad?" Mecca's voice edged along his consciousness. "The paramedics are coming."

"You hear that, Jim? They're going to come and fix you right up. Don't worry about Jenny and Carolyn. I'll make sure they're safe. I promise."

Jim's body went limp, and David's heart froze, panicked, but the rattling breathing went on. Each intake sounded like it used all the energy Jim's body could muster. David held his friend's limp, clammy hand, not caring that blood covered his shoes, his knees and his own hands.

"Go get some towels," he said, looking up at his daughter. At least it would get her out of the room. "We can try to stop the bleeding."

Mecca looked around the room, saucer-eyed, and swallowed so hard, David heard her gulp. When her gaze swung back to him, he could read the question in those eyes. *"How much can there be left?"* He said nothing to the unspoken question, she turned and rushed out of the room.

Jim's breath rattled, and David looked down to see his friend staring at him with wild eyes. David gripped his hand tighter, reached out with his own life force and felt for Jim's.

The bloody room dropped to the background as the Cavern unfolded over the scene. The cave was cool and almost empty. It was like an old grotto that had been an underwater beauty, but was now reduced to a brittle cave with only a sad, trickling stream of water slipping along its smooth floor.

David couldn't keep the soft groan from his lips as he realized just how close Jim was to being gone.

"I'm not going to let you die," he whispered, as he released some of his own life energy into that hollow cavern. In his mind's eye, the strong golden wave rolled away from him and splashed against the wall of Jim's soul center. It trickled down to the ground and began to drain away.

"No."

He released another small burst of energy, watching it illuminate the cave and then slip down the walls to the diminished stream. David let a larger bit of himself go, feeling the subtle weakening of his own energy as he tried to feed his friend's life force. It didn't matter. Each time he sent his energy out to Jim, it slipped away within moments. Jim's life had been shredded; David couldn't feed it energy faster than Jim lost it.

"I brought the towels." Mecca's whisper brought him away from the Cavern.

Golden light pumped out of the open wound in Jim's neck just before David shut the mental door to the Cavern, the two visions merging for that one moment. Jim still stared at him, but the fear in his eyes had gone. Did he understand what David had tried to do?

He took the towels from Mecca, keeping his other hand firmly on Jim's. Sirens howled in the distance as he laid one towel with care on his friend's throat. A red blossom bloomed on the ivory material, like a rose.

Jim's hand twitched in David's grasp. He took a long jangling breath and whispered, "Save—"

Then it was over.

Jim's hand fell limp and his eyes stared through David. The rose on the towel bloomed for another minute, then it too stopped.

Despair slid into David's heart. How could they fight this woman who had no regard for life?

One thing became clear in those minutes before the siren stopped at the front door. Mecca was right: Emilia wouldn't stop hunting either of them. Running wouldn't help.

He stood, his belly a mixture of regret and apprehension, with a seed of anger thrown in to take root. Behind him, Mecca loosed a sob. He turned and pulled her to him, holding her tight against his chest. Her body shuddered with her tears, but she didn't pull from him. Whatever he'd done to make her angry earlier had been washed away in the blood in this room.

Banging on the door.

"I need to let them in," he said to her, his voice low. She disentangled herself from him without looking down and left the room. He followed, fear for her heavy on his heart.

They spent three hours with paramedics, then police officers, explaining a version of the situation over and over again. Yes, he'd been talking to Mr. Barron while driving with his daughter. There had been a loud sound in the background. Mr. Barron grunted and then went off the line. He could still hear sounds, so he rushed over, but this is what they'd found.

No, they didn't know who might have done this. Yes, he'd call if he thought of anything else.

The entire time, he expected Emilia's goons to show up.

When the police finally allowed them to leave, the night had blackened, which made the walk back to the van a long one. Luckily, they hadn't been asked about their vehicle.

David wondered if one of the detectives would eventually think about the father and daughter who'd gotten there without any transportation. He'd worry about it when the time came, he decided, as they reached the van and climbed in.

"Do you still want to fight them?" he asked, as the van's engine rattled to life.

Mecca didn't respond. He looked over and she was studying her finger.

Red flakes of dried blood scaled her fingertips. He didn't know when she'd touched the blood. He reached and laid his hand on her forearm. She looked at his it, but didn't raise her gaze to meet his. The hot splash of a tear landed on his knuckle.

"If you want to fight them, we will. If you want to run, we can." He wouldn't run, though. Not after this. He would make sure Mecca had a safe place to stay, and he would track down Emilia Laos and drive a stake through her heart with his bare hands, if that's what it took.

"I don't think we can. Did you see what she did to him? She slaughtered him."

David put the van into gear and began the trek out of the subdivision and back to the highway. How could he protect her from this? Even if he killed Emilia Laos, who else had the woman told about Mecca? When would it end?

"Then let's not worry about that now," he said. "How about we go check on Jenny?"

Mecca lifted her gaze at the mention of her best friend. "We can't let her get Jenny." Her voice was small, like it'd been when she was a little girl.

"We won't. And after we know she's safe, we can decide what to do."

"Okay." Her system must have been shot. Too many traumas over too short a time.

They drove in silence as he pulled onto the interstate, heading south, and the silence hadn't lifted as David pulled off an exit and turned left down Edgewood, passing hipster bars and eateries.

Farther on, old shells of buildings with peeling paint and warped doors lined both sides of the street like soldiers, sad old veterans being ravished by time and neglect. No homeless in this neighborhood. The gathering of young thugs on the corners saw to that.

He took another left onto Euclid, the line of demarcation between the haves and the have-nots. As he entered the Little Five Points area, brightly painted pastel homes popped up on the right and the left, then gave way to rows of New Age shops, mom-and-pop bookstores, the occasional hole in the wall joint with great pizza/fries/beer, depending on what you were looking for. And, of course, the bars.

A variety of people came out to Little Five at night. Being so close to the ASU campus meant college students could be found here day or night. In the brick plaza, men and women with tattoos, or Rasta braids, or brightly colored hair — sometimes a combination — sat around and begged for money in exchange for music or poetry. One woman had a precariously balanced folding table covered with rough woven blankets. Splayed across the surface was every manner of trinket. David drove past.

"Where are we going?" she asked.

"I need to meet with someone. We're going to have to throw them off the trail. They're probably watching the airport, at the very least." Channeling Jim with those words. Hadn't he said the same thing about David's house and credit cards when he'd given David the money from the lamp?

"I left Josie's car at the cabin."

"We'll get it to her, don't worry."

He looked over and worry tickled at the edges of his mind. Still focused on her fingers, Mecca stared at them with an intensity he'd never seen. Had she lost it or was steeling her resolve? Would he be able to tell the difference between the two?

A twinge of guilt slapped at him for thinking this way about his daughter. How would he have reacted at twenty if these things had happened to him? Though perhaps he wasn't the best person to compare to, really.

David found a parking space down the street from Sara's house and fed the meter a few coins he found in the van's ashtray. He decided that parking with Mecca's side on the curb had been a very good idea when she flung the door open without even looking up. A young girl with spiked hair—purple, tipped in neon green—jerked out of the way.

"Hey, watch it, bitch!"

David came around and put himself between the two, but the girl just kept walking. He leaned in toward Mecca's ear. "Are you going to be okay?"

She nodded, but didn't say anything.

He put a hand on her back and directed her toward Sara's house. Emilia Laos had hinted that she knew about his past. Had she told Mecca? Was that what had been upsetting her at the cabin?

He didn't know whether putting the two parts of his life in the same room together was the stupidest idea he'd ever come up with. He thought it might be. But he didn't have a choice. He needed to get Mecca out of public. Sara's would be the safest place for her.

This can work, he thought as he rang the bell.

Chapter Nineteen: Mecca

A woman about her own age opened the door. Small and compact, pale, with short, tight curls of black hair, she wasn't really paying attention as she opened the door. A cell phone, poked into the front pocket of her faded jeans, buzzed. She pulled it out long enough to check the display, then crammed it back into her pocket.

When she finally noticed them, her vivid green eyes lit up. She broke into a smile and held the door open. "Hey! Is this Mecca? You found her!"

Mecca tried to decide how her dad could be friends with someone so young. Someone who probably went to school with Mecca, considering where this chick lived. When and where would he have met her? And why did her smile look familiar?

And what did she mean by "found"? Had her dad told this *stranger* about what had happened? Mecca's heart rate sped up. How much had he told her?

"Yes and no. She actually got away herself." Pride swelled his smile. "Mecca, this is Sara."

"Hey," Mecca said.

Sara grabbed her hand and shook it fiercely with her own thin fingers. "It's great to finally meet you! And I'm so glad you're safe. What happened? They didn't hurt you, did they? Come in!" Sara just about pulled her over the threshold.

"Thanks." Mecca looked at her dad. Seriously. How much did this girl know? *And when am I going to get my hand back?*

He followed them in and pushed the door closed. "Sara, I need a connection."

She finally got an eyeful of him and gaped, dropping Mecca's hand. "What the hell happened to you?"

Mecca looked at her dad's clothes. He'd washed his hands and face before they'd left the Barrons' house, but his clothes were a mess. Blood stained the knees of his jeans and the sleeves of his blue jacket. Fine red drops splayed out in a mist pattern along the front of his shirt. The reminders brought acid up from her belly. She turned toward the living room.

"I'm okay. There was an accident at a friend's house."

"The councilman?"

She wasn't watching, but she guessed he'd nodded. Mecca's nerves jangled every time Sara spoke. It seemed like every other sentence out of her mouth was something she shouldn't know. Or Mecca preferred she not know, anyway.

"I'm sorry," Sara said. She sounded like she meant it. That was something at least. "We need to get you some clothes. I don't have anything that would fit you, but we can probably find something in one of the mother earth stores around the corner. It'll be cotton and you'll look like a hippie, but there are worse things. And man, your face. I don't even know what to do with that."

She sure can talk. How does he know *her?* Mecca sat on the arm of the threadbare sofa and watched them.

"Thanks," her dad said. "I still need a connection though."

"Head downstairs. It's all up and running."

"Sara," Mecca said, watching the woman closely, "you look familiar. Do you go to ASU?"

"Yep, computers. You?"

"Yeah. You really look familiar."

Her father interrupted, his voice tight and edgy. "Okay, Sara, show me which machine you want me to use, would you?"

Sara looked at him sidelong, her left brow arched. "Certainly, if you need me to show you again."

"That would be good," he said as he walked to a doorway beneath the stairs. "It's been a long day."

Mecca followed them down. The narrow staircase down opened out into a large room with a red concrete floor. Books lined the walls and an island of electronics took up the middle of the room and one entire wall.

It reminded her of a movie, where the underground resistance has a secret bunker from which the charismatic hero— or heroine, of course — commanded the valiant troops. At one time, she could have seen her father as the charismatic hero. Now, though, she wasn't so sure.

"You can use that one over there," Sara said, pointing to the desk in the middle of the room with a dual flat panel monitor set-up. "What are you wanting to do?"

Her dad sat down in the oversized leather chair and pulled the keyboard tray out from under the desk. "We need to do some traveling, but I want to make sure to throw them off track."

"Who?" Sara asked.

Mecca wondered how he would answer. She still couldn't tell how much Sara knew about the situation, or even about her own Gift. *Their* Gift.

"The people who kidnapped Mecca. You know I'm not going to go into detail, Sara. It's too dangerous."

Sara shrugged and flopped down into the chair at the other desk, which had an entire wall of monitors. "Whatever," she said. "If it's so dangerous, it's not going to matter what I know or what I don't."

Mecca wandered over to one of the overstuffed bookshelves and ran a finger along the wood. "Dad. We don't have our passports." It was weird the bits of information that decided to come up at random times.

The tack-tacking of the keyboard stopped.

"Shit," he said.

"Are they in your office at home?"

"No, the safety deposit box at the bank. Damn it."

"The bank's closed."

"Yes."

Would they end up staying the night here? Where else would they go? Mecca didn't want to be in the house longer than she needed to.

The keyboard tacking resumed, and her dad said, "I'll get them in the morning. I should be able to get in first thing. We'll be out tomorrow night."

A low chirruping sound came from her father's jeans and he pulled the cell phone from his pocket. Concern, then anger slipped across his features as he listened to the caller. "Yes," he said. "We'll be leaving tomorrow night. I'll see you there." He clicked the phone off and then looked at her.

"That was Uncle Ken. He's going to see if he can get Carolyn and Jenny to go to Amsterdam."

"I thought they were in London?" Mecca asked.

He nodded and turned back to the monitor. "They are."

Emilia must have sent someone after them. But what good would that do? Jim was dead. Mecca tried not to think too hard on that. Maybe Emilia was trying to frighten them.

Or flush her and her dad out.

Mecca took the stairs back to the living room, her palms leaving damp streaks on the handrail. The sudden urge to sit and be alone overwhelmed her. Grateful to be able to put a closed door between herself and her father, along with the strange girl he'd inexplicably befriended, Mecca sank into the old, blue sofa that dominated the room.

Decorated in typical college décor, with mismatched furnishings and an array of scattered books, Mecca realized with surprise that she felt at home here. She craved the normalcy that this living room promised, with its oddly tilted recliner and scuffed wooden coffee table.

Safety. Normalcy.

But she could never be this normal again. Perhaps she'd kidded herself all along that she could be like every other girl in the world. She should have known the moment she put her mom in the hospital. Nothing could be normal for her. Ever.

"Mecca?" Sara's voice came from behind her, from the doorway to the basement. "I thought maybe you'd want something to eat or drink. I think I've still got some muffins in the kitchen."

"No, I'm okay. Thanks." She was hungry, but she didn't think she could eat. Every few minutes, memories of Jim Barron's study, or the sound of his breathing, or … a million other things about those moments, would flitter through her mind. She didn't know if she could keep anything down.

The door closed, but she still felt Sara's energy in the room. Quiet footfalls approached.

"David's still looking at travel sites. I think he's going to book you guys flights to a bunch of different places. You'll each need a suitcase though. Flying without luggage can make them look really closely at you. Not always, but better not to take the chance. I can give you clothes for your suitcase, but I don't know what we're going to do about him, except buy him a bunch of hippie clothes."

"How do you know my dad?" The question came out before Mecca had even thought whether it was a good idea to ask.

Sara came around the sofa and perched on the edge of the recliner. From the way she sat, she'd had lots of practice balancing on the precariously slanted chair.

"He was married to my Gran a long time ago."

Anxiety stabbed through Mecca's heart. "What's your last name?"

"Harrington. Why? Did he tell you about me?"

Mecca shook her head and Sara's smile faltered a little. Mecca felt even more confused now. Harrington—the name of the last woman the papers said that her father killed. If he really murdered those women, how could he still be in contact with the families? Why would he take that chance? How could he live with himself?

A bright thought crept in.

Maybe he didn't really kill them. Who could say that the reports Emilia fed her were even factual? Emilia could have told her anything—probably *would* have told her anything—to get her cooperation.

"Yesterday," Sara said, "was actually the first time I'd met him in person."

"Really?"

"Yeah. We're online buddies though. It's not like he hangs out or anything. We talk about techie stuff a lot, what with him getting into the whole 'hacking' thing." She grinned at Mecca conspiratorially. "He plays with it, but he's not serious."

Mecca barked out a laugh. She'd said the same thing when he'd told her he was interested in "computer security." Her dad knew his way around a computer, but the Department of Defense had nothing to worry about from David Trenow.

"I'm glad he got in touch with me yesterday though. And I'm glad he found you." Sara's green eyes held Mecca's gaze. "He was really worried. Even I could tell, and I'm definitely not a people person." The quirky grin tugged at the corners of her mouth again.

"Thanks." Mecca didn't know what else to say — she didn't even know how she felt — and they drifted into an awkward silence. Mecca's thoughts jumbled through her head.

She liked Sara, but Sara linked her to her dad's past. It confirmed, at the least, that he'd been married to a woman named Harrington. Mecca didn't want to ask Sara how her grandmother had died.

After a few minutes, Sara got up. "I'm going to go check on him. Do you need anything?"

"No, but thanks."

"Okay. Come on down if you feel like it."

An hour and a half later, her dad had purchased plane tickets for ten destinations around the world. They sat at the kitchen table, a modest spread of Quarter Pounders and Chicken McNuggets scattered across the surface. Sara had picked them up, along with a pair of brown cotton pants and a white tunic for her dad that reminded Mecca of Hari Krishnas at the airport. He only needed a sprig of daisies.

Mecca munched on a few fries but nothing else. She still didn't trust her stomach. Not just because she'd witnessed her best friend's father die a terrible, bloody death — that was bad enough, but also because she'd finally come to face the reality that her father had probably killed those women. Watching his nervous moves and pinched eyebrows, she knew that the last thing he wanted was for her to spend much time with Sara.

She wished that she felt angry and betrayed, instead of this nothingness that sat on her shoulders like a vulture. Between learning about her dad's past and watching Jenny's dad die, Mecca figured being numb shouldn't be a surprise. Shock. It's normal. Natural.

But it still made her belly hurt.

"I think I'm going to go to bed," she said. Relief sailed across her dad's features for a split second before he fixed the concerned look back on his face.

"Okay, honey. You can take the spare room and I'll sleep on the sofa."

Sara made some noises about getting extra sheets and pillows and showing her the way, but Mecca'd already stood and found herself through the doorway before Sara finished speaking. Mecca made her way upstairs and into the bathroom, closing the door tight behind her and throwing the lock on the knob. Through the wood, she heard Sara climb the stairs, the tread too light to be her dad.

In front of the mirror, Mecca braced herself against the porcelain pedestal sink and hung her head.

Exhaustion crept through her limbs, weighing them down, making her eyelids droop. She twisted the faucet for the hot water and there came a tap on the door.

"Mecca?" Sara's voice came through. "I put out some clothes that might fit you. You're way taller than I am, but maybe there's something you can use. I also left a duffel bag in the guest room too. For the airport."

"Okay. Thanks."

Sara seemed to be on-board for this jaunting all over the globe thing that her dad had devised. But it was a bad idea. They couldn't save Jenny and her mom. They couldn't save anyone.

Not by running away.

Steam floated from the sink and fogged the mirror. Mecca's reflection became a dark, blurry outline, all her features indistinct. It matched her mood: unfocused.

She leaned over the sink and pulled a handful of water up and onto her face. Her nerves tingled with the almost-too-hot temperature. If it could wake her up, if it could un-blur the outline of her mood, her thoughts, maybe she could figure out some alternative to jetting around the world, waiting for monsters to slaughter them.

--->>><<<---

She slept heavily, but not for long. The bedside clock glowed 12:47 a.m. when Mecca jolted awake from a nightmare where Jenny and her mom had been turned into zombies. She didn't understand it, but it scared the hell out of her, all the same.

The answer came to her as the dream receded to float in her subconscious.

She would go back.

It all came clear in her mind as she swung her legs out of the warm bed. The only way to truly escape from them would be to destroy them.

They would expect her to run. They would expect her and her father to try to save Jenny.

She wouldn't be trapped on their terms, she decided.

Mecca pulled on a shirt and pair of jeans that Sara had left on the dresser. The jeans barely came to her ankles, but they would do.

If Emilia expected her to run to Europe, then Mecca would do the opposite. She'd confront the Visci in their own yard. But she'd do it her way.

Her feet, still tender and a little swollen, only fit into the sneakers Josie had brought her yesterday morning after she loosened the laces as much as their length would allow. She winced, but tied both as tight as she could handle, doubling the knots.

Beyond the curtains on the window, Mecca saw darkness, save for the streetlights which always shone after sundown in this neighborhood, so near the university. The street below looked clear.

Now she wished she hadn't left Josie's car at the cabin. How would she get back to the house where she'd been held captive? Enough time to figure that out later. Now she just needed to get out of *this* house.

She crept out of the room and closed the door behind her, listening for any sounds coming from below. Down the hall, a light peeked from under a closed door.

Sara.

What was she doing awake?

Mecca tread with light steps to the stairs and tiptoed down. Halfway to the main floor, she heard her dad snoring. It made her smile as she thought of all the good-natured teasing she and her mom had put him through over his freight-train snore. Then she remembered that she shouldn't be smiling.

Maybe she could take the van. Where would he put the keys?

Probably in his jeans.

She couldn't see anything in the gloom of the living room, where someone had drawn the curtains closed against the streetlights. A minute ticked by and her vision adjusted to the shadows.

There, on the corner of the coffee tables. The keys.

The van's shocks left a lot to be desired; Mecca bounced along the potholed road away from the university. The ride smoothed out as she turned onto Moreland. She thought she could recall the route to the house. She was pretty sure.

She didn't have a plan of action. Going back to the house had seemed like a good idea when she'd woken up. Now, as time got shorter, she thought maybe she hadn't thought it through enough.

In the back of her mind, she knew she wanted to destroy Emilia. It would be the only way to be free of her. But how? She tried not to think too hard on it, hoping something would come when she wasn't paying attention.

She'd thought briefly about waking her dad to come with her, to help. But he still wanted to run. Sure, he'd made noises about rescuing Jenny and her mom, but really he wanted to run, she knew. Mecca didn't understand this hidden side of her dad — the side that thought running away would solve this problem. But the only way any of them would be safe would be with Emilia's death.

And if she was being very honest — and why not? She was probably going to die soon anyway — a part of her didn't want to see him fight them. She didn't want him to use the Gift against Emilia. That would mean everything must be true. Everything.

In her heart, she still didn't want to believe it.

She took the exit after Stone Mountain and turned at the third light. The Sonic on the street corner served as her landmark. She passed subdivisions and strip malls, groceries and video stores, all their parking lots dark, except Kroger. God bless the twenty-four-hour grocery store.

After fifteen minutes, suburbia gave way to pasture and ten minutes later, Mecca recognized the strip of road that would lead to where she'd been held. A hot panic flashed through her and she sucked in a lungful of air. She pulled onto the shoulder and cut the engine. The van shuddered to silence.

Counting her breaths, she waited for the unease — she didn't want to call it panic — to settle.

She knew she would only have about a mile to walk before she came to the wooded edge of the property. Another ten minute jog, and she'd be at the back gate. She remembered Jenny's dad, lying on the floor of his office, blood droplets spraying his chin as he tried to breathe through the gash in his throat.

Mecca let the horror well up and incite her anger.

Yeah, that worked.

She pushed open the steel door and dropped down to the ground.

Chapter Twenty: Claude

Something pulled at him. An internal pull, like the need to find something previously lost. It told him someone of his own blood should be nearby.

Claude looked across the pens, but didn't see anything out of the ordinary. Only filthy cattle making pitiful sounds and an ungodly stink.

He'd sent Salas to check on Will, as Emilia had asked. She'd decided to oversee the details at the maze herself, rather than leave it to one of the younger ones who'd never attended a Maze Gathering before. Claude thought the pull he'd felt indicated Salas's return, but the tall Egyptian didn't materialize.

Claude looked more closely at the occupants of the pens. Dirty and thin, every one. At least the hunters had found young ones this time. The last Maze Gathering he'd attended had featured old, tired men and women. He'd hardly considered it sport at all.

Another tug.

Who is that?

None of the cattle should pull at him. Only —

"Ahh," he said, as he considered the only other human who carried his blood.

The girl in the pen nearest him shrank back. The tangy smell of sweat and excrement came through the bars as she moved away from him.

"My girl has come home."

--->>>≪≪---

"Will is resting," Salas said when he returned to the pen area. Tall, with skin the color of pale molasses and a toned but slender frame, Salas intimidated most people, including the cattle in the pens. Claude found it to be one of his most useful talents.

Claude nodded. "Mecca is here." When Salas looked around, Claude clarified. "She's on the grounds. I don't know exactly where yet. I expect we will be seeing her soon."

Claude had taken to grooming one of the horses, a dapple grey with an uneven white marking right between his eyes. The musky scent of the animals made Claude's nose twitch.

"What would you like me to do?" Salas asked.

"Nothing, right now. This will necessitate a change in my plans for the Gathering. I will not be participating in the Maze."

"What will you tell Emilia?"

Claude shrugged. "I'll work something out. But if Mecca happens upon the Gathering, I don't want her seeing me in the midst of it. It would ruin things."

"I understand. She would no longer see you as a potential ally," Salas said. "Do you think Emilia knows she is here?"

"I suspect not. I substituted my blood for hers many times. I don't think she has as strong a bond as I do. But that remains to be seen, I suppose."

Salas nodded. "It's getting close to time. I've laid out your clothes for the evening, if you wish to dress. I will get one of the cattle handlers to hose these beasts down." He waved a hand toward the pens.

"Very good. Guests should be arriving soon."

———※≪≪———

The silk slid against his skin like the light touch of a lover. It brought him back to memories of Rome and its bathhouses—glorious times. Claude sighed as he fastened the buttons on the well-tailored shirt. The present—which had been the future then— hadn't turned out the way he'd hoped. However, silk shirts did indicate a significant improvement over togas.

He pulled on the light linen jacket that Salas had placed on his bed and looked himself over in the mirror. He took a moment to fasten his hair back with an antiquated leather thong, his accessory of preference. From the dresser, he took an ancient silver coin. It depicted two men on a chariot, one holding the reins on a pair of horses, the other with a bow outstretched. Though it predated Claude's birth by many hundred years, he always carried it with him. It had been his mother's.

Claude dropped the coin into the pocket of his matching ivory slacks. Into the other pocket went his small key ring with the security fob attached. Before leaving his room, he turned on the concealed alarm he'd had Salas install when they'd arrived. The Egyptian had many, many talents.

Emilia caught up with him at the elevator three minutes later. She'd taken the time to change as well, having donned a pair of dark silver, form-fitting slacks and a sheer, brick red, button-down blouse. Her sleek, black hair framed her face in the most exquisite way. For a moment, Claude felt the old lust well up in him, but he tamped it down. He had no place for those feelings any longer.

"Everything is ready?" he asked.

The elevator doors slid open, and she answered as they stepped inside. "Yes. This will be a successful Gathering, I think."

"Your Gatherings are always successful."

She flashed a smile. "And you'll be playing tonight?"

"I don't think so."

She raised one thin eyebrow. "No?"

Claude leaned a shoulder against the lift wall. "I didn't see any that struck my fancy. You know I prefer my meals a little more plump. That's one of my complaints about this place, this era. Everyone must be so thin. It's like feeding on a dusty skeleton."

"But the object isn't to feed," she said with a smile.

The doors opened with their soft sound and Claude motioned forward with an open hand. Emilia stepped off the elevator, the fabric of her slacks swishing with the movement. He loved the style she'd adopted since coming to Atlanta. Very polished and elegant. A far cry from the young, demure peasant girl he'd discovered so many years ago crying over her dead mother's body.

"Are you concerned about what will be said at the assembly?" he asked.

Gaiety drained from her face, and her brow tightened. "I'm concerned more about what I *won't* be hearing. I know we have purist sympathizers among the leadership, but I don't know how deep that support runs. And I doubt they will be candid in front of the half-breed who controls the largest city in the south." Her scowl made her face ugly.

"Yes, it wouldn't benefit them to voice their opinions about that in front of you. Though their tongues may be looser later, after a bit of drink and revelry."

The lift doors opened and he rested his hand on her back as they entered the second floor's lit hallway. Her muscles tensed when they approached the room where they would meet with the Visci who controlled other southeastern cities.

"I may be more successful in finding out who supports which faction," Claude said.

Emilia stopped, mid-step, and Claude almost strode past her. When he stopped and turned she scrutinized him, openly. He only stared back at her and waited. In this time, with the open slaughter of anyone not of pure blood, he knew she distrusted everyone.

"Yes," she finally said. "I would appreciate that."

--->>><<<-

They surrounded a sturdy, mahogany conference table, Emilia and a dozen or so others who controlled various cities across the southeastern United States. They came from as far north as Virginia and as far west as Louisiana. Claude, and five other non-official attendees, stood against the walls. Two looked like bodyguards, but the rest seemed to be companions.

Not all of the leading Visci were in attendance. Many didn't often travel away from their cities, so there were a number who were never expected. But one who always attended Gatherings had not come to Atlanta: Tony Mercado, from Miami. Claude wondered whether Mercado, a pure blood, had stayed away for political reasons. And he wondered, also, whether this would be the start of something no one would be able to stop.

They dispensed with the ordinary business, then Thomas Eli, who ruled in Charlotte, brought up the topic Claude knew would have most of them shifting in their seats.

"We've had three more killings." He stood, a short man with flaming red hair, ruddy skin and eyes the color of deep ice, which flashed with anger. "Two mixed bloods and one full. We are assuming that the full blood was murdered in retaliation for the two last month."

Emilia bristled. At least Eli hadn't called them half-breeds—those who came from a pairing between a Visci and a human. Claude supposed that was the only good part of what Eli said.

The random murders of mixed blood Visci had begun in the northwest and moved to New England within a decade. The killings in Charlotte, only 200 miles from Atlanta, hit closer to home for Emilia than any others. Claude watched closely.

"These extremists need to be rooted out," Eli continued. "One more killing and I will lock the city down."

"How do you plan on finding them?" This came from Arabella Connelly, from Memphis, a beautiful mixed-blood with a classic southern drawl. "Even if someone is of pure blood, that doesn't mean they're fanatics."

Eli sat down. "I don't know. But these murders must stop."

"They've become more organized, I think. The purists, I mean," Arabella Connelly said. She had everyone's attention. "Last month, we caught a human as he was fixing to set a house on fire. The house is owned by—well, it don't matter whose house, but she's of mixed blood."

"A human?" Wide eyed, Eli shifted to the edge of his seat, leaning on the table. "Who brought a human in?"

Arabella, a petite, delicate woman, looked down for a moment from where she sat beside Eli. Claude admired the calculated move, which made her look demure and refined.

"We later found out that he had been hired by Jarot Kendling, a purist who'd moved to the city from

Seattle." She pushed a lock of sandy hair back from her face. "We tried Kendling, of course. Quietly."

The room remained silent. Claude studied each face around the table. In their own ways, he suspected they were all coming to the same conclusion. War could not be avoided. It was coming, whether the leadership wanted it or not. And from more than one of the faces Claude could see, some didn't seem to mind.

"Where is Mercado?" Eli broke the silence with his accusatory tone. Others around the table exchanged glances, but eventually all eyes turned to Emilia.

"He didn't respond to the invitation," Emilia said, her voice flat.

"He's a pure blood," Eli said. The muscles in his neck tightened and his face reddened. One hand curled into a fist on top of the table. "This is an insult!"

Murmurs enveloped the room. Many of those gathered nodded, including Arabella Connelly. Others remained silent and still. Claude understood the benefit of choosing either reaction. However, he thought those who remained silent, in this assembly comprised mostly of Visci with some human heritage, could be construed as having purist sympathies.

Emilia raised a hand. "If it is, Thomas, it is my insult to attend. I will speak with Tony when I am able. I'm certain he did not mean for his absence to be a slight."

This had a calming effect on the room, though Thomas Eli still glowered but at no one in particular.

"We all must attend to our own cities," Emilia continued. "And we will need to be creative in dealing with the threat of extremism. I believe that most of us simply want things to remain as they have for centuries. Some may disagree, however." She scanned the room, settling on each face for a heartbeat before moving on. "Violence against Visci is not tolerated unless sanctioned by the city elder. This has been our rule of law. These purists who have resorted to killing other Visci have begun working outside of our established order. Therefore, they must answer for their actions. For their crimes."

No one disagreed. No one spoke. Just by the stances they took in their chairs, Claude could see that most agreed with Emilia's assessment. But not all.

"We must think of creative ways of finding the criminals among us, but we have to adhere to our laws. Discover them and bring them to trial." She paused and then smiled at the group. "So let's adjourn now. We will have a pleasant evening at the Maze Gathering, then we will go to our respective cities and consider how we might find those who would kill others of the Blood and bring them to justice."

When Eli began to bluster, Arabella Connelly put her hand on his forearm, leaned over and whispered to him. He looked around the table, wild-eyed, then sighed and leaned back in his chair. Arabella stroked his arm and smiled at him.

"We are all concerned, Thomas," Emilia said. "And I suspect we will need to work together on this, in the end. But for now, let's enjoy the night."

Chapter Twenty-One: Mecca

At the back of the property, the stone wall cut through the forest about two hundred yards east of the back gate. Tree branches from both sides canopied over the wall. Mecca scrambled up an oak tree and inched forward onto a thick branch. Darkness made the ground seem farther than ten feet below.

The branch extended a couple beyond where the barbed wire topped the wall. Mecca crawled along, her movement slow and deliberate. The oak, old and sturdy, held her weight without bending until she'd gotten past the sharp wire. The branch sagged as Mecca hung and then she dropped to the ground. Pain twanged the soles of her feet in memory of her escape, but she ignored it.

She sprinted away from the wall but then slowed to a walk, her pace dictated by the darkness of the night and the heavy leaf cover. A chill breeze brought gooseflesh up on her skin. She wished she'd thought to bring a jacket.

She found the fire road that would lead her back to the main house. Mecca didn't walk along it, but beside it, retracing her earlier steps when she'd fled her captors. At least it felt better to have shoes on this time, even if her feet still stung from her first trip through.

To keep her mind off her dad — and whether what she was doing was stupid or just crazy, she concentrated on not tripping over the exposed roots and fallen branches. The filtered moonlight threw gruesome, misshapen shadows against tree trunks and bushes. Leaves crunched beneath her rubber soles.

Mecca stopped and leaned against a tree, the cold seeping through the thin shirt covering her. She closed her eyes and wondered what she'd do when she got back to the house. Should she sneak in? Maybe she should sit outside until the sun came up. Would it be safer to go in during the day?

Mecca sank to a crouch, her back against the tree. "What was I thinking, coming back here?"

What did she hope to accomplish? She didn't even know how many people Emilia kept in the house. Were they human or Visci? She didn't know the floor plan. Hell, she may not even have made it out the first time if Claude hadn't given her directions.

Why had Claude helped her escape, for that matter? Did he know she'd be returning? He couldn't. Not really.

Could he?

When she thought of him seated in the library, reading, her belly flip-flopped. And what the hell was *that* reaction all about? It pissed her off.

"Too many questions." Her brain hurt, thinking about it.

She pushed off from the tree, stood and strode along the side of the fire road. She'd deal with whatever she found when she found it. Maybe it would get her killed, but she'd take a few of them down with her, damn it.

Her decision felt very final. But that was okay.

Another five minutes went by before she realized that music floated on the air, light and bantering, from the direction where the main house lay.

Without warning, she stepped into the small clearing that made up the guest house's back yard. She hadn't realized she'd gone this far. The walk turned out to be much shorter going in than it had been coming out.

Here, near the well, the music sounded louder, closer, a tinkling mix of drum machine and strings. Not something Mecca would choose to listen to, but it sounded tight in the night air.

As she crept around the guest house, the enormous tract of land behind the main house came into view. Festooned with party lights, the slate patio looked like it came off a movie set. Lanky, but beautiful, men and women milled about in their *haute couture*. Plants in thick stone pots glittered with the twinkling bulbs below a canopy set on the lawn in case of rain.

The first time she'd come through here, she'd passed a very high hedge. Now it stood, decorated with the same white lights and Mecca could see a gap centered in the length of it about eight feet wide. Beyond the eight foot gap, she could see more hedge inside. The end closest to her turned back at a ninety degree angle. The lights in the hedge only seemed to go a few dozen yards toward the back, but Mecca could make out the shadow of the hedge much farther than that. She couldn't see the end in the darkness.

A hedge maze? Seriously?

People milled about near the entrance, sipping on dark red wine in fine crystal glasses. It looked like any formal evening party, but everything about it made the hair on Mecca's arms stand up. Tucked in moderate safety behind the corner of the guest house, she watched for several moments, trying to find Emilia or Claude among the guests.

One familiar face caught her eye. The tall, dark-skinned man who'd been with Claude in the library. He stood, speaking with a woman who looked no more than seventeen. He inclined his head toward her as he spoke, and she tilted her own back and laughed. The sound didn't reach Mecca's ears over the low thrum of the music, but she recognized the flirting between them. Moonlight made the scene look romantic, but it didn't allay Mecca's sense of things being Not Quite Right.

She scanned the crowd once more and then made her way back around the guest house in silence. She wanted to get a closer look at the back part of the hedge, so she followed the line of the cottage until she reached the other side.

As she suspected, though the lights only went a short way, the hedge itself extended for dozens of yards toward the woods in the back. On this side, she saw another open gap just like the one in the front. A lone man, dressed in conservative slacks and a dark blue button down shirt, hung around the gap, a rifle held comfortably in one hand.

As quietly as she could, Mecca doubled back through the cottage's yard, into the tree line.

Emilia had armed guards on the hedge. What did that mean? Mecca wanted to get a look at the back. The more she saw of it, the more it made her think of a maze. Hedge mazes creeped her out. All mazes creeped her out, really. They reminded her of that movie with Jack Nicholson where he went crazy in the snow-bound hotel.

She made her way around and had to go several yards out of her way to stay within the safety of the tree cover. The back of the hedge came into view, small ground lighting casting hazy illumination on the third entrance to the maze.

It *had* to be a maze. No other explanation fit.

Four hundred feet back from the hedge, a barn squatted in the clearing. Dark green paint tried valiantly to cling to the weathered wood, but seemed to be losing the battle. A few windows scattered along the walls, the pale wood of new shutters pulled tight, not giving Mecca a view inside.

She ducked deeper into the shadows of the woods. A few more people gathered here, but not the elegant guests of the party. These men and women dressed as workers and each wore a pistol in a waist harness. Most were busy setting up portable fencing which made a corridor from the front door of the barn to the maze's entrance. It reminded her of corralling bulls and horses at a rodeo.

The hair on her arms rose again and dread crept into her veins. *What are they planning?*

Moving with as much care as she could, Mecca crept through the woods toward the back of the barn. What were they corralling here? The horror of possibility tugged at her mind's corners. She pushed it away, resolute that she wouldn't jump to conclusions.

But there's really only one thing you're going to find here, Mec. You know that.

She ignored her own voice in her head and found herself looking at the backside of the barn. Large double doors dominated this wall, locked with a silver padlock, but a smaller, person-sized door with a knob was tucked near the right corner. Surprised that no one guarded this side, Mecca decided to take advantage while she could.

She launched into a sprint and covered the few dozen yards in several seconds. Her skin tingled with adrenaline and danger.

Up close, the barn didn't look in any better repair. The weathering of the wood left gaps between some of the slats. Mecca peered through one. Inside, the only light came from a single bare bulb hanging from a rafter. Where horse stalls would be along the left wall, she saw cages, with several dark shapes inside. They looked like people, but Mecca couldn't tell for sure.

That tickling horror nibbled on her conscience again.

A loft extended above the cages and she could make out squared bundles up there. Hay, probably, but she didn't really see Emilia as the farming type. Across the way from the cages, proper stalls lined the wall and the sounds of horse drifted to her ears. She didn't think anyone else wandered around inside. Only those in the cages and the horses in their stalls. She tried the doorknob and was shocked to find it unlocked.

Clouded in shadows, the interior reeked of sweat, hay, manure and urine. Mecca wrinkled her nose while she waited for her eyes to adjust to the gloom. Beneath the soft snorts and whinnying of the horses, she heard shuffling and the dim sounds of crying coming from the cages. She picked her way over, concentrating in the murkiness so she wouldn't trip over some discarded piece of farm equipment.

A gasp came from the first cage just as Mecca reached it. A woman's face pressed against the bars. She looked young, maybe Mecca's age, but her skin, her clothes, everything about her was filthy. Blonde hair hung in dirty tendrils around her face, accenting the high cheekbones in a way that would have been beautiful if the girl's face weren't so gaunt.

Aghast, Mecca turned her gaze to the rest of the people behind the bars. Two cages butted up against one another, each with a small handful of people. The one closest to her held women, all in different stages of filth. Mecca counted seven. Two sat on the dirt floor and paid her no mind. The others, save for the girl who gasped, cowered away and huddled together like frightened children.

The second cage held seven men, all just as dirty as the women. Also like the women, most looked young, in their late teens or early twenties. Scattered around the small cage, some stood and others sat.

They reminded her of cattle. And she felt guilty at the thought.

One man, older than the others, squatted in the corner facing out, facing her. His eyes looked black. He lifted his head in a half-nod to her and his voice, though quiet, carried across the murky darkness.

"Come open the cage. The guard outside has the keys. You can get them from him." His voice, monotone, didn't carry the confidence to back the words he chose, and he remained squatting in his soiled and tattered clothes.

"No!" whispered the blonde girl, frantic. "Go, run away. Get help!"

The words set the women to twittering in panic. Mecca only caught bits and pieces of what they said, her own terror creeping beneath her skin like ants.

"She can save us!"

"No, no! You won't survive…"

"She'll never get those keys."

The young woman with the gaunt face reached out a skeletal hand. Mecca jerked when the cool fingers brushed her elbow.

"Run. You should leave us and run as fast as you can. Send help back."

"How long have you been here?" Mecca asked, lowering her voice to match.

"I don't know. Weeks. Maybe months."

"All of you?" Mecca looked again at the other women in the cage. Two had found some bravery still in their hearts and had stepped forward to listen. They weren't as emaciated as this girl, but they looked horrible. Like refugees. Mecca's stomach roiled.

"I haven't been here more than two weeks," one said, her voice cracking.

Mecca looked back at the blonde who first spoke. "What's your name?"

"Alicia."

"I'm Mecca," she replied absently as she studied the door of the cage. Not even high enough to walk through upright, it only spanned half the height of the cage and sat on a sliding track. No hinges to work with. A tarnished silver padlock hooked through the eye of the closure. Mecca tugged on it, though she knew it would hold. It did.

"They're going to come and take us somewhere tonight. They talked about it when they were in here earlier," Alicia said. "It's going to be soon. You should hurry."

Mecca nodded, pushing away the mental image of these captive people being herded into the hedge maze. She understood what the corral was for now. But once they were in the maze, then what?

Accustomed to the shadowy dimness now, Mecca looked around. Five stalls took up the wall across from the cages, but only two had horses in them. Though both were beautiful, one grey and the other white with black spots, Mecca didn't have time to admire them.

The barn entrances in the front mirrored those in the back, with large double doors in the center and a small door in the right corner. She guessed the doubles were padlocked like the others, so she made her way toward the corner.

When she glanced back, she saw that all of the women and the men had stood and crowded toward the fronts of the cages, watching her. Even the older man stood with his face between the bars, his dark eyes following her every move.

Their hope powdered the air like the scent of a too-sweet flower, trapped in the filth of decay.

The responsibility weighed heavily on her shoulders. She had no doubt that these people would die if she left them here. She didn't know exactly how, but she knew in her heart that Emilia wouldn't keep them like this only to let them go. Did they understand that? She thought the older man might, at least.

She pressed her ear against the door and winced when a splinter of wood jabbed against her lobe. But she kept her position and listened to the sounds of work on the other side. Still putting up the fencing, she guessed, but they had to be almost done by now. What else would take up their time before they came in here and pushed their captives to the slaughter? For surely, there was to be a slaughter.

The smooth latch moved easily under her hand and she cracked the door two inches. Voices became louder, words more distinct. She tried to separate the different conversations, hoping to hear someone mention the night's plans.

Without warning, the door pulled away from her with a jerk. A monster of a man towered over her with thick shoulders, a solid middle and Paul Newman blue eyes. The beauty of those eyes was no match for the nasty look on his square face.

"Who the hell are you?"

Mecca stuttered and stepped back into the barn as he pushed his way through the doorway, his huge body barely clearing the frame. Dark curls framed an awkward and ugly face, with a large, bulbous nose that had been broken more than once. He reached a massive paw toward her, but she ducked to the left and broke away.

The women in the cage behind her let out a collective gasp, then broke into a cacophony of shouts that echoed around the high ceiling.

Mecca wanted to tell them to shut up, that they'd bring more attention, but she could barely stay out of reach of the gorilla after her. He moved faster than she expected him to and when he lunged for her again, his fingers wrapped around her upper arm, half over her sleeve. The squeeze of his grip sent jolts up her arm.

Mecca sent her energy out, into him, even as she struggled, trying to escape his iron hold. She envisioned seeing him a withered corpse at her feet but his strength kept distracting her. Her energy gushed into the Cavern. Warmth suffused her there.

Warmth.

With her surprise, her energy recoiled, slammed back home and sent her reeling.

She shifted her body around and suddenly his broad, sloped forehead clouded her entire field of vision as he head-butted her. Her head snapped back and stars exploded in front of her eyes.

She stumbled. Something hard got under her heel, and she railed backward. His hand lost contact with her as she fell. She tried to catch her balance, but everything moved twice as fast as she could. Her head slammed against the side of the first horse stall, sending a crackling white pain down her spine. She fell in a pile on the dusty floor.

Human.

He was human.

Chapter Twenty-Two: David

"Wake up."

The quiet voice filtered through the dark buzz of dead sleep.

"She's gone. Wake up."

David's heart double-pounded, and he jolted upright. One curtain had been pulled back to let in the silver light of the street lamps. Sara stood a few feet away dressed in bright green cotton shorts and a black shirt with the words *Bella Morte* in ghostly white script on the front.

"Are you awake?" she asked.

David nodded, pinching the bridge of his nose as he swung his legs around and his feet hit the floor. Sleep still covered his mind, catching his thoughts the way feet get tangled in a blanket. "Who's gone?"

"Mecca. I thought I heard the front door a little while ago, and when I passed the spare bedroom, that door wasn't closed all the way. She's gone."

His limbs turned to rubber, and panic rose in his chest. Mecca couldn't be gone. She had no place to go. Maybe she went for a walk. That made no sense, but his fear hoped for it. "Damn it. What time is it?"

"After one," Sara said as she flipped on the overhead light.

David closed his eyes and pressed his fingertips against them and then he sucked in a deep breath to calm his heart. When its thudding slowed, he opened his eyes. The almost-bare coffee table mocked him. The cell phone he'd borrowed from Sara sat near the corner.

His keys.

Gone.

He dropped to his knees and to look under the table. Panic wrapped around his heart like a boa constrictor. His stomach lurched. Not finding the key ring, he turned and shoved his hands into the cracks around the sofa's cushions. He pulled out an elastic hair band and a Snickers wrapper, but found no keys.

"God damn it, Mecca!"

Sara perched on the chair arm and watched him. "They're not in your pocket?" she asked, her voice patient, but not hopeful.

David patted his jeans, though he knew they weren't there. "No. I laid them on the table before I went to sleep. They kept poking me in the hip."

"So where'd she go?"

"And that's the question. I don't know."

He didn't think her so naive as to try to go back to their house or her dorm. Jim's house held nothing. Perhaps she went back to the cabin. But no, he didn't think so. Not the way she'd been talking about not running away, about confronting them and fighting—

"Shit."

Sara pulled a foot up onto the chair arm, rested her chin on her knee. "What?"

"I think she went back."

"Back to where? Your house?"

"No. Back to the place they held her."

Her brows furrowed, the confusion very clear on her face. "Why the hell would she do that?"

"It's complicated." David rubbed his hands over his face, the stubble on his cheeks scraping his palms. He just wanted to crawl into a soft bed and sleep for a few years. Was that too much to ask?

"Of course, it's complicated. Jesus."

The edge in her voice made him look up. She hadn't moved from the chair, but her stance changed. She held herself more rigid, her lips pursed, jaw tight.

"I suppose you're going to want to borrow my car now," she said.

The first step of the nebulous plan in his head *had* been to borrow her car; she hit that one out of the ballpark. But she didn't look all that willing to loan it right now.

"Yes," he said. "I'd hoped you'd let me use your car."

"Okay." She slipped from the chair and walked to the stairway.

"Okay?"

"Yes, okay, you can use my car. I'll get dressed. Because I'm coming with you."

--->>><<<---

She'd changed into a pair of blue jeans with ragged hems at the ankles, but kept the Bella Morte shirt. Over it, she wore a beat-up, dark red, Adidas windbreaker. She'd wet her hair down, and its small curls shone deep black.

"No. This is dangerous," David said, as he stood. He'd had no choice but to wait for her to change, since she had the keys to her car. "I am not taking you."

"So you're going to what, knock me in the head and steal my keys? Call an Uber?" Sara stood with one hand on her cocked hip and an eyebrow raised.

"Of course I'm not going to hit you," he said. He completely ignored the Uber comment. "Why are you pushing this now? I just don't want you to get hurt."

Sara stepped toward him and brought her face as close as she could, being a full foot shorter. Her breath smelled of spearmint.

"I've helped you, with no questions asked, ever since you messaged me yesterday. I've cracked your hard drive. I've given you a place to crash." She counted each item on a finger of her raised hand. "I've loaned you equipment. I've welcomed your daughter here. You haven't even offered to tell me what the hell is going on. You're the only family I have besides my mom. I *want* to help you." She tilted her head to the side and gave him a tight smile. "But I'm not the type of girl to wait for a man. I was patient, but I'm done now. So, you want my car? I have no problems with that. But I'm going with you one way or the other. Don't forget who found that address for you. I can find my way there on my own, you know."

David couldn't stop the ominous dread dragging itself up his spine like a corpse pulling itself out a grave. But this dread had never really died, had it?

This was going to end very badly.

"Sara, please. I'm just trying to keep you safe."

"That's not your job," she said, drawing a jangly set of keys out of the jacket pocket. "Are we going?"

His nerves bounced along with the keys. He darted a hand out and snatched the key ring from her. "If you go, you'll do what I tell you, when I tell you." He didn't bother keeping the frustration from his voice.

She shrugged.

"I mean it, Sara. I will dump you out on the highway if I have to."

"Okay, okay. Whatever."

The old Chevy Cavalier puttered along, barely reaching the 60 mph speed limit without shaking itself apart. Now David knew why Sara had such great computer equipment. All her money went into the techie stuff, not practical things, like tune-ups and new tires. At least she'd put gas in the car.

They'd ridden in silence since pulling out into the late-night traffic. She didn't fight when he insisted on driving. He estimated they'd get to the house by 2 a.m. He didn't like the idea of trying to get in at night. While the cover of darkness would prove helpful, the idea of running into a group of blood suckers in the dark didn't give him warm-fuzzies.

"So, why would Mecca go back there?" Sara asked again.

"It's complicated."

"You said that already. I'm a smart girl. Explain it to me."

David sighed. He could feel the situation moving beyond his control. Bringing Sara here, even if he left her in the car and down the road, could expose her to Emilia's people. Not telling her about them—would that protect her, or would it make her more vulnerable? He had no idea, in truth.

"I don't know that you'd believe me if I told you." David turned onto the two lane blacktop highway that would lead them to Emilia's estate. Ten minutes. "I've learned that there are things out there I never imagined could exist."

Sara didn't respond, but the weight of her stare told him that he had her full attention.

"The other night, Mecca was bitten." He had to tell her something, but David didn't know how much. If he told her about the Gift, could he keep his own secret?

"Bitten by what?"

"A person." Was the man a person? Again, no idea.

"Okay…" She drew the word out, so it had three syllables.

"Look, I told you it's complicated. When we get there, I'm going to park just off this road. I want you to stay with the car. I'll need you on the outside."

"Absolutely not. I'm going with you."

David frowned. Sara glared at him, her jaw set and her eyes flashing with intensity. Her attitude sparked the rising tension in him. His blood burned, his face flushed. He stomped on the brakes and jerked the wheel to the right. Sara tilted forward before the seatbelt locked and held her in place. The car shuddered and bounced as it went from sixty to twenty, then down to a slow crawl. Three cars whizzed by.

David slammed the gearshift into Park and turned in his seat to look at her startled face.

"I told you when we left that you're to do what I tell you, when I tell you. I'm not fucking around, Sara. I appreciate everything you've done, but this is my daughter's life we're talking about, and your own too, even though you don't realize it. This isn't a game. So if you don't want to sit in the car and wait for me, you can get your ass out right now and walk back. Your choice."

He leaned across her and yanked on the passenger handle, shoving the door open with his fingers. The smell of pine filled the car.

She stared at him. Her indecision rolled off her and hit him like a heat wave. David looked out the windshield at the street, anxious about the time wasted sitting here. But she was going to listen, or she was going to get out. He looked back at her. Finally, she slammed the door shut and trained her gaze through the windshield at the dark roadway.

David caught the relieved sigh before it left his lips and shifted the car into Drive. He waited as four luxury vehicles — two Jaguars, a Cadillac SUV, and a Dodge Viper — raced past, then he pulled onto the two lane road.

Five uncomfortable minutes later, David spotted the tree-lined drive to the estate. He pointed it out to Sara but didn't slow. As they passed, he looked up the long driveway. A line of cars, including the Jags, the Caddy, and the Viper, waited to be checked in at the guard house just inside the gate.

"They're having a party," Sara said.

"It looks that way." David tried to figure out what it meant for Mecca. Was she already in there? Had they caught her or had she blended in with the party-goers?

He drove another mile down the roadway and pulled over. Gravel crunched beneath the tires. He put the car in park and turned to Sara.

"I'm going to go check things out. If I can find a way in, I'm going in, so don't freak if I don't come right back. You've got your phone, right?"

She nodded.

"Okay, I'll call you in an hour to check in. If you don't hear from me, go home. I'll find my way back." He pulled out his phone and put it on vibrate. "Call if you need to, but only if it's an emergency."

She watched him slide it into his front pocket, her expression hard and indignant.

"Look, these people aren't fooling around. They killed a close friend of mine. Left him bleeding out on his office floor." David's voice thickened. He swallowed a lump in his throat. "He died while I knelt beside him, unable to save him. I'm not being a hardass just to be a hardass."

Sara's face paled as she listened. She toyed with the zipper of her jacket.

"I couldn't live with myself if something like that happened to you. So please, just stay in the car."

She didn't respond, but her wide eyes told him that he'd gotten *something* through to her, at least. He unfastened his seat belt and opened the door.

"Good luck," she said as he got out of the car. "Be careful."

David stooped over and looked in the open door. "I will. And thanks. You too." He closed it, sprinted around the car, and into the trees along the side of the road, relieved that she'd finally agreed to stay there.

Maybe he could pull this out of the weeds. But first, he needed to find Mecca.

It took a ten minute jog through the pines to get to the base of the pavered drive. David crossed and stayed in the trees on the house side as he made his way up the hill. A line of cars extended halfway down the driveway. He crept along the pine needle carpet. Each footfall brought the sweet, decaying smell to his nose.

The line of cars moved forward. As he got closer, he saw the front car's driver side window open. The angle hampered his line of sight, but David guessed the driver was getting his entrance validated by the guard.

Bringing up the tail of the line, third back from the gate, the black Cadillac Escalade rolled forward several feet. Through the tinted windows, David could just make out a man's silhouette.

As he lifted the handle, the back passenger side door opened with only a click, and David slid in as the man turned to look at him, surprise etched on his face. Before he even had the door closed behind him, David thrust his left hand forward and grabbed the man's upper arm from behind as he slammed the gearshift into Park. He shot his energy out, feeling for his captive's own life energy.

Sure enough, David felt the cold Cavern where the driver's soul should have been, along with the small ball of human life held captive there. Letting all the frustration of the day out, his own energy encircled the ball, and he pulled it with all his force.

The man shrieked in anger and pivoted. He reached out with his left arm, his hand just reaching David. Fingers encased his throat and clamped down. David tried to suck in a breath, but no air could bypass that vise around his windpipe. The edges of his mind went fuzzy. Time slowed.

David concentrated all his focus on ripping the stolen energy away. He felt the little ball dislodge, but not completely.

Panic met panic as the man tightened his grip further, his eyes wild. David's heart pounded double-time. His lungs screamed for oxygen. The pressure in his head threatened to overwhelm him; his vision wavered.

Don't let go. You can't let go.

He closed his eyes, and let the instinct of his energy take him. Bright colors swirled along the insides of his lids. He pulled again at the energy he could almost see. Pulled hard. If he could just get the soul out.

The colors dimmed, and he felt his hold slipping. He ignored everything, but his objective. One last surge — it was all he had.

The silk-covered arm beneath his hand shuddered. As the stolen energy finally broke free of the man's hold on it and tore into him, the sudden jolt almost threw David back against the seat.

The fingers around his throat loosened; he drew in a raging breath. His throat burned and he coughed, gagged. The double slam of getting his breath and the energy from the driver all but knocked David over. He couldn't let go of the man's arm if he wanted to. Every muscle in his body had locked.

The life force suffused him. His skin tingled and gooseflesh rose. He filled his tortured lungs with breath after breath, the adrenaline from almost suffocating adding to the high that washed over him. The arm beneath his fingers shrank. David opened his eyes.

A living skull looked back at him, its own eyes wide with the realization of its death. Its jaw moved but only a gritty whisper came from its dried out throat. The eyes dimmed, as the last of its energy coursed through David. The skull toppled from the neck, landing with a dusty thud on the floorboard at his feet.

David swayed, trying to gain control over the pulsating levels pouring through him. The outside world came into focus, and he realized the line ahead had begun to move.

He itched to get out and run the energy off, but instead, he pulled the skeleton into the back and then climbed over the console into the driver's seat. He shifted gears and eased the Caddy forward. Two cars waited in front of him.

He realized he'd arrived sadly underdressed. He put the car in Park again and stretched back, maneuvering the black silk dinner jacket off the remains behind him. He let the bones scuttle to the floorboard.

The line of cars moved forward again. One car left. When the Jaguar in front pulled away from the guard house and proceeded up the long drive, David drove slowly through the gate.

He stopped beside a man in black at the door of the tiny guard house who held a clipboard. A clear cord ran up the side of his neck to his ear. Close-cropped blond hair looked like thick peach fuzz on his head. He looked all of twenty five.

"Good evening, sir. May I have your invitation, please?"

Shit.

David reached into the jacket with his right hand, but found nothing in the pocket there. Trying to seem natural, he patted his right lapel and felt something smooth beneath the fabric. He slipped his left hand in and found a thin, heavy note card. He drew it out and glanced down to confirm it as an invitation.

The anxiety that gripped his heart eased as he read the words "Maze Gathering" in gothic script along the front. He handed it out to the guard.

"Thank you, sir. One moment please." He compared the invite to his list. "Thank you very much, Mr. Jerome." He handed the invitation back through the window. "Please enjoy your evening. There is parking at the top of the hill and to the right." The young man took two steps back and waved David through.

In his rear-view, he saw the metal gate rolling closed. He didn't like the trapped feeling that it gave him. But he'd made it in; he'd accomplished that much.

Now, to find Mecca.

Chapter Twenty-Three: Mecca

Mecca came to with a sneeze. She groaned. Something thudded inside her head and banged against her skull. She suspected it might be her brain. But she didn't rule out a sledgehammer.

The dirt floor pressed against her cheek. The smell of manure was strong down here. She pried one eye open. Several pairs of bare feet stood a yard away.

"She's awake."

"Leave her be."

The whispered voices tickled her mind and brought back memories of women in cages. And men.

"That's what she gets for being so stupid." A familiar man's voice.

"Shut up, Ray." *Alicia?* "She wouldn't be in here if you hadn't wanted her to steal the fucking keys."

"She's a big girl. She made her own decision."

"Asshole."

Mecca raised herself on unsteady arms. The pounding in her head didn't ease. She squinted against the glaring overhead light. Someone knelt beside her, put a hand on her back.

"Just sit up for now. You took a good bang to the head."

Mecca raised her gaze and recognized the pretty but filthy young woman who'd encouraged her to run. "Alicia."

"Yes. Slowly now." Alicia supported Mecca's back and arm as she eased herself into a sitting position.

"Thank you." The throbbing settled at the base of her head. Mecca reached back and winced. The light touch of her fingers across the knot there brought a flash across her vision. Memory of her battle with the gorilla returned to her. She groaned.

"They dumped you in here with us when you passed out. Said they needed to report to some woman."

Shit. "How long ago?"

"Only a few minutes. You haven't been out long."

Mecca struggled to her feet with Alicia's help. "We need to get out of here."

"She's a smart one," Ray said.

"Shut up," Alicia replied. She turned her attention back to Mecca. "Don't listen to him. He's a dick."

The room tilted and went out of focus. Mecca's knees gave out, but Alicia held her up. Mecca didn't know how, though, since the girl looked skeletal. She kept a very close check on her Gift. She could easily kill Alicia because of her own weakened state.

"Here." A dark-skinned woman with thick, black hair offered a small tin cup half full of water. A battered silver collar wrapped around her neck from just below her chin to where her neck met her shoulders. None of the woman's dark skin could be seen.

Mecca looked closely at Alicia. She wore one, as well. All the women had silver necks. In the other cage, light from the bare bulb above glinted off silver there too. How had she not noticed those earlier?

Mecca took a tentative sip of the water, expecting it to be foul. The cool, fresh liquid cascaded over her tongue, surprising her. She sipped a few more times before handing it back. "Thank you." The young woman retreated to a corner of the cage.

Refreshed more than she could have imagined, Mecca steadied herself and straightened up, taking most of her weight off of Alicia. The room righted itself and seemed to settle.

"They'll be coming for us soon." Alicia's breath tickled Mecca's ear. "I heard them talking about adding you to the maze. They had to tell the woman though. They don't seem very smart, the guards. They said something about seven men and seven women. You would make eight. They weren't sure whether to put you in or not."

Seven men and seven women? What the hell did that mean?

"It'll be bad, if they have eight." The voice came from a very young girl, not more than fourteen, Mecca guessed. She squatted in the far corner, swaying forward and back. With short, mousy, brown hair and crooked glasses, she looked like the class nerd. "He requires seven lads and seven maidens."

"Who?" Mecca asked.

"The Minotaur."

Mecca looked at Alicia, who lifted her shoulders in a shrug. Mecca felt the gazes of the other women in the cage.

"Ever since she heard about the maze," Alicia said, "Tina has been obsessed with the notion of us being fed to a Minotaur. She says that the legend was that every year seven men and women were sacrificed. I don't know. Is it coincidence that they're so focused on there being seven? But a Minotaur? I mean, come on." Alicia smiled, but no certainty touched her eyes.

"I don't think it's a Minotaur," Mecca said. She released her hold on Alicia and stood on her own. Each passing moment brought more strength back, though she gave up on any relief from the hammering in her head. She looked across the small group of faces, all different, but all harboring the same emotions: fear and also hope.

She stepped away from the group, keeping a hand on Alicia's arm, drawing her along. Mecca leaned in, ignoring the stale tang of sweat and body odor coming from the other woman's skin.

"You're not going to want to believe it, but if we're going to make it through this, you need to know."

Alicia watched her with calm patience. Mecca supposed that she'd learned that from being here, caged.

"It's not a Minotaur, but they obviously are playing with that idea. They're—well, they call themselves Visci, but they seem an awful lot like vampires to me."

Mecca waited for a reaction, but Alicia's expression didn't change. After a moment, the blonde said, "I know. I saw them kill a girl after I first arrived. No fangs, but they suck the blood, all the same."

"If you know, why do you let Tina believe it's a Minotaur? Why haven't you told the others?"

"Does it really matter whether it's a Minotaur or a vampire? Do we stand a chance either way?" The resignation came across clearly in her tone. Alicia knew she was going to die today.

"Are you giving up?" Mecca lowered her voice, reigning in her frustration. "You really want to die in filth and stink?" She touched the edge of Alicia's torn sleeve.

"I don't want to die at all. Do you have any idea how strong they are?" Alicia's eyes flashed. "What the hell am I supposed to do against that?"

Glad to hear emotion filtering into Alicia's voice, Mecca continued. "We can fight them. If we all stay together, we can take them down individually. Or maybe even two at a time if the men will join with us. I'm hoping the maze will put the Visci at a disadvantage too."

Alicia looked at the gaggle of women and then beyond, to the cage holding the men. Her brow creased in thought, and she frowned before turning back to Mecca. "Do you really think we can get away?"

"I can't say for sure. But we don't have to go easily. We don't have to hand ourselves over to them."

She leaned closer. "I also have a weapon. I can hurt them. If we get everyone on board and stay together—"

A clattering outside the barn doors caught everyone's attention. A moment later, one of the massive wood doors swung open and three men stepped into the light. Alicia stiffened at Mecca's side.

"Okay, all of you," said the tallest one — the gorilla, who had the square face, stubble-covered chin and the scar from his left eye, across his nose, to his right cheek. "Everybody out."

Whispers scuttled through the air among the captives. Murmured questions of freedom. Sniffling prayers to whoever might be listening.

"Everybody can get out," the man said, the nasty grin on his lips made uglier by his scar. "But there are rules."

Herded down a narrow path formed by portable fencing, toward the entrance of the maze, Mecca walked with the huddled group of filthy men and women. The air smelled fresh compared to the staleness of the barn, and she took a long, deep breath. Alicia's arm looped through hers, and they stayed hooked together like two links in a chain.

Scar, as Mecca had taken to thinking of the gorilla, spoke to them as if they were children.

"Once you go into the maze," he said, "you're gonna want to be the first one out the other side. Because the first one out gets to go on home. And I know you all wanna go on home." The malicious twinkle in his eye made Mecca wonder whether going home would really be an option for any of them.

"What about the rest?" Ray asked. Mecca had learned from Alicia that he'd been a captive almost as long as she had.

That ugly smile crossed Scar's lips again, and Mecca shuddered.

"That's not something you really want to know," Scar said. Whispers rippled through group of captives.

Behind her, Mecca heard Tina's voice. "The Minotaur."

Mecca turned and looked at the girl, who hugged herself with rail-thin arms. "There's no Minotaur, Tina. But you stay with us when we get inside, okay?"

Tina nodded, silent.

Off to the side, a whooshing sound caught all their attention. One of the guards held a large, industrial hose; water gushed from the nozzle.

"Okay," Scar said over the noise of the water. "Get going!"

With his signal, the water-bearer turned the hose on them, sending up screeches and surprised yelps. Mecca reached for Tina, pulling the smaller girl between her and Alicia.

They rushed along as the group surged forward, toward the maze, everyone soaked to the skin within moments. The dirt-packed ground quickly became a muddy pit. People slid as they ran, grabbing each other for purchase, only to drag others down as they fell into the sludge.

A long wooden pole came out of nowhere and cracked one of the fallen men across the back. He yelped and scrabbled to his feet.

"Go on!" The veins in Scar's face bulged as he yelled at them. "Run!" He swung the pole back again — it was a rake, Mecca saw. Another icy blast from the hose made her turn away amid the scream and yells of the others. She dragged Tina along, hoping Alicia hadn't fallen.

Once inside the maze, they could go right or left to escape the hits and Mecca dashed to the right. The guest house would be on this side. More of the captives scrambled into the relative safety of the hedge, away from the relentless spray.

Alicia made it in the midst of a small group of women. She came to where Tina and Mecca stood near the corner. Mud covered everyone, at least to the knees, much higher for some. Those who had fallen looked like swamp creatures. The only sounds for a minute were harsh breathing and the chatter of teeth.

Metal lamps, like tiki-lights, stuck out of the ground at each turn of the hedge, dropping soft light onto the grass. They gathered together once they got around the first corner and out of sight of their captors. The soft music Mecca had heard when she'd first approached floated in on a small breeze, faint and muted.

If they just followed the right-hand wall, Mecca decided, they would eventually find the side exit that she'd passed on her way in. It had been lightly guarded. Mecca thought they could easily overtake the one man and then she could lead everyone out to the fire road.

Ray, the older man from the cage, shouldered his way through the group almost at a jog. "I'm getting the hell out of here!" He knocked into Tina as he came by. She landed on her backside. As she went down, the crunch of her teeth made Mecca's jaw ache in sympathy.

Alicia helped Tina up as four men followed Ray and then two women behind them. Mecca looked around the corner in the direction they went into the maze, but they'd all disappeared from sight. She turned back to those remaining, now two men, both young and slight, Alicia, Tina, the dark skinned woman who'd shared water with her in the cage and two other women.

"When I came in, I saw an entrance to the maze on the side. There was only one guard but he does have a gun. If we can get out of here, I can get us to the road." Mecca kept her voice low, not sure what lurked beyond the leafy walls that surrounded them.

She hoped they would all make it out alive, but she had no intention of holding her breath. Tina tugged at her hand. The girl looked up at her, grey eyes haunted. Mecca leaned and strained to hear Tina's voice.

"We'll stay with you, because you make eight." She peered back toward where they'd been herded into the maze. Light from the tiki torch glinted off her silver collar. "But we should go. He'll be coming soon."

The Minotaur.

Mecca had an idea of what they'd be facing, and it wasn't a Minotaur, but she wondered if Alicia had been right. Did it matter whether Tina believed it to be the Greek mythical creature or the mythical horror monster? Mecca looked at the women and men surrounding her. They all watched her with anticipation and hope, tinged with the raw look of fear behind it.

Mecca wasn't sure she was ready to be a savior.

The light music in the background turned to carnival music, louder and brash. Sinister. Whoops and cheers came from the front of the maze. Mecca felt those around her shift uneasily, like antelope surrounded by lions. She didn't blame them. Whatever was going to happen had just started.

After a minute, the music changed back to the softer, electronic sounds from earlier and the cheering quieted.

"Listen," Mecca began. "If we stay along the right wall, we will eventually hit the side exit. We may run into some dead ends first, but sooner or later, the exit will turn up. Is everyone okay with that?"

Many heads bobbed and a thin hand lifted to get her attention. The young man looked as dirty and underfed as the rest of the captives, but a dark intensity shone from his deep blue eyes.

"What happens if we run into the Minotaur?"

Mecca squeezed Tina's hand before she answered. "There isn't a Minotaur. But I think what we're going to find is much more dangerous. And there's probably going to be more than one." Mecca nodded at his heavy, silver collar. "I don't know why they protected your necks, but I don't think it's for anything good. We're going to be fighting vampires." For all practical purposes, this was true.

The ragamuffin men and women exchanged glances and Mecca felt the tide of emotion shift from fear to disbelief. Modern world sensibilities replaced captivity's mental anguish. Murmurs filtered through their small group.

"You're kidding, right?" the young man asked. "Vampires?"

"I'm not kidding," Mecca said.

"Why are vampires less believable than a Minotaur?" Alicia's voice silenced the whispers. "We need to move. We need to get out. And we need to stick together if we're going to do that. We can argue over monsters later." She pushed forward, bringing Tina as well as Mecca along with her.

They walked along in silence, standing two or three deep, a quiet group of shadows in the dim light of the corner torches. The sharp scent of green touched Mecca's nose. The hedge didn't seem to being moving with the season, like the trees of the woods. She reached for a leaf, rubbed her fingers on the waxy surface. Evergreen.

They came to a corner and stopped. A ripple of whispers slid through the group. Mecca and Alicia exchanged glances. Mecca released Tina's hand and said, "Stay here. I'm going to look."

Her heartbeat thrummed in her ears as she crept forward. She decided then and there that she hated hedge mazes. She crouched low and then peered around the leaves. Breath caught in her throat.

She hadn't expected to see anything, but on the other side of the long, horizontal pathway stood a young man, his neck free of any collar, silver or otherwise. Short and stocky, with broad shoulders and close-cropped, black hair, he looked like any college football player. The way he cocked his head made her think of a dog.

Mecca pulled back with very slow movements. When she looked to the group, she laid a single finger over her lips and made brief eye contact with each person. Wide eyes and nods met her gaze.

She wiped her sweaty palms on her thighs. They wouldn't be able to turn this corner and get around to the next one if he didn't move. She peeked around the hedge again. He paced a ten foot line with slow steps, almost like a guard. Like a toll.

Warm fingers touched her arm, and she jumped. Alicia patted her forearm and gave her a smile and then looked around the side of the hedge. Mecca felt the young woman's body stiffen. When Alicia had seen enough, she leaned in so her lips almost brushed Mecca's ear. The pungent smell of unwashed skin touched her nose. Alicia's voice came to her in a low hum.

"You're not wearing a collar. You look like one of them." They locked gazes for a long moment until Mecca understood what Alicia meant. When Mecca nodded, Alicia stepped back with the others.

Alicia had a very good head on her shoulders. Even if it meant Mecca was screwed.

With bravado she hardly felt, Mecca straightened her back, lifted her chin and strode around the corner.

"What the hell?" he said. He narrowed his eyes at her. "How'd you get this far back so fast?"

"I'm just that good."

His voice reminded her of wool, scratchy against her skin. "Bullshit."

She gave him a flirty grin. "Emilia put me in the side entrance. She likes me."

He took a moment to consider this as his gaze slid up and down her body. Just the look in his eye made Mecca feel slimy.

"Yeah?" he said. "Where's your bag?" He patted a brown burlap hump on his hip: an oversized fanny pack, adhering to him like a tumor.

What the hell was that for?

"Damn! This is my first time. Was I supposed to bring that in? It's so ugly."

Laughter grumbled from his throat. "Not planning on winning then, hm?"

"I guess not. Unless you want to lend me yours." She sidled toward him and melded her lips into a seductive smile — at least she hoped it looked seductive.

Distrust fogged his eyes, but he grinned. "What's in it for me?"

"What do you want?" Another step closer.

"Hmm. Such an interesting question. I could ask for a lot of things."

"Yes, you could."

He watched her with an appraising look in his eye. "I hate to leave a damsel in distress." The condescension dripped from his words. "How about when I win, I give you my pouch, and you can have whatever might be left in the maze?"

"That's very kind of you." She wanted to punch him. "What do you need to win?"

"Four players. Well, five counting you. Four hearts should be enough to win." He smiled, showing teeth so white they almost glowed in the shadowed maze.

"And you'd give me the pouch after you're done? You'd do that?" She'd gotten within a few steps of him. He didn't move away.

"Sure I would." The gleam in his eye told her he'd prefer to do other things instead.

"Well, I don't know." She slowed her speech down, laying on the sultry tone. "I guess that probably breaks the rules. Do you think we can get away with it? Teaming up like that?"

"Can't know till we try, yeah?" His lips curled up in a feral grin. "You in?"

Mecca paused, made like she was thinking it over. "I guess it's the only way to get a prize. Okay, deal. Shake on it." She offered her hand, wrist limp.

His skin was like cool leather against hers. She didn't hesitate. Her energy shot into him, searching for the Cavern, trying to find that little spark of life that didn't belong to him.

He felt it. Felt her.

He tilted his head, something like a dog does when spoken to, and then he yanked his hand away. Mecca's heart rattled her ribcage as her energy came home, thrown back by the break in contact. She'd thought she could hold onto him. Thought she could weaken him enough to be stronger, to bring him down.

He looked like an animal; as if he wanted to rip into her, tear her throat out. "What the fuck did you do?"

"Nothing," she said, innocence in her voice. "I shook."

"No, you didn't." He looked her up and down, but entirely differently than before. He pointed a long finger at her. "You look like a half-breed to me. Maybe *you* should be wearing a collar."

Mecca shook her head and took a step back. Maybe she could lure him into coming closer, if she played like she was afraid. It wasn't much of an act. Terror iced her veins. For each step she took away from him, he moved forward.

Thorny branches poked her back and thighs. Nowhere else to go.

One corner of his mouth lifted, though she couldn't call it a smile.

A high-pitched shriek tore across from the other side of the maze, chilling the air. She'd never heard a scream so filled with terror. It stopped abruptly, and the maze fell to silence. Mecca's gut wrenched, but her attacker only broadened his non-smile.

"You'll scream like that too, little lady."

Condescending bastard. Now he was just pissing her off.

A white blur flashed across her vision, and pain exploded in her jaw. The coppery taste of blood flooded her mouth. She reeled back into the hedge. Branches stabbed against her, and some part of her brain registered the sound of fabric ripping before she bounced forward and tumbled to the grassy ground.

He pounced on her, tossing her on her back. Her head hit the ground hard, squarely on the knot from her run in with the stable wall. Bright lights flashed across her vision. Sharp pain bounced around inside her skull to join the dull ache already there. She couldn't even get her limbs to move. The man straddled her waist and pinned her arms at her sides beneath his knees.

He leered down at her as Mecca finally pushed the dazed feeling away and gathered herself enough to struggle. He wore scratchy wool slacks — *who wears wool in Georgia, like ever?* — so her bare arms were no help to her, restrained underneath. When she bucked beneath his weight, he grinned.

"I'm sort of glad you don't have a collar. It'll make this a lot easier." He leaned over as he spoke, and the warm, spoiled scent of bad breath washed over her. It struck her funny that something so frightening would have regular, garden variety halitosis.

Her laugh sounded like a bark.

He frowned and then snorted before leaning down. His lips brushed the side of her neck gently, like a lock of lover's hair. His tongue, wet and warm, snaked along her skin. Then she felt a single pinprick.

Mecca turned her head to face him and then jerked forward, taking a trick from the Scar's playbook. Her forehead crashed into his temple, and stars brightened her vision again. He swayed for a moment and satisfaction coursed through her.

Swift movement near the hedge caught her eye. Silent, the rag-tag group of captives moved as one, rushing from their safe spot around the corner. They slammed into the man on top of her as one entity, bowling him over onto the ground earning them a surprised yelp.

Mecca watched, stunned, as they held him down; seven scrawny, filthy humans pinning a struggling Visci.

"Hurry!" Alicia called to her in a fervent whisper. She strained against his thrashing left leg. "You said you needed to touch him. We can't hold him for long."

Mecca, her head throbbing all over, pulled herself onto her hands and knees and crawled to where he lay prone, still fighting. He snarled and redoubled his efforts, but he had half a dozen people almost lying on him. Even super-strength wouldn't help him against those odds.

Gnashing his teeth, he leaned up and tried to bite Tina, who had his left arm pinned with the help of two others. She jumped back with a cry and landed on her tailbone. Girl kept falling on her ass.

Mecca dragged herself up and swung a leg over, straddling him the same way he'd sat on top of her. She ripped open his button down shirt. He had a broad chest, covered with a light carpet of black, curly hair. She laid both hands on the cool skin of his chest, the wiry hair tickling her palms. When she looked into his eyes, the animal hatred she read there came through her like a knife. But it didn't matter. She mirrored it back as she sent herself into him.

She sought the Cavern, slid into that big, hollow place and searched for the little ball of human energy she knew she would find somewhere. Closing her eyes made the search easier. She concentrated while he tried to wrench away from the dozen hands holding him down. Behind his growling, she heard the wondering murmurs of the other captives.

All the thoughts and sounds fell back when she spotted the golden ball of energy in a nook of the Visci's Cavern. Its edges shone a bright green. Mecca had never known whether the different colors meant anything. She saw and also *felt* the stolen humanity there, as if it wanted to reach out and embrace her. Silver tendrils bound it to the Cavern wall. That this stolen energy kept this monster alive made her ill.

Her own energy, a golden brilliance edged in deep blue, encompassed the little piece of life, and she gently tugged at it. Her taking of the energy could be more controlled this time, since she wasn't fighting for her life.

It must not have been a part of him for very long, or maybe he was young, because the energy ball came away from him easily. Mecca wrapped her own energy, her own life around it and drew it away.

She looked at him again and judging from the widening of his eyes, Mecca figured he felt her taking his life. She didn't try to do it fast; she didn't try to make it painless. He wouldn't have given her that consideration when he had her on her back.

The farther away from the Cavern she took the stolen energy, the more wild-eyed he became. His thrashing intensified, but his strength was waning; Mecca didn't feel like she was riding a mechanical bull any longer.

He let out a yell, but he slammed a hand over his mouth.

Silence settled, only interrupted by the gentle, filtered music coming from the front of the maze. She never broke eye contact with him. He'd already shrunken in the few minutes since she'd straddled him. His body felt like an old man's beneath her.

She watched him closely as the energy ball broke free. It came away from him the way a flower pops from its stalk.

The life force rushed into her, but not the slamming crash of Hayden in the parking lot. This time it washed over her like a wave on the beach, overpowering, but not violent. It filled her and pushed back the thumping pain in her head until it was only a nagging tickle. Surprised, but grateful, she sighed her relief.

A last look of fear swept over him before he began to fade. His movement stopped and finally, his eyes, sightless, stared past her. Then he began to really shrink, cave in on himself. The dry smell of dust hit Mecca full in the face.

She finally stood, her feet still on either side of his emaciated hips. She looked around her. Ashen faces stared back, some with terror etched on their features, others with confusion and a few, like Alicia, with awe.

Mecca felt like a zoo exhibit. No one spoke. No one smiled. They only stared.

She moved to one side of the corpse and then knelt down and unfastened the hip pack from around his waist. At least it would help her in faking out any others they might run into.

She glanced back at the group again. They hadn't changed position at all. She just had to get them out of the maze and tell them how to get to the road. She could handle being a circus freak until then.

"Come on," she said. "Let's go."

Chapter Twenty-Four: Claude

Edward Bingham leaned forward, his voice lowered, spittle flecking his lips. "I think it was those damned purists." He shifted his weight from his club foot. Edward's enormous head sat on top of a thick neck, and oversized, milky eyes made him look as if he couldn't blink. His grey hair, thinned and stringy, hung like threadbare theatre curtains. "They killed Hayden."

Emilia's brow crinkled. "Who would that be, Edward?"

Claude listened to the exchange between Emilia and Hayden Bingham's father. He had hoped to glean more about Emilia's plan before the obligatory hostess duties overtook her. Mecca's presence still sang in his blood; she lingered nearby.

Now, however, he knew with Edward's terse accusation, any information would no longer be forthcoming. Emilia would be too preoccupied with the current situation.

"I don't know, right offhand," Edward said. "I mean to say, I don't have any *names*, as it were." He pushed glasses with thin metal frames up the bridge of his nose.

Claude thought the glasses were an affectation. He didn't think Edward could see properly with or without them.

"But the war has come to Atlanta. That much is obvious."

Emilia raised her slender hand. A diamond-studded tennis bracelet slid down her forearm. "You shouldn't jump to that conclusion. Are you even sure he's been killed? Hayden always had a way of disappearing."

"Of course I am! Do you think I didn't feel it? He died in horrible agony." Edward's plump face contorted, the corners of his lips turning downward. He blinked several times, very quickly, thin membranes of eyelid barely covering his huge eyeballs. "And confusion."

"Oh dear," Emilia said. "I hadn't heard anything about it. Of course, Hayden rarely checked with me."

"Yes, well, it wasn't for lack of trying on my part, I'll have you know."

"I have no doubt of that, Edward. After the Gathering, I will put a call in to—"

For half a second, the room brightened. Claude's senses overloaded. Edward Bingham's yellow linen suit made him into a lemon; the silver of Emilia's sequined halter called down the starlight. The scent of pine choked him. Then things settled back to normal. Claude hoped his surprise at the change didn't register on his face.

Emilia's pause lasted less than half of a second. Claude may even have missed it if he hadn't felt the same sudden, intense rush.

"—my contact at the police department and let you know what I hear. In the meantime," she continued, "please don't rush to conclusions. Hayden was not without enemies, as you well know, both human and Visci."

"I know it must have been the purists." Edward bristled, straightening his back. "Hayden may have had enemies, but none that would kill him. I'm sure of that. No, it had to be one of them."

Emilia exchanged a glance with Claude, her lips pursed into a tight, pale line. He knew she wouldn't tell Edward about Mecca. She would let Edward's accusation of Hayden as a casualty of war go on. If the rumor escalated though, it really *would* bring the war to Atlanta.

"We can't let them overrun the city, Emilia," Edward said, leaning in. He clearly had no idea that Claude was a "purist." Perhaps his sense of smell was as bad as his sight.

"No one's going to overrun the city." She laid a hand on his forearm. Her skin looked dark against the pale yellow suit jacket. "After the Gathering, I'll find out what happened to Hayden. You have my word."

Edward took her measure. "All right. But mark me: this won't end well."

"Let me look into it."

Edward nodded, a tight, brusque movement and then turned away. He left them with brisk steps, the limp from his club foot pronounced without his cane. He lurched with each step.

When Edward moved out of earshot, even for their advanced hearing, Emilia turned to Claude.

"Mecca's here. She's in the maze."

The surge of energy he'd felt had told him the same thing about Mecca's location, but he fixed a look of surprise on his face. It wasn't entirely false. He had no idea how she had gotten into the maze.

Now he wished he'd taken part.

"How could she have gotten into the maze?"

"Just before the Game began, I received a report from the guards that they caught a young woman snooping around. They put her in with the offerings."

The stupid sheep! He felt his advantage floating away.

"You'll kill them for that, I hope." He scanned the crowd, searching for Salas. "And so they released her with the others. She is being hunted."

"Yes, yes, and yes," Emilia said, almond eyes intense. Her voice lowered even further. "I believe she's killed one of the players."

That explained the surge in Claude's senses. His link with her, through his blood, caused him to feel a fraction of what she felt when she drained the energy from someone. It was quite intoxicating. He wondered how strong Emilia's surge had been. Was her tie to Mecca as full as his?

"I'm going in to find her," Emilia continued. "I can't have one of them killing her, and I certainly can't have her killing all of them."

"Edward might find out that it wasn't a purist who killed his son, after all."

Emilia watched him closely for a moment. What was she thinking? Finally, she nodded. "Yes. But that's a problem in itself. I don't want him thinking it was a purist either. I don't need additional unrest in my city."

"I understand. I'll post extra guards on the maze exits and instruct them not to shoot escapees. I'm assuming you don't want her killed."

"No extra guards," she said. "I don't want people alerted. Everything needs to seem as normal."

"As you wish. Though when they see you going into the Maze, they'll know things are not as normal."

"I don't intend them to see me. I'll go around to one of the side entrances. Have Salas find Will and tell him." She left his side without waiting for his agreement.

Through the French doors, he spotted Salas, speaking to a young woman he'd never seen. When the manservant saw Claude approach, he wisely separated from her, redirecting his attention to his master. He stepped out onto the patio to join Claude.

"What's happened?" Salas asked. "You look as if you've seen someone burned at the stake."

"Mecca's in the Game. She's killed someone." He looked around Salas to study the Maze.

"Are you sure she's not in the house somewhere?"

"No. I don't think she would kill for killing's sake. In the Maze, she would be doing it to keep herself alive." The more he considered it, the more he thought Emilia was right. "She has to be in the Maze. And she's killed someone in there. In all the history of Maze Gatherings, no offering has ever killed a player." Claude rubbed his palm over his face. "Things have just gotten much more complicated."

"What will you have me to do?"

"We have to find her before Emilia does. She's gone into the Maze herself."

Salas raised both eyebrows. It was the extent to which he ever showed surprise.

"Yes. I suspect she's going to try to talk to Mecca, maybe subdue her. I don't know. But we need to get to Mecca first. I think she will respond to me."

"Well, if she really is in the Maze," Salas said, "this is going to go badly. Everyone will know."

"Yes. Especially if she's killing players. And I'm sure Emilia is thinking the same thing." He shook his head. "I should have participated this year."

"You couldn't have known."

"No. But it would make this much easier." Going into the hedge would be dangerous for Salas, being human, with or without a collar. "If I go into the Maze on the east side, it might be possible to find her without drawing attention from the party or Emilia. If that's the side Emilia's chosen to enter, I'll have to convince her I'm there to help her."

"If you run into any of the players, they will recognize you."

"I'll have to take that chance, I think."

Salas looked toward the house. "Oh no."

Claude followed his gaze. Through the glass of the French doors, he looked at every face inside the room before he realized what Salas had seen. Standing near the wall, a man with graying hair and broad shoulders wore a mis-tailored suit coat over a long white tunic, brown drawstring pants and gym shoes. The man's eyes seemed familiar. When it came to him, Claude sucked in a breath.

David Trenow had not been on the guest list.

Chapter Twenty-Five: Mecca

Alicia walked close to Mecca. The rest of the group, including Tina, lagged eight or so steps behind. The young girl had fallen even farther back, toward the tail of the bunch.

"They'll come around," Alicia said.

"It doesn't matter. My only concern is getting all of you out of here alive. I don't care whether they like me or not." Mecca continued to brush her hand along the leaves that made up the hedge wall to their right. Even when it curved around into a dead end, she knew if she just kept touching it, stayed with the wall, she'd have to find the side exit. That was the trick of these things.

"You freaked them out, is all."

Mecca couldn't tell who Alicia was trying to convince. She looked at the young woman sidelong. "Really, Alicia. I don't care. If they want to stay separate, that's fine. As long as they don't get too far behind."

"When we find the way out, how long will it take for us to get to the road, do you think?"

"About half an hour, depending on how fast you go. It's not difficult to find, but you do have to be careful." Mecca couldn't decide whether a large group along the fire road would be a help or a detriment.

"Especially now. They may have people patrolling the woods. You'll need to stay together, in a group."

"Wait a minute. You're coming with us, right?"

"No."

She put her hand on Mecca's arm. "What? Why not?"

"I have something to deal with here, at the house."

"Mecca, I don't think that's a good idea. You should come."

"I can't. I've run once already. Running won't help me."

They had to be close. It felt like hours since they'd entered the maze. Mecca's shoes squished as she walked, and her clothes were still soaked, making the cool night air even colder. Sara's jeans hung like a weighted curtain from her hips, heavy and cold.

If they got out of here alive, she wouldn't be surprised if they all came down with pneumonia. That would be irony.

Mecca had lost all track of direction and distance as they twisted through the Maze, hitting dead ends and doubling back. They always kept a hand on the right wall, so she knew they'd have to find that side entrance by the woods. It was taking forever though. And with the group of stragglers now afraid to get close to her, Mecca thought they might not make it. She picked up the pace.

The Maze took a sharp turn to the left and as she peeked around the corner, she was glad of the distance between her and the others. Ray's corpse lay on the ground, spread eagle. His eyes stared at the night sky, wide open, his lips curled back from his parted teeth.

She heard the soft whispers of the group as they all came to a stop, waiting for her to lead them onward. Ray's chest, covered in red blood and gristle, lay open to the night air, a yawning hole where his heart had been.

How could she parade them past this?

"What is it?" Alicia whispered near her ear.

A squeal from behind startled them both. Mecca jerked around just in time to see a thin arm and leg disappear around a dark green, leafy corner they'd already passed. She felt sick to her stomach as she rushed back, past the single file group of refugees staring wide-eyed. They'd started crowding forward, scuttling away from that corner. She scanned the faces as she ran. Who was missing?

A faint mewling sound came across the still night air and Mecca stopped short of the corner. The mewling stopped with a high-pitched squeak and a sickening squelching sound. *Oh God.*

The image of Ray's corpse burned her mind. Alicia, who'd been following just after, jostled into her. Mecca's shoulder raked the corner of the hedge as she stumbled forward. She tried to catch herself and keep from landing on the ground. Pointed little branches scraped her palms. She recovered just as she came around the corner.

Tina lay on the ground. Hovering over her, a young woman knelt with her hand embedded in Tina's chest, just below the ribcage. The woman's brown hair formed a veil around her face and Mecca couldn't make out her features. It didn't matter. She couldn't keep from looking at the glistening, wet, red ring encircling woman's wrist.

The racket Mecca made coming around the corner of the hedge got the woman's attention. She met Mecca's gaze with bright dusky blue eyes. They looked hungry.

Chapter Twenty-Six: Victoria

Victoria couldn't believe her luck. First this child, who'd been easy to overcome with a simple snap of her neck, and now another comes barreling around the corner. That would bring her total to six. If she wasn't in the lead, she had to be close.

She'd already gotten her fingers around the heart, but the heart would keep. Victoria couldn't have this new one running away. The cavity she'd made in the child gave a wet slurp as she pulled her hand out, empty except for a thick coating of blood. The rich smell of lifeblood, the blood of the heart, infused her mind as she got to her feet.

Can't let this one get away.

The girl, dark skinned with hair in a ponytail, watched Victoria, wide-eyed, one hand against the dark green leafy wall. Little red blooms of blood spotted the right shoulder of her white t-shirt. She looked as soaking wet as all the others, her jeans very dark, hanging low around her hips. But she didn't wear a collar.

What did that mean? Victoria didn't remember seeing this one when the Games began, so she couldn't be one of the players. She *had* to be an offering. She must have somehow escaped the band of metal around her neck.

Victoria thought the collar was more symbolic anyway. They were no more difficult to kill for not being able to feed from their necks.

Too much thinking. Time was running short.

Victoria lunged, covering the three yards between them before her prey had a chance to run. The look of surprise on the girl's face before they hit the ground was priceless, and Victoria laughed. It came out maniacal, but she chalked that up to the adrenaline. She ended up on top of the girl, lying full against her.

As Victoria scrambled into a straddling position, the girl thrashed, now fighting for her life.

A thrill coursed through her veins. It always surprised Victoria how much she enjoyed it when they struggled. She wouldn't be able to just snap this one's neck though. Not with all the flailing. She wouldn't be able to get a good enough hold. She'd just have to do it the messy way.

"Get off me!" The young woman beneath her bucked her hips up, and Victoria tilted, off balance. Maybe she had underestimated this one.

Her prey bucked again, but this time, Victoria leaned forward and rose up on her knees. She pinned the woman's wrists to the ground. Someone flashed past her, toward the body she'd left on the ground. She didn't have time to see if it was another player, but if anyone stole her heart, they'd have to answer.

Something invaded her. It was like a worm had gotten into her head and was squirming around, looking for something.

She jerked backward and released the girl's wrists. But those hands sought Victoria, and when her fingers wrapped around Victoria's forearm, that same wriggling feeling came again, but stronger and harder. Insistent. It made her think of a giant, wet slug.

Victoria tried to pull away, but the girl kept her hold, sitting up when Victoria tried to stand. The worm in her head split off into different directions, reaching into her chest and her belly. It curled around her insides, alien. The metallic scent of ozone filled her nose.

The girl stared at her — no, through her. *Into her.* Her deep brown eyes, open wide, focused on something just past Victoria. Or rather, something at the back of Victoria's own eyes. It made the girl look crazed.

Victoria jerked her arms, and they tore from the girl's grasp. She got to her feet, and the girl followed, reaching out again, not afraid. When she pushed the girl's shoulders — Victoria couldn't very well call her the prey anymore; those roles seemed to have changed — small, dark hands grabbed at her again, even as the girl propelled backward. She caught hold of Victoria's right hand, and her momentum pulled Victoria forward.

What had been a worm, now became a colossal boa constrictor. It coiled around her insides and heaved backward. Her gut was being wrenched out.

Panic blinded her in a way it had never done in her life. The girl had gone to her knees, but her hold on Victoria's arm had gotten stronger somehow.

Victoria kicked at her. The angle was bad, and what should have been a solid kick glanced off the girl's shoulder instead. She felt drained, like she had the night she'd fed off a dying heroin addict. It had put her stomach in knots, and she'd felt half-dead herself for two days.

But this was worse. So much worse. Whatever the worm pulled on was close to breaking free. She could feel it stretching away from her. The strength she lost had gone to the worm, and it had redoubled its labors. And she was losing her remaining strength too quickly.

The girl still looked beyond Victoria, her forehead wrinkled, her jaw clenched tight.

And then the thing inside her broke free.

Chapter Twenty-Seven: The Maze

Mecca lay on the ground, staring up at the sky spotted with silver stars. She could see thousands. The energy from the Visci woman pulsed inside her, throbbing against her skin, her bones, her organs. She knew she had to get up, to get everyone moving again, but she needed just this minute or two.

She had to get control of this raging energy. She'd never taken in so much in such a short period. She felt like a live wire.

The night breeze caressed her skin as if the air itself were alive. A low keening came from somewhere behind her. Shuffling feet off to her left. And a strangely rotten smell of apples in the air.

Mecca wanted more time to lie, but she rolled onto her belly and pushed herself up and onto her knees. They had to get moving.

The keening came from Alicia, who rocked over Tina's body, her arms wrapped around herself. She stared at Tina's chest, gaze glued to the glistening red hole. Light from a torch in the corner shimmered off a tear. Mecca closed her eyes and willed herself not to gag at the raw meat the Visci woman had left behind. Like a fist, her belly clenched and unclenched.

She leaned over, putting her head on the cool ground and drew a deep breath, the clean smell of the grass beneath her incompatible with Tina's grisly remains.

Mecca raised up and crawled over. Alicia didn't notice her approach, or didn't acknowledge it. Her stringy, dirty blonde hair swayed as she rocked. Mecca heard the cushioned footfalls of others approaching them.

"Alicia," Mecca said, her voice low. It took effort to speak quietly. The energy made her actions hard to control. She knelt up. "We have to go."

"Can't leave her." Alicia's voice couldn't be called a whisper. It was barely a breath.

"You can't do anything else for her. But the others need you. We have to get them out of here."

"No."

Mecca laid her hand on Alicia's forearm. Energy jumped through the connection, leaving Mecca less... full. She jerked back. Alicia's rocking stopped, and she stared at Mecca with glittering eyes.

"What did you do?"

Mecca looked at her hand. "I—I don't know." She hadn't drawn energy. The energy had left her and gone to Alicia. "That's never happened before."

"I feel different," Alicia said. "Stronger, maybe." She put a thin, almost frail hand on Tina's shoulder. "If you could do that for me, can you help her?"

"I don't think so," she said. She was being honest. The glazed eyes, the hole in Tina's chest, these things told Mecca that the girl was well beyond anyone's help. "Alicia, we have to leave her. She wouldn't want you and the others to get caught too. She would want us to go."

Alicia stared down at Tina's face and wiped a tear from her cheek, leaving a clean spot, pale beside the filth on the rest of her face. She leaned forward and kissed Tina's smooth forehead, then whispered in her ear. Mecca thought it was an apology.

She helped Alicia to her feet, careful to keep the energy in check. Until she understood what she'd done, she didn't want it to happen again.

They'd lost two of the women. When the Visci grabbed Tina, they'd run into the maze together. That left them a group of seven, counting Mecca herself.

Anxious energy crowded the air among the refugees. They no longer hung back, but crowded forward, as if trying to stay in as tight a knot as possible. No one wanted to be the last in line.

When they finally reached where they'd been when Tina disappeared, Mecca stopped. "I don't know how to keep from going through here."

"What is it?" Alicia asked.

"Ray."

"He's dead." Alicia's voice had a resigned tone.

Mecca only nodded.

Emilia had tried to portray herself and her kind as people with their own agendas and strange needs, but just trying to get along. No danger to humans. Controlled.

But this sort of sport—this sort of *game*—they played with humans as prey. Prey. Worse than a horror movie: there was no guarantee anyone would survive in the end.

Blood rushed to her face. She curled her hands into tight fists. Even if she had been considering Emilia's offer before, this experience showed Mecca the true nature of the Visci and of the beautiful but deadly woman.

"I can't look at him."

When Mecca turned around, she found Alicia had shifted and now faced the rest of the group. Ghostly faces looked at her, pale and washed out. The entire group fidgeted, some shifting from foot to foot, as if ready to run, others wringing their hand. One woman had all the fingertips of her right hand in her mouth, gnawing on the nails.

"I don't want to see him," Alicia repeated. "I can't."

"There's no other way to go." Mecca's heart dropped into her belly. They were never going to make it out of here alive. "We're close. We're almost there. We have to keep moving."

Alicia's shoulders and chest rose as she took a hitching breath. When she turned back to Mecca, her eyes red-rimmed and swollen. And then Mecca realized. It wasn't Ray — it was Tina. Ray would just make her see her friend in her mind all over again.

"I can't look at him. If I have to go by him, fine, but I can't look at him."

"All right. You can hold on to me and stay facing the hedge."

They formed a chain, with Mecca in the lead, then Alicia, each holding the hand of the next. Everyone faced the hedge except Mecca. She didn't have that luxury. Someone had to watch the other entrances to this pathway. She didn't want to be surprised.

There had been way too many surprises already.

Ray's body seemed worse than when she'd seen it earlier. More grisly. The red of the blood leapt out at her. The stench of copper reached her nose. She hoped the others didn't smell it. It occurred to her that she might be more sensitive with having absorbed so much energy. She hoped so.

They inched along quietly. A scream broke the night air. They all froze. It came from deep in the center, it sounded like. It rang out, long and high pitched. And moving.

Whoever it was had managed to run.

Mecca's group shifted from a single file line to a small huddle as everyone crowded together and exchanged glances. Hope etched the features of more than one of the women.

They were being too optimistic. Whoever was running was making too much noise. Whichever Visci was after her would be able to track her with no problem. Mecca listened to the voice with a sense of inevitable doom.

And she wished she hadn't been right.

Mecca let her eyes close as the screaming rose to a screech, only to be cut off violently. The silence that followed felt huge. Heavy. Ominous.

The death sounds didn't reach them — the squelch of a fist plunging into a chest; the ripping sound of a heart —

Mecca was just glad the silence was the only sound. It meant that particular Visci was relatively farther away. She tugged on Alicia's hand. "Let's go."

Alicia looked at her blankly, tears following the trail on her cheeks cut earlier at Tina's side. Mecca glanced at the others and saw similar gazes.

"Come *on*," she said and pulled again. "We have to go."

Alicia hitched in a breath and gave a little head shake. Then a nod. "Okay. Yeah." She looked back at the others. "Come on. We're almost there."

Mecca knew Alicia had no idea whether they were almost there. Mecca didn't even really know, though she thought they should be. But Alicia was present and ready to move. And for that, Mecca was both grateful and impressed.

She led them along the leafy wall, everyone silent, save for an occasional quiet sob. Mecca didn't begrudge them their sorrow. Or their fear.

They reached the corner, which led again to the right. Peeking around, she saw a short pathway, then another turn to the left. When they were all safely in the short end, Mecca looked around the next corner — would the corners never end, for fuck's sake?

A shot of adrenaline coursed through her so fast, she clamped her lips shut to keep from laughing.

A long branch of the Maze led farther north. Halfway down it, on the right, was an opening. The narrow wedge through which Mecca could see out of the opening showed the trees of the forest.

They'd found the exit!

"There it is!" Mecca said, trying to keep her voice low. She turned to the others, who were ready to bolt forward. They reminded her of sheep who'd been spooked by a predator. That wasn't really so far from the truth, she figured. "We're almost there. But we can't run. I know there's a guard at this door. And he has a gun, so we need to be really careful."

They all gathered in the corner, and Mecca straightened the canvas pack that hung on her hip. "I'm going to see if I can get him."

Alicia put a hand on her arm. "Be careful."

"I will. We're almost done. We'll make it." This was the first time Mecca had really thought this might be true.

Alicia said nothing. The defeat in her eyes remained, but behind it Mecca saw a spark of hope. That hope spurred her forward.

"Okay, the rest of you stay here." Mecca lowered her voice as much as she could. "I'm going to try to get him down or get his gun from him, whichever works. Alicia, can you stand by the entrance so you can hear? If I need help, I'll say your name and then you" —she pointed to the entire group— "come running. I think we can all take one of them on our own, if we have some surprise. But it's also possible they posted more guards, so I want to see, first."

Heads bobbed their agreement. Mecca moved quietly toward the entrance, Alicia behind her. Every hushed crunch of grass beneath her feet sounded like thunder in her ears. She *really* hoped that was just sharper hearing. Just as she reached the opening, she glanced over her shoulder. Alicia gave her a small nod.

Mecca straightened her back and strode around the hedge, her step bold. The guard, tall and thin, faced the woods, his back to her. A nasty-looking rifle barrel leaned against his shoulder, pointing at the sky. A whistled tune came through the air.

She'd planned on bluffing her way through until she could find a way to incapacitate him, but now she modified those plans and quieted her tread. Mecca's gaze shifted between watching the guard and scanning the ground for anything she might step on.

The man took two steps forward, the tune on his lips at odds with the crickets singing in the woods beyond. He seemed oblivious to anything behind him. He obviously didn't expect anyone to be leaving the Maze.

He continued whistling — a show tune from *Cats*, Mecca thought — though she just knew at the last minute he would turn, shoot her, and it would be over.

But he didn't.

She managed to get within arm's length of him without alerting him to her presence. She pulled back and brought her foot up squarely between his legs. A whoosh of air left his lungs in a strangled cry, his legs folded, and he went down on his knees. The rifle slid from his hands and toppled to the ground.

Mecca sprinted the few steps to where it fell and snatched it up. It looked like something military, out of an action movie. She pointed the business end at the guard. Other than that, Mecca had no idea how to use it. She didn't even know whether the safety was on. She hoped he didn't realize that.

"Alicia, come on. It's clear!"

Her group of rag-tag refugees dashed out of the Maze, Alicia in the lead. By the time they reached her, the guard had regained his breath and straightened up, though the pained look never left his eyes and his face remained pinched. But there was no fear there.

"Emilia's going to be very unhappy that you were so easily overtaken," Mecca said.

"What are we going to do with him?" The question came from a female voice behind her, but Mecca didn't know whose.

"We can't take him with us," Mecca said.

"Kill him." Alicia's voice carried on the air, hollow and emotionless. She looked at the guard without compassion.

"We can't kill him." Mecca took a step toward her.

"Why not? He helped kill Tina. He would have killed us if he'd seen us before we saw him."

Murmurs of agreement came from the others.

If she handed the gun to Alicia, Mecca suspected the man would really end up dead. Alicia's emerald eyes were like hardened little gems as she watched him.

"I'm not a murderer," Mecca said. A week ago, she'd never dreamed of even hurting anyone. Now, she'd killed three people, maybe four, if Will hadn't survived.

But all were in self-defense. And all, except Will, were Visci.

The guard at the barn had been human. Will was human. Mecca guessed this guard was probably human. Visci didn't seem to need guns.

The group of women watched them in silence for a moment. The tension felt real, pushing against Mecca's skin like hot steam.

"No?" Alicia looked at her, those eyes still cold and hard. "We just watched you kill two people. What are you then?"

Mecca didn't know how to answer that without sounding petulant, so she said nothing.

The guard jumped to his feet and rushed Mecca, catching her across her middle with his shoulder. She flew backwards and her tailbone hit the ground first, jarring every bone in her body, making her brain rattle in her head. Her breath fled, leaving her gasping and almost panicking. She couldn't get enough air. She ended up flat on her back as he wrestled the rifle from her hands.

Her ears rang from the rattle to her head, but from a distance, she heard shouting and then the weight of his body disappeared as the women dragged him off her. Mecca gasped, trying to refill her lungs. She pulled herself up to a sitting position.

A few feet away, the small party encircled the guard, who'd curled up in a fetal position on the ground. He covered his head with his hands, trying to protect himself from the bare-footed stomps and kicks raining down on him. A blur of black came from above and the crack of gun butt against skull overrode the shouts of the group, silencing them and ending the kicking.

Alicia held the rifle by the barrel, almost like a baseball bat. She raised it and slammed it down on the guard's head again and again. His arms went slack and a moment later, the end of the butt came away wet in the moonlight.

Alicia kept swinging.

"No! Stop!" Mecca pushed herself up to a standing position and everything swayed lopsided for a moment before righting itself. She staggered to Alicia, the others stepping back to allow her through but doing nothing to end the rage. "Alicia, stop!"

The young blonde, eyes wild, raised the gun again and brought the butt down squarely on the top of the guard's already bashed-in skull. Mecca had no doubt he was dead. His chest didn't rise with breath; his body only moved when Alicia hit it.

Mecca put one hand on the gun and the other on Alicia's shoulder. She was amazed the rifle hadn't gone off and shot Alicia as she swung. "Stop now," she said. "He's dead. You killed him."

Alicia looked at her. It took a moment for Mecca's words to register, but the blank look on her features finally shifted into understanding. "Good," she said. "He killed Tina."

Mecca took the gun from Alicia's hands. "No, he didn't. But it doesn't matter now." She looked around to get her bearings. They'd moved about twenty yards from the Maze. The woods were still another eighty yards away. Mecca could see the path to the guest house a ways to the north.

"We need to get him out of the clearing so no one sees him." She held the rifle out to one of the women who shied away. "Hold this, damn it. You were fine beating on him when he was down, now hold this fucking gun so I can get your mess out of the way."

The startled woman took the rifle by the barrel and held it at arm's length. Mecca bent and grabbed the guard's right foot. She nodded at the lanky young man. "Grab his other foot and help me." The boy jumped forward and together they dragged the body the distance to the tree line, with the remaining group following at a short distance. Alicia came up behind, her face expressionless again.

"Leave the gun here with him," Mecca said after they'd tucked the body behind a short, straggly bush. She turned her back on the knot of people and tried to keep her mind away from the fact that she'd become an accessory to murder. Actual murder.

"Shouldn't we take it with us?" came a random voice.

"If you have any idea how to use it, bring it. I don't care." There came murmuring from the group and a fair-skinned woman took the rifle and looked at Mecca, who only nodded. "Come on. I'll lead you to the path that will take you off the property."

Mecca took them along the tree line, staying just inside the edge for cover. They didn't move as fast as she'd liked because all of the others were without shoes. She knew how they felt, but she tried to keep them going faster anyway. When Emilia found out that they'd escaped, the hunt would be more than a party game. It would be an all-out rampage.

They reached the path to the guest house. She had hoped to let Alicia take over from here, but now Mecca wasn't sure she could be trusted. Mecca would have to take them to the guest house clearing herself, show them the beginning of the fire road, then head back to the main house.

Twenty minutes later, the path opened out. She saw the guest house — a cottage, really — through the trees, windows all dark. It looked deserted. *At least we're getting one break.* She stopped the group before they reached the end of the path.

"Let me check and make sure it's clear before we go." She spoke to everyone in general. "You can't see it from here, but on the other side of the house is a small road. That will lead to a back gate. There will be a guard, maybe more than one, so you'll need to figure something out before you get there."

They looked at her with blank faces, but she just shook her head and turned away. She did her part. They could make their own way from there.

Mecca saw no movement in the clearing, so she stepped out quietly. The dark guest house remained quiet, and she was grateful. Her nerves were so frayed, so jangled that she found herself jumping at any sound that came from the woods. The image of the horrible hole in Tina's chest kept coming into her head, no matter how many times she tried to push it away. Mecca rounded the corner of the guest house and stopped short.

Near the well, a figure stood motionless.

Small, the silhouette looked like a woman, but she knew that had no bearing on the danger. Mecca took a slow step backward, moving for the corner of the house. Relative safety.

"Mecca?" The whisper barely made it to her ears, the voice familiar. "Is that you?"

"Who are you?"

"It's Sara."

What in the actual fuck? Relief made her insides feel loose and wobbly. Mecca knew that Sara really couldn't be of any help, but just having someone from the outside, someone normal, here in this crazy place made her feel better. She closed the distance between them quickly and yanked the other woman into a hug. When she pulled back, she asked, "Why are you here?"

The surprise in Sara's face didn't fade as Mecca released her. "I came with your dad."

She didn't see anyone else in the clearing. "Where is he?"

"At the house. He came to find you."

Oh God. Now what was she going to do?

"Mecca?" A whispered voice came from behind her.

She turned and motioned for the group of refugees to come forward. "Come on out. She's a friend."

"What's this?" Sara asked, waving a hand at them.

"I know we hardly know each other, but I need you to do me a favor."

"Um, sure." Sara peered past Mecca as the group assembled behind her.

"They need to get out of here. Can you take them — wait. How did you get past the guard?"

The confusion and surprise finally melted as Sara grinned and pulled out something gun-shaped. "I tasered him!" She looked satisfied with herself. "It didn't knock him out, of course. I had to give him a good wail on his jaw with his gun. But I got to use my taser! "

Mecca looked at the small, pixie-like woman, with her lop-sided smile and child-like enthusiasm for tasers and laughed. She tried to keep it from sounding crazy. But it felt really good not to be terrified for a moment.

"So what happened? They look like... Well, they look rough."

They really did. "I'm sure they can explain it as you go."

The moment dragged out as Sara studied her. "You're going back in, aren't you?"

"Yes. I have someone to deal with. And Dad's in there."

"Okay," she said. "I know I can't talk you out of it, but tell your dad I tried to." She gave a gentle smile. "Be careful."

"I will."

Sara looked past Mecca at the women and two men. "We've got a little bit of a walk in front of us. Come on. Let's get going."

Mecca watched them, a pixie leading escapees to freedom. When they'd disappeared into the trees, she turned back the way she came.

Now, it was time. She was done fucking around.

Chapter Twenty-Eight: David

"Good evening, Mr. Trenow." A man stepped up from the side, wispy blond hair pulled back from his face. He looked to be in his late teens with a slight build. His delicate features reminded David of a young girl. He didn't extend a hand to shake, but said, "My name is Claude Kassinzi."

This was the man who'd helped Mecca escape. Though he didn't look dangerous, he *felt* dangerous. The hair on David's arms rose. His nerves, already on edge, wanted to spring from his skin.

"Good evening. How do you know who I am?"

Claude's lips turned up in a smile, but his teeth remained hidden. "You resemble your photos. A bit older, perhaps, but unmistakable. There are a few others here who may recognize you. You must be careful. But if you want to save your daughter, you should come with me. I have a proposition for you."

What the hell was this? David clenched his fists and forced himself not to show a reaction beyond the clipped tone of his words. "Where is she?"

"We don't have much time, Mr. Trenow. If you will please follow my man, Salas, there." Tall and broad shouldered, Salas filled the doorway which led to the hall.

He knew this could be a trap. But what could he do? How else would he find Mecca in this crowd, in this huge house? His feet felt heavy, as though his shoes were filled with sand, but he forced them to move toward the door. Claude fell into step behind him.

Salas led them a short way down the hall before he opened a heavy-looking oak door on the right. When the lights came on, David saw a small sitting room furnished in classic pieces, including a wide Queen Anne chair as the centerpiece. Floor to ceiling windows covered the far wall, flanked by thick, royal blue, velvet curtains. The room smelled like lemon Pledge. Strangely normal in a weird place among weird people.

David stepped in and though Salas stood near the wall and seemed to ignore them, he couldn't help but feel as if he'd just walked into the world's biggest mouse trap. If that man had a gun, David didn't have a chance.

"I am going to make this quick, Mr. Trenow, because I was not being dramatic about time being short." Claude closed the door behind him and paced into the room. "Right now, Mecca is being hunted. I believe she's holding up well, however, bigger hunters are now entering the game. She's killed at least two people, most likely in self-defense." He tilted his head and gave David a pointed look. "She doesn't seem the type to kill for no reason."

David's mind fogged with questions. "How do you know? That she's killed someone?"

"I've established a link with her. I can feel when she has an influx of energy. Perhaps she didn't actually kill anyone. But I doubt it." Claude remained so still, David found it unnerving.

"Where is she?"

"Out on the grounds somewhere, but I can't say exactly where" Claude said. "As I said, we don't have much time. I want to cut you a deal."

"I won't let you hurt Mecca."

"I have no interest in hurting Mecca. I would, however, quite like someone with your talents available to me."

What the hell? "You're with Emilia."

Claude smiled again, lips closed in a thin line. "Not as such. I have been honest in our talks thus far, so let me be plain now. I will make sure that Mecca walks out of here alive and free. I will further ensure that none of our kind will ever hunt her down again. In exchange, you will make yourself available to me as needed."

"For what?"

"Nothing that would be adverse to you, I think." A slight quirk upward of his lips. "There are certain people of my own race with whom I have some difficulties. You would only be employed to deal with those individuals."

"Kill them, you mean." David's voice had lowered, registering the tension that coiled in every muscle. To the side, he saw Salas pull himself into a straighter posture.

Claude shrugged, the move refined, almost dainty. Yet David felt nothing but raw power from him.

"I could kill you now," David said, ignoring Salas, who bristled.

"You could try, yes. You might succeed, certainly. But a moment later, you'd be dead." Claude nodded toward where his big bodyguard stood. "And who would save your daughter? Emilia will have her at all costs if I do not intervene. If we are both dead, there is no one left to save her." He paused for the briefest of moments. "Again, Mr. Trenow, we do not have the luxury of time. I need your decision. Now."

"So if I say no, you will kill her?" The thought of Mecca dying at the hands of these creatures almost made his breath stop in his lungs.

"I would do nothing of the sort. But if you won't agree to assist me, then Mecca is the only one I have left to persuade."

Either I become his murdering lapdog, or Mecca does. David still couldn't rule out this man killing his daughter. Because he couldn't see her ever agreeing to these terms. "How do I know I can trust you?"

"Well, I suppose you don't. But logically, if I betray you, you have no incentive to work for me. So it really is not in my best interest to go back on my word, is it?"

"And Emilia?"

"I'll handle Emilia. Do I have your agreement then?"

"You vow nothing will happen to Mecca?"

"She will be left alone to live out her life."

"All right, fine." *You just made a pact with the devil, old boy.* The words came into his head in his father's voice. But if he could save Mecca, he would make a pact with Lucifer himself.

"Very good," Claude said. He had been very still through the entire conversation, and now his body went into motion, impossibly fast. He passed David and reached the door so quickly, David lost focus on him. "I believe I mentioned we are a bit pressed. It's time to find your daughter."

--->>><<<---

With Claude leading, David in the middle, and Salas taking sweep, they moved through the crowded party rooms and out into the night. The smell of clove cigarettes hung in the air as people milled about the patio, talking about who would win the Game, and making wagers on their favorites.

David didn't understand what the Game was, but he didn't think it could be anything good.

Claude led them off the patio, onto the lawn, and then along the back of the house. A large hedge ran parallel, several dozen yards away. David saw an opening in the front as they passed, and it suddenly became clear. A maze. Who had a maze in their back yard these days?

He wanted to ask about it, but something kept him from speaking. He didn't want to interact with Claude more than he had to.

David looked back. Salas followed behind, the tall man crouching somewhat. The sides of his suit jacket flapped as he moved.

David didn't think he'd be able to take Salas in a fight. Broad-chested and thick with muscles, Salas looked like he might have been a boxer or perhaps a football player. Just as David turned his head back, the left side of Salas's jacket swayed open and David caught sight of the butt of a pistol at his hip. His attention again on Claude, David thought the gun would make another good reason he wouldn't be able to take Salas in a fight.

They walked quickly, staying near the edge of the house and moving away from the party. Where were they going? Maybe this was the real trap. Maybe Claude would get him out in the darkness and that would be it.

When they reached the edge of the tree line near the corner of the house, Claude motioned to follow — as if David had stopped — then moved into the darkness of the woods. Leaves and pine needles crunched beneath David's step as he slid into the coolness.

"I didn't want to stay close to the maze," Claude said in a soft voice. "It's all open space. Nowhere to take cover. It won't take long to get over there if we need to but this way, our approach isn't obvious."

"Who are we hiding from?" David asked. If Claude was so powerful, why did he have to hide?

"Emilia is looking for Mecca. She said she was going to come this way. Mecca is familiar with this side of the property, so I don't think it's unreasonable to think she might be here. In any case, we will be able to keep an eye on Emilia without her seeing us. She is the biggest threat to your daughter at this time." Claude pushed his way through the thick underbrush.

David followed close behind. He was close enough that he could reach out and touch Claude. And kill him. But with Salas at his back, with his gun, David didn't like the odds. He also reasoned that Claude seemed to have a plan to save Mecca from Emilia. It might be best to let him live in order to rescue Mecca, first. David would have plenty of time and opportunity to touch Claude later.

Chapter Twenty-Nine: Mecca

Mecca left the guest house and made it halfway back down the path toward the house and the maze, when Emilia stepped in front of her about fifty feet away. At first, she looked like a mirage. A silver, glowing angel in the leafy darkness.

How in the hell did she find me?

"I didn't expect you to come back," Emilia said. "I thought I would have to track you down."

"How did you know I was here?"

"You should have figured that out by now." Emilia smiled, but kept her distance. The smart thing to do, considering she wore cocktail attire and had a lot of exposed skin for Mecca to latch on to.

"Don't play games with me. Tell me or don't tell me."

"We're linked. I can feel you, especially when you kill."

The guard's bloody face flashed across Mecca's mind's eye, and she winced. But she hadn't killed *him*. Emilia must have meant the two in the maze.

"When someone rips out a child's heart, she deserves to be killed. This is an evil game you play here." Mecca kept her voice flat, holding in the anger that bubbled just below the surface suddenly. The light from the stars didn't penetrate the oil-black darkness of the forest. The path felt closed-in, claustrophobic. The smell of decaying leaves and pine needles hung heavy on the air.

"Yes, I'll grant you that it is archaic. But it's a tradition among my kind. It's somewhat barbaric, but it is expected, and so I accommodate."

Mecca shuddered.

"Why did you come back?" Emilia asked.

"To kill you."

"Oh?" Surprise registered on Emilia's face for a second with her raised brows, then disappeared. "I suppose I should have expected that."

"But you didn't."

"No, I didn't. Because of our bond." She smiled again. "You shouldn't entertain those sorts of thoughts about me."

In some ways, you are mine already. The words came into Mecca's head with Emilia's voice.

"What the *fuck*?" Mecca reeled back and put a hand to her forehead. "Get the hell out of my head!" Thoughts of the dinner on the balcony slipped through her mind. How she'd felt drawn to, almost compelled by Emilia. Mecca glared at her. "Your blood. You *really* put your blood into me!"

"Yes."

Energy, her own and what she had taken from the two Visci in the maze, prickled below her skin, mingling with her anger. Scenes from her captivity and her escape flew through her mind.

Emilia hadn't moved from her spot on the path. "It will protect you. It will keep you young and strong."

"I don't want it. I told you before that I don't want it."

I'm sorry. It wasn't really a choice. Emilia's voice edged along Mecca's mind, grating like metal on metal.

"And Claude?"

"What about Claude?"

"You put his blood into me too?"

"No." Emilia's brow creased just above the space between her eyes.

She doesn't know. Mecca laughed out loud.

Emilia regarded her and Mecca realized she could feel a hint of the woman's edginess in her head.

"Oh, this is great! You don't know." She laughed again. "The bond you're talking about?" She stopped smiling and narrowed her eyes at the woman in front of her. "It's stronger with Claude than with you." Even as she said the words and got satisfaction from Emilia's reaction, fear crept into her belly. If her bond with Claude was stronger, what could he make her do? But it wouldn't help her to let Emilia know that. "You didn't even know it."

Emilia made no reply, but Mecca could see her working out the details as her gaze hardened.

"Enough."

"Your lackey, working behind your back. I wonder how else he's betrayed you." She lifted a hand. "Oh, wait, I already know."

Emilia made fists at her sides. Anger radiated from her and pushed against the edges of Mecca's mind.

"Do you know how I escaped? Did he tell you?" She shook her head. "No, I can't imagine he did." As she goaded Emilia, the energy in her rose higher with her adrenaline.

"Mecca, it's time for you to come back with me."

"He gave me directions out of the house and off the grounds. He sent his little buddy — well, big buddy. That guy's huge — to distract the guard at the back gate so I could get out." She kept her tone light.

Emilia raised her right hand. Without warning, a sharp pain bit into Mecca's thigh. A small dart embedded there, having plowed through her jeans and into the muscle. She reached down and pulled it out.

Inertia flooded her body. The forest swayed in her vision. She blinked several times to straighten it out and put a hand out to the tree beside her, steadying herself.

This is like déjà vu.

She stumbled but did not go down. The energy in her battled the drug from the dart. Everything took on a glittery, silver glow. She blinked again and tried to clear her vision. She realized, too late, that Emilia had closed the distance between them and grabbed onto her arm. To help her or put her on the ground, Mecca didn't know. But Emilia had been careful enough not to touch her skin directly.

Mecca leaned forward and tried to lay a hand on Emilia's forearm. Everything had doubled, and she couldn't tell which forearm was the real one. Time had become herky-jerky.

Something large crashed through the woods on her left. An animal? She found that caring wasn't an emotion she had.

She reached out again and this time felt cool, soft skin beneath her skin.

Emilia jerked away just as Mecca sent her energy out. Her life force slammed back into her, ejected.

"Mecca, stop fighting me."

Horrified, Mecca found herself doing as ordered. Her arm fell limp at her side, and she couldn't raise it again. *Move, damn it! You're not going to get another chance!*

"I don't want it to be this way, but I'm not afraid to break you if I need to," Emilia said. She lowered Mecca to the ground. "Will, help me."

Mecca felt as though someone had put a lead blanket over her. She could sit up, but couldn't get any of her limbs to do as she wanted them to. Will's face swam into her field of vision from the left, where the crashing sound had come.

"Mecca!" A voice from the woods. "Move!" Claude's voice.

The blanket lifted.

Mecca still felt doped, but her body seemed to be more responsive as she raised her hand and clamped onto Emilia's bare upper arm. The Asian woman registered surprise again, but this time it wasn't so quick to get away.

Mecca shot her energy out into the Cavern. She found a shining ball of golden light there, but the Cavern itself was cold, dead. Grey tendrils — dozens — rose from the ground and covered the ball, keeping it bound.

The smell of smoke infected the air, but Mecca could see nothing of a fire.

She'd never seen the Cavern so clearly. She didn't know if it was because of the connection between them or because of all the energy she'd taken in earlier.

The walls stood grey with age, the same color as the things that held the golden ball in place. Craters pockmarked every surface, some deep, others shallow. It looked as though droplets of water had slowly eroded those areas, even though that was impossible for some. Water doesn't drip upward.

Mecca sent her energy to surround the bright ball of light. The taste of a fresh snowfall flooded her mouth. Another surprise. She'd never had a taste in the Cavern before. She didn't know what that meant and didn't have to time work it out. She tugged at the ball, but the greyness held it tight.

"No!" Emilia shoved Mecca away and fell onto her backside with the strength of her push. She looked dazed for a long moment.

Mecca propelled forward, but strong hands wrapped around her. Will's scent — musky and dark — enveloped her. He held her tight to his chest.

"Will, let go!" Mecca struggled against his grip. His hold on her was too strong.

"I can't. I'm sorry." And she heard the regret in his voice, real.

She groaned. "I'm sorry too." She sent her energy into him and followed the warmth of his soul to the Cavern. It was easy to find. The ball of light glowed gold, with silver veins pulsing through it. Again, she tasted fresh, clean snow on her tongue. She still didn't understand it.

Mecca slammed her energy into his, like a metaphysical head butt. She felt the jarring hit to her soul and staggered. She didn't want to kill him. His grip on her loosened as he swayed too. She did it again and hoped this wouldn't do real damage to either of them. She had no way to know.

He broke his hold on her and stumbled down to the ground, more than dazed. With their break in contact, Mecca's energy came back to her. Emilia, pine needles stuck in the sequins of her dress, was just pulling herself to her feet.

"Mecca, stop." Emilia's voice rang with authority.

When Mecca realized that her body had no response for Emilia's words, she lunged at her. As soon as she felt skin to skin contact, she let her energy loose into the other woman, straight to the Cavern.

She wasted no time tugging but circled the ball of light at its base, concentrating on sawing through the grey vines. At their bottom, where they merged with the wall of the Cavern, they had to be two inches in diameter. Mecca put more energy into the sawing, moving quickly, desperately.

When the first tendril popped, Emilia's screech assailed her ears.

She managed to get one more ropey vine dislodged before Emilia threw her off. Emilia's strength awed her.

Mecca sailed six feet through the air and landed hard on her right leg. A mind-numbing crack and a knife of brilliantly and fiery pain in her shin tore a scream from her. Her heart pulsed as thumps of agony.

"It's not too late, Mecca. I don't want it to end this way." Emilia's face looked drawn, old. Her beautiful acorn-colored eyes, world-weary, fixed on Mecca.

"I will not be your pawn. You're a monster."

"If I am a monster, then we are sisters."

A gunshot tore through the night air, and Emilia staggered, a fine red spray jetting from her thigh. Her right leg folded beneath her, and she went down, an enraged shriek on her lips. Mecca searched the forest beyond the path but saw nothing. She didn't even know which direction the shot came from.

A gun can't kill her. Can it?

But it didn't matter. Mecca pulled herself over to where Emilia lay and pounced on the woman. Her leg screamed in her head, but she ignored it. She had to.

Grabbing the downed Visci by the bare foot, Mecca again found her way to Emilia's Cavern. With the vines holding the soul down weakened, with Emilia herself on the ground and bleeding, Mecca surrounded the ball of light with her own life force again and heaved. The tendrils stretched this time, extending.

Emilia kicked out and clawed around her, searching for a weapon. The side of Emilia's foot connected with Mecca's right shoulder, another bloom of torture erupting from her body.

She lost her grip with that hand, but not before a single grey vine snapped. Mecca's hope surged anew. The struggle lessened only a little bit as another tendril popped and after several moments, the rest gave way slowly, one by one.

Emilia screeched. In the Cavern, the shriek echoed and deafened Mecca. When it hit her, Emilia's energy threw Mecca just as hard as Emilia's physical push had. Again, Mecca flew through the air, both in reality and in the Cavern. In the real world, she came down on the same leg. Bright red and blue fireworks burst in her head.

The sound of fire roared in her ears, popping and crackling. Suddenly, a vision overlaid the forest, like when she looked at the Cavern with her eyes still open. A burning village, thatch roofs engulfed with flame, people fleeing, screams filling the air, the smell of burning meat. Rice fields eaten by fire.

She sees this through the eyes of a child. Tastes the acid terror in the back of her throat. A woman burning, the child's mother. Strong hands sweeping her up onto a horse. Brown eyes in a pale, young man's face. Wind in her hair, but the smell of smoke and death does not — cannot — leave her nose.

Mecca felt nothing but the wind and the roaring grief and fear. Then the light dimmed, the vision faded, and everything went black.

—➤✦◄—

The searing, enveloping pain woke her, a scream on her lips.

"I'm sorry. I know it hurts." Will's soft voice filtered through the haze.

Mecca opened her eyes. Will's face wavered, and she blinked hard, nausea gripping her belly. Behind him stood her dad and… Claude. Another tall figure stood farther back, nearer the trees. She couldn't see him clearly, but she bet it was Claude's big man.

"I'm going to use one of the tranquilizer darts. That should help."

Mecca waved the idea away and pulled herself up onto her elbows. An agonizing flood threatened to bring on the blackness again. "Where is she?"

Will tilted his head to Mecca's left but said nothing. She saw hurt in his eyes.

Five feet away, a desiccated corpse lay, engulfed by a dirty, silver sequined gown. Nothing recognizable was left of the beautiful Asian woman. It could have been a mummy from a museum.

"I've got to try to set your leg," Will said. "It's going to hurt, but I'm hoping the tranquilizer will help. Then I need to look at your shoulder. I think it may be dislocated."

Mecca heard his words, but they were like a garbled radio message. She looked at her father. Even in the darkness, she could see the startling blue of his eyes. No matter what he'd done in the past, she would still always love him. But she didn't know if she'd ever be able to look at him again.

A sharp sting got her attention. The bottom half of her pant leg had been cut off and Will now removed the needle he'd just stuck into her calf.

It suddenly came to her that the white and red bit sticking out of her leg was her own bone. Bile burned the back of her throat, and she turned her head just in time. Only liquid came, but it stung every cell as it gushed out, soaking the leaves and pine needles.

Will threw the used dart back into a canvas bag at his side and then reached toward her head. The tenderness in his touch as he brushed her hair back startled her.

"You should probably lie down," he whispered to her, resting a hand on her good shoulder. "I'm not going to do anything drastic, but this is going to hurt."

"He better not make it worse." Her father's words filtered through Mecca's cloudy brain.

"He's very well-trained," Claude said. "Let him work."

Mecca lay back with Will's gentle, insistent pressure on her shoulder. The other shoulder throbbed. She closed her eyes. The tranquilizer dart, her second of the evening, left her floaty. She felt his hands on her leg, touching gently, putting things on either side of her calf.

"Are you okay so far?" he asked.

"Mmm," Mecca said. Colored lights flashed behind her eyelids.

Tight pressure around her leg just below her knee made her pop her eyes open. Will hovered over her. A little wrinkle gathered over his eyebrows as he concentrated. It surprised Mecca that he would be so intent on helping her, the one who killed his — what? Mistress? His focus seemed unbreakable as he tied something else around her leg at the ankle.

The aching pain became sharp again, thrumming through her torso and into her head. Her belly clenched with a sudden wave of nausea. She gagged.

Her dad cursed and Claude said something to him that she couldn't made out.

"Turn, here, turn." Will slid a warm arm under her shoulders and carefully tilted her up and to the side.

Mecca retched, all of the muscles in her abdomen contracting together. Bile stung the back of her throat, but nothing came up this time.

"Deep breath, Mecca. Come on. It'll pass. Don't worry."

Her vision went fuzzy as Will continued to give her encouraging words. She closed her eyes and trusted him.

Chapter Thirty: Mecca

The world returned to her through voices.

"You are not taking her back to that house!" Her father's, in a hushed but very firm tone.

"She'll be safe there with Emilia gone. Or do you want to drag her through the woods?" Claude.

"I'm glad you're awake." Will's voice, quiet, not far from her ear.

"I don't really want to open my eyes," she replied.

She felt him chuckle behind her, his body supporting hers in a reclined position. In her darkness, his scent surrounded her.

"I don't blame you," he said. "They've been like this since I finally got you settled."

"How did you know I was awake?" Could everyone read her mind?

"Your breathing pattern changed, and you tensed when you heard them." She heard a smile in his voice. "I spent quite a while learning how you sleep and wake."

"Oh." Heat rushed her cheeks. From anyone else, that would have been creepy. But it wasn't from him. "How long was I out?"

"Just long enough. I was able to get your shoulder back in its socket and I did what I could for your leg. We need to get you to a hospital. There's a high risk of infection with that sort of break. And we're not exactly in a sterile environment."

"She's awake?" Her dad's voice came closer, along with the rustle of pine needles.

She opened her eyes to see him kneeling beside her. "Hi Dad."

"Hi, honey." He smiled and the light touch of his fingertips on her arm tickled. She didn't know if that meant he'd used his Gift or not. "How are you feeling?"

"Not the greatest, but I think I'll live."

He smiled. "You did great back there."

"Thanks, I guess. How did you get here?" The groggy feeling from the drugs seemed to be wearing off a little bit. It made thinking easier, but pain thrummed a steady beat in time with her heart.

"I came to find you."

"You found me."

"Yes, though not as soon as I wish."

"Well, it's done now." She looked back over her shoulder at Will and smiled, then she pulled herself forward, away from him. God, her shoulder hurt. "Thanks for playing furniture, Will. I think I can sit on my own."

He scrambled from behind her and stood. "All right. I'll give you two some privacy."

Her father gave her a tender look and said, "We're going to get you out of here. Do you think you can walk with help?"

"Yes. In a minute." She really had no idea whether she could or not, but she wanted out of these woods. Mecca's heart pounded even harder in her chest and before she spoke, she wasn't sure she wanted to know the answer. But it came out anyway. "Did you kill your wives?"

His eyes widened, but then he looked down for a moment and swallowed. When he met her gaze again, he asked in a voice barely audible, "How do you know about my former wives?"

"Does it matter?"

He regarded her. "No, I guess not."

The soft murmur of conversation floated on the night air. Will and Claude had been joined by Claude's guard, the tall figure Mecca had seen earlier but not recognized. She looked back at her father.

"Did you?"

He gazed out at the trees. Mecca didn't ask again, only watched him. He'd aged at least ten years since they'd been at the cabin. His shoulders slumped and the lines on his face, which had looked distinguished before, now just looked like a roadmap. His eyebrows had just begun to grow back.

He took a deep breath, his chest expanding as his lungs filled. He looked back to her and then hesitated again. When he finally answered, his voice was quiet.

"Yes."

Her soul shattered. All along, she'd seen the evidence, weighed it intellectually and come away with the idea that he had to have killed them. The photos, the way they all died: nothing left much doubt.

But in her heart, in her soul, she hadn't believed it, couldn't believe that her father — the good man, the good husband — committed those murders.

She pulled her arm from under his hand. "How? I mean, I know *how*" —she stared at him pointedly— "What I want to know is how *could* you? All those women…"

"I don't know. I was different then."

That was his excuse? He was different? Mecca's anger kindled. "You're a murderer."

He bowed his head but didn't respond.

"And Mom? Did you murder her too?" Numbness stole over her.

He jerked his gaze up, agony in his eyes. "That was different."

What the fuck did that mean? "Did you kill her?" Her voice scaled up with each word. Old guilt welled in her, warring with the new revelation that maybe she *hadn't* been the one. "*Did you*?"

"We had talked about it before she ever got bad enough to go into the hospital."

Still not an answer. "She knew you had the Gift? She knew about the women?"

"No! She knew about the Gift, but she didn't know anything about my past."

He reached out again, but Mecca slapped his hand away.

"Please understand, Mec. When I met your mom, she changed something in me. I wanted to be a better person for her, a better man."

Her skin felt hot and tight and a little buzzing pain had started behind her eyes. The possibility that she hadn't killed her mother felt foreign, but she couldn't deny the relief it brought. Her eyes burned with a need to rage, to cry, but she wouldn't. Not here.

"Drinking less is becoming a better man! Picking up your dirty underwear is becoming a better man. Not *murdering* women — that's just... I can't even." She jerked her gaze away. She couldn't look at him anymore.

"The cancer had gotten really bad," her dad continued, as if she hadn't even spoken. "I know you remember the hospital, but you never knew just how much pain she was in."

She did remember the hospital: the smell of clean and sick all mixed together, the white sheets, the tubes and beeping monitors, the cold coil of fear in her belly every time she went to visit. She hated that place.

"When your mom first started going through the chemo and was sick all the time, she told me that if it ever got so bad that she couldn't come home, she wanted me to —" He choked on the words. He looked down, his face hidden from her and resumed, voice thick with tears. "She wanted me to help her go peacefully. She wanted me to let her go."

Grief overpowered her, and tears burned from her eyes. Sorrow stabbed her as strong and sharp as when she had been only twelve. The hole in her heart echoed her loss like the biggest, emptiest cavern.

"I didn't want to," he said, now looking into her eyes. His own cheeks glistened in the moonlight, soaked with his grief. "I wanted her to fight and win. I wanted her to be there for your prom and your high school graduation and the tenth grade science fair you won. I wanted her to see the woman you've grown into."

"I don't want to hear any more." The buzzing behind her eyes had become a hammering. She felt her grasp on her own self-control slipping.

"Please, Mecca, you've got to understand."

She pushed him. "No, I don't! Do you know how long I've lived with the belief that *I* killed her?" Her voice sounded screechy. When Claude and Will looked over, she lowered her tone. "That because I couldn't control it, she died?"

"What?" His surprise and shock looked genuine. "Oh, no. Honey, it wasn't your fault. The cancer made her sick and it's what killed her. Your Gift didn't."

Mecca tried to swallow a sob, but couldn't. It rattled through her ribcage and her lungs, from the deepest parts of her. The tears came down and she couldn't fight him when her father encircled her with his arms.

Chapter Thirty-One: Mecca

In some ways, she found the room similar to the one she'd had in Emilia's house. Only not locked. When they'd arrived at the Emergency Room, they'd taken her right away and admitted her. They'd taken her to surgery not long after.

Now she lay in another hospital bed with a cast up to her knee. They gave her a sling for her arm also and told her to use it to give her shoulder time to heal.

Her dad hadn't left the room since she'd been admitted except to go to the bathroom and get coffee. Usually not at the same time.

She had trouble looking at him. She kept seeing the grainy newspaper photo of Susan Harrington. Sara's grandmother, she realized. She wondered if Sara understood his role in her grandmother's death.

Probably not. It was best to leave her with her ignorance, Mecca decided.

"The people from the maze that you brought out are all okay," her father said. "Well, the jury's still out on the one girl. But I guess with some therapy, she should come around." He must have meant Alicia.

"Okay." She was glad they were okay, but none of it really mattered anymore.

"I ended up having to tell Sara everything. I don't know whether she believed it all, but I told her."

"You told her everything, huh?" She just stared at him, blankly. After a moment, he got it.

"No. Not *everything*. But everything about your ordeal."

Mecca shrugged. "You probably should have told her before it was all over. Then she may not have wandered onto the grounds. It could have been a lot worse for her."

"Yes, it could have. But I don't think knowing would have stopped her."

"Did you tell her about the Gift?"

A faint flush settled on his cheeks. It looked strange there. He shook his head. "I thought it best not to mention that."

"I suppose so. Tell her thank you for me, for showing up when she did."

"I will. She's asked about you several times and sends her best wishes. She wanted to get you one of those big balloon arrangements, but I talked her out of it."

He smiled, but the sparkle in his eyes was missing. Mecca didn't feel like smiling back, so she didn't.

"I have to go by her place later and return a couple things. I'll give her your thanks then."

He'd been babbling for the last hour. She really just wanted him to leave. She needed time to process everything that happened.

How had things changed with Emilia gone? Would Claude step in? And why would Claude leave her and her dad alone when Emilia wouldn't?

A name her dad said caught her attention. "Will told me he would stop by a little later. I guess he's clearing some things out of Emilia's place."

The mention of his name made her smile for the first time since she'd woken up.

"He's going to stay at the house for a week or two until he can figure out what he'll do now."

Mecca wondered that too. She didn't know whether her dad knew about Will's tie to Emilia. But the way Mecca understood it was that once Emilia's blood in him faded or was used up, he would age to his natural life span. And Emilia said he'd far exceeded that time and would die. There had to be a way to keep that from happening.

"You're very quiet," he said.

She looked straight at him for the first time since he'd admitted to killing his previous wives. "I'm waiting for you to tell me whatever you're beating around the bush telling me." She was tired of the small talk.

He brushed a hand over his buzz cut. "Okay. I'm going to be going away for a while."

"Why?"

"I've got some work to do."

"What kind of work?" She shifted in the bed to sit up more. He was hiding something specific. She wanted to scream.

"Just some stuff I need to take care of."

"More secrets?"

"Some secrets are better kept." He didn't shift his gaze away from her.

How could he be keeping *more* secrets? What the hell else could there be?

She didn't know whether she would ever be able to trust him again.

A tentative rap interrupted them. Will's face appeared in the partially open doorway.

"Is this a bad time?"

"Not at all," Mecca said. She couldn't keep the anger from her voice. "Dad's just leaving."

He didn't argue with her, but stood and nodded to Will as the younger man stepped into the room. A blue nylon backpack perched on Will's back.

"Come by the house whenever you'd like," her dad said. "I have a spare key for you whenever you're ready."

"Okay. Thanks a lot."

He just nodded and left the room.

"This wasn't the best time, was it?" Will asked as he pulled a chair over to her bedside.

"As good a time as any." Mecca smiled. She couldn't help it. Something about him brought that reaction.

"How are you feeling?"

"Like I had the hell beat out of me from the inside out."

"Well, I suppose you did." His smile wasn't perfect, a bit lopsided and one of his side teeth was crooked. But the flaws made it more endearing.

"I like that you're asking me for yourself, rather than for her."

The gentle way his lips curved up made her feel good.

"I like that too." He reached over and brushed his fingertips across the top of her IV-bound hand. The tingle washed through her. Nothing supernatural, at all.

They sat quietly for a little bit, not looking at each other, but it didn't feel at all awkward. Finally, Mecca spoke. "The doctor said I should be healed up in a couple months, all together. I guess that's okay."

"It could have been worse."

"Yes, I could be dead."

He nodded, his sea green eyes bright.

"Will, what are you going to do now?"

"Hang out with your dad, I suppose." He looked very serious for a second, then a grin lit his face.

She laughed. She couldn't help it. "Don't be a smartass. You know what I mean."

Will shrugged off his backpack and let it fall to the floor beside his chair. "I don't know. I guess I'll just take it one day at a time and live until I die."

"Isn't there some way? I mean, can't we do something?"

"Claude has already said he won't take me in. I'm really not interested in approaching any of the others in the city. I didn't really want Claude either, but at least he's the evil I know."

Mecca wasn't sure that Claude *was* the evil Will knew. But she didn't want to argue the point. "How long do you have?"

"I've no idea. We never tested it." That lopsided smile again.

"Maybe I can help you. Maybe my Gift…"

"I suppose we could try, but I don't think it's the same thing at all. Be honest. After feeling what you felt of her and of me, do *you* think it would work?"

She didn't think it would. She hated that he knew she didn't.

"Don't worry," he said. "I've lived a very long life. Longer than any man could expect."

"But you were a prisoner."

"That doesn't mean I didn't have a good life." The flippant grin had gone, replaced by a kind smile. "Besides, what would I do now anyway? My era is long gone."

"You could continue your medical training. You could become a doctor!" Mecca hated the desperation in her voice. Jesus, she sounded like a whiny teenager. But dammit, she didn't want him to die.

Will rested his hand on her arm. His palm warmed her skin. "Are they releasing you today?"

Both glad and annoyed at the change in subject, she nodded. "I think so, this afternoon."

"Okay. How about I go by your dad's and get my key, and then I'll pop back here and sit with you until they're ready to cut you loose. It'll give you some time to rest too."

"Okay. Don't let my dad come with you though. It's bad enough I have to stay there until I can get around on my own again."

Will nodded as he stood up and grabbed his backpack. He stared at her, his expression tender. When he leaned down, Mecca closed her eyes. His lips brushed against her forehead. When she looked at him again, he was smiling down at her.

"Get some rest. I'll see you later."

"Okay." She watched him retreat to the door. "Will?"

He turned back, one corner of his mouth tilted up with the remains of his half-smile.

"I still want to try." She flushed hot and quickly added, "With the Gift, I mean."

He tilted his head and a soft brown curl slid along his forehead. The half-smile turned into a full one. "Okay. We'll try."

The End

Did you like what you read? Please be sure to go back and leave a review! Reviews are how authors get readers. The more good word of mouth about the book, the better it is for the author! So leave reviews for authors you love! ☺

Jivaja on Amazon:
https://amzn.to/2Pgp6sF

Would you like to be kept updated on news, appearances and new releases?

Sign up for updates:
http://www.venessagiunta.com/sc-signup/

Turn the page for a sneak peek at Book 2!

Sneak Peek

Want a sneak peek at what's in store for Mecca in the next book?

------➤➤◄◄◄-

"He's at the bar, sitting on the corner. Red shirt, black pants. He looks like a throw-back from the eighties," Will said as he closed the car door and settled into the driver's seat. They'd parked in the side alley, just to stay out of the way. "Oh, he's bleached his hair, but otherwise, he looks just like the photo."

Mecca smoothed her blouse. She'd chosen the cami top with a black leather mini skirt. For two weeks, she'd practiced walking in the four inch heels. She still favored her bad leg, but with care, she wouldn't limp. If this didn't get his attention, nothing would.

"Are you sure you want to do this?" Will asked.

"Yes. I'll get him out here, get him on the ground, and you can use your modern medical miracles there" —she nodded at his black medical bag that they'd gotten on eBay— "to get what you need from him. Then we'll rid the world of him for good."

Will didn't meet her gaze.

Mecca sighed. "Don't tell me you're feeling guilty. They're monsters!"

"I know. Just go on. Let's get it over with."

She spotted him, right where Will said he'd be. She smoothed her skirt and put on her best saunter in his direction. She'd only gotten halfway there when he stood and pushed through the crowd in the other direction. She followed, trying not to be obvious.

He disappeared into the men's room.

"Dammit." Of fucking course.

Mecca changed direction and found a spot near a pillar where she could see the bathroom door.

"Can I buy you a drink?" The voice came from over her shoulder. When she glanced back, a man easily twice her age—maybe three times—shifted his gaze from her ass to her eyes.

Gross. "No, thanks. I'm waiting for my boyfriend." She returned her attention to the bathroom door. It hadn't opened. She half-turned to her would-be suitor, who hadn't yet left.

"He lets you out in that?" The guy smirked, his thick lips curling up into a leering grin.

"Seriously, if that's your best line, you need to fast forward into the current century."

He scowled. "Bitch."

"Yeah. Now go on."

He groused under his breath but turned away. She was glad he hadn't made a scene. She didn't want that sort of attention.

When she brought her own attention back to the bathroom, the men's door was swinging shut and a tall figure slipped into the crowd. As she watched him move away and toward the door, she recognized his walk. She looked back at the bathroom door. It remained closed.

"Oh no. No, no, no." Mecca rushed after the retreating figure, shoving her way through the crowded bar.

She could only think of one reason she would see him here. One reason why he'd have been in the bathroom with the monster she was after. Her bad leg throbbed as she stopped treating it carefully.

She broke through the crowd and out the door into the cold night air. Her breath steamed in front of her.

"Dad!"

He turned, and her heart sank. It was him.

"Mecca." He looked up and down the street. "What are you doing here? And why are you dressed like a hooker?" He hurried to her.

"You killed him, didn't you?" She barely kept her voice a whisper. Past his shoulder, she saw Will jogging toward them from the car.

The wide-eyed, open mouthed look on her father's face would have been funny if the situation weren't so dire.

"Why were you even here? How did you know who he—" Mecca broke off. She looked from her dad to Will, who'd just made it to them, and back to her dad.

Things clicked into place. One reason why he'd be here. Why he'd kill the Visci in the bathroom.

"Claude."

Will lifted one shoulder but gave a single nod of agreement.

She looked into her dad's eyes. "You're working for him."

He didn't look away but didn't respond.

"That's why Claude's left me alone, because you took my place. You're his assassin."

"It's the only way for you to live your life safely."

"I'll never be safe as long as he's alive. Neither will you or Gramps or Uncle Ken."

"I'm not worried about us. Our lives are mostly done. You are the one who's important."

"I can't believe you're killing for him." She gave an exasperated snort. "I don't know why I can't believe it," she said, only half under her breath.

"What were you doing in there? And again, looking like a hooker?" He reached out and fingered the strap of her camisole.

She jerked away. "I don't look like a damn hooker. And even if I did, none of it is your business."

"I think we need to move this off the street," Will said, stepping between them.

"No," Mecca said. "We're done here." She gathered her anger and leveled her gaze at her father. "I will kill him and every one of them I come across. You can warn him or not. I don't care. But as long as you're his pawn, I don't ever want to see or speak to you again." She spun on her heel and winced as sharp electric pulses arced up her leg. But she didn't stumble. There was that.

She was already sitting in the passenger seat, fuming, when Will opened the driver's side door. She didn't look up as he slid in.

"You shouldn't be so angry at him."

"Please just start the car. I'm freezing."

The motor hummed to life and Mecca pointed all the heater vents toward her. She thanked the car gods that the engine was still warm.

"He's only trying to protect you."

"I don't want to talk about it. I just want you to help me keep my promise. I want to kill them all."

Will's hand froze on the gearshift, and he looked over at her sidelong. "Are you sure that's what you want to do? You know how they are. What they do. You're basically declaring war on them."

"I've never been more sure of anything. We get what you need to keep you alive and then they die. Will you help me?"

He put the car into Drive and pulled out of the parking space. "Yes," he said, after a time. "I will."

PATREON |

Back in the old, old days, artists were supported by wealthy patrons who took care of their living expenses so that the artist was free to create their art.

These days, though, not many of us are so wealthy as to support another person fully, but you can pledge a few dollars a month to help your favorite creatives focus on their art.

Patreon is the platform from which you can do this. Plus, you get cool rewards based on your support level!

So if you like what you've read and would like to provide additional support to *this* creative, please check out my Patreon and sign up at the level you're comfortable with.

See you on the inside! ☺

https://www.patreon.com/VenessaG

Venessa Giunta

Venessa Giunta is a writer of weird things. She holds an MFA in Writing Popular Fiction from Seton Hill University and has worked on the editorial side of publishing for a decade. Her non-fiction essay "Demystifying What Editors Want" can be found in the book, Many Genres, One Craft. She is active in convention life, having held a number of organizational positions over the years and is currently Second to the Director of the Writers Track at Dragon Con, a SF/F fan convention with more than 80,000 attendees.

Venessa lives with her hubby in Atlanta, Georgia, and shares a home with three cats who all seem to think they rule the castle, but none of which pay the mortgage.

Follow her on Twitter @troilee or check out her website at http://www.venessagiunta.com, where you can find lots of good info for writers, especially.

CPSIA information can be obtained
at www.ICGtesting.com
Printed in the USA
FFHW022040230419
51962145-57364FF